How to Find What You Need... Online or Offline

The Creative Guide To Research

Robin Rowland

Franklin Lakes, NJ

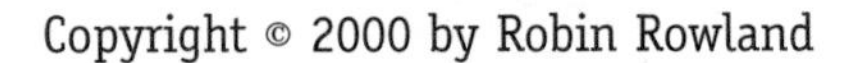

THE CREATIVE GUIDE TO RESEARCH
Cover design by Barry Littmann
Printed in the U.S.A. by Book-mart Press

To order this title, please call toll-free 1-800-CAREER-1 (NJ and Canada: 201-848-0310) to order using VISA or MasterCard, or for further information on books from Career Press.

The Career Press, Inc., 3 Tice Road, PO Box 687,
Franklin Lakes, NJ 07417
www.careerpress.com

Library of Congress Cataloging-in-Publication Data

Rowland, Robin.
The creative guide to research : how to find what you need—online or offline / by Robin Rowland.
p. cm.
Includes bibliographical references (p.) and index.
ISBN 1-56414-442-9
1. Information retrieval. 2. Research. I. Title.

ZA3075 .R69 2000
001.4—dc21 00-037882

Acknowledgments

Writing *The Creative Guide to Research* was a journey in which several paths I have traveled came together. I thank all my students and my colleagues, both at Ryerson Polytechnic University School of Journalism and at various conferences and seminars, who showed me what works and what doesn't work in teaching Internet research; all my friends and co-workers at CBC.ca and *The National* and *The Magazine* at CBC Television News who provided advice and support; and all the members of the Writer-L list, whose collective wisdom I have absorbed during the past several years. In addition, I want to thank all the fellow "newsgeeks" I have met at the Computer-Assisted Reporting conventions since my first in San Jose back in 1994.

On this specific project, I want to thank the following:

Dan Bjarnason, Jet Belgraver, Ian Kalushner, Sonja Carr, Pam Clasper, Martin O'Malley, Harvey Cashore, Sig Gerber, and Declan Hill, all at CBC; Duncan McIntosh, Rob Sawyer, Tanya Huff, David Hayes, and Chris McKhool for their advice and the interviews; and Anna Karagiannis for not being intimidated by the piles of paper and books in my home office.

At Narrative Train II, at Boston University, I want to thank Mark Kramer for organizing great conferences in 1998 and 1999, as well as for taking time during last-minute preparations for an interview. Many thanks also to Mark Bowden and Steve Biel, whom I met at the 1999 conference.

I also express my gratitude to Jon and Lynn Franklin for making Writer-L a pleasure to read five days a week and Lynn for the e-mail; Nora Paul, who invented the ultimate 5W lists, for permission to use them and for her advice throughout the years; Bruce DaSilva, Todd Lewan, and Ted Anthony at the Associated Press; and Ira Silverman for sharing his memories, as well as the callbacks.

Mike McGraw, of the *Kansas City Star;* Steve Lawrence and C. Lee Giles of the NEC Research Institute in Princeton, N.J.; Bob Port at APBOnline; Jerome Loving at Texas A&M; and Steven Pressfield, Bill Brewington and John Sawatsky all have my appreciate for their assistance. I also thank Writer-L members Walton R. Collins, Mark Pendergrast, Aaron Elson, Christopher Hadley, and Sol Stein.

Others who gave information, interviews, e-mail, advice, or support include Louis Rosenfeld and Samantha Bailey at Argus Clearinghouse, Marshall McPeek (WKYC-TV), Erik Piepenburg (MSNBC Chicago), Elizabeth Weise (*USA Today*), Alice Bishop (The Freedom Forum), Court Passant (CBS News), John Hendren (AP), Robert A. Harris (Vanguard University), Eric Nadler (*Seattle Times*), Kevin Donavan (*Toronto Star*), Kelly Crichton, Hester Riches, Fred Langan, and Kimberly Brown (CBC), plus Barbara Vandegrift, Tom Glad, John Griffith, Bill Dyer, and Jared Mitchell.

My collaborator on *Researching on the Internet*, Dave Kinnaman, has been a wonderful source of advice. Jim Dubro's work with me on *King of the Mob* and *Undercover* gave me the opportunity to do all that research, which served as a great training ground for this book. Eric Rankin at CBC's Pacific Rim Report who said yes to the River Kwai documentary, which again led me to new research.

Finally, thank you to Margot Maley Hutchison, my agent, who found a home for the book, and Stacey A. Farkas, my patient editor.

Contents

Introduction

What's It All About?

The Creative Guide to Research is a primer for research in the new millennium.

Approximately six years ago, on December 15, 1994, Netscape Communications officially introduced Netscape Navigator 1.0 by opening up its FTP site to anyone who wanted to download the software. By doing so, Netscape became the "killer ap" that opened the Internet as we know it today.

The Internet has always been a research tool. It was created in 1969 so that scholars, scientists, and engineers could log into remote computers and complete their research quickly.

Tim Berners-Lee, who created the World Wide Web, first wrote what he referred to as a "play program" in 1980 called *Enquire*, short for *Enquire Within Upon Everything*. In his book, *Weaving the Web*, Berners-Lee says: "The Web arose as an open challenge, through the swirling together of influences, ideas and realizations from many sides, until, by the wondrous offices of the human mind, a new concept jelled."

Research today can also be described as a "swirling together" of information: data found on the Web, messages on an e-mail listserv, traditional first-hand accounts from one-to-one interviews, peer-reviewed studies found in scholarly journals, and startling revelations found in dusty documents hidden for a generation in the dungeons of the world's government archives.

I call this book *The Creative Guide to Research*. As we enter the 21st century, I believe that there is the need for a book that tells the creative individual about the resources out there in the world of research.

There are research guides by academics for academics and scholarly students. There are books on reporting by journalists for journalists. There are books on Internet research, chock full of software tips and URLs. There is little out there for the writer of narrative nonfiction, the dramatist, the actor, the fiction writer, or the musician who is looking for solid, fact-backed inspiration.

What if we put it all together? That's what this book is about: how each field of research can learn from another.

The French term for net surfers is *les internautes*, which best describes what the researcher is trying to do. *Les Internaut*es calls up the image of the ancient Argonauts seeking the Golden Fleece, as well as today's astronauts and cosmonauts, exploring "the final frontier."

So consider yourself an Internaut, an explorer, an adventurer, not only in the virtual world of the Web, but beyond.

Who is this book for?

This book is written for creative people who do research: writers of all kinds; journalists in print, television, and online; actors and directors; students; creative and innovative academic scholars; television producers; police officers and other professional investigators; artists and musicians—anyone who is seeking information, both online and offline.

For those students who believe "everything is on the Web," this book will show you a wider world and tell you what there is on the Internet beyond the Web. Then I will take you further, away from the computer screen, to libraries, to archives, and on the road.

For those researchers, journalists, and scholars who believe there is nothing worthwhile on the Internet, this book will show you what there is on the Web, mailing lists, and newsgroups, and how to evaluate the material you find.

For those who type a few words into a search engine, hope for the best, and then find frustrating page after frustrating page, this book will show you how to take command of your Web searching and find better information, faster.

For those researchers who go to their favorite search engine, usually a major portal, only to find that the marketing department has once again changed the interface and you have to learn it all over again, this book will give you some basic principles for Web searching that will withstand the whirlwind of the dotcom marketing wars.

When I use the terms *Internet* or *Net*, I am referring to all the aspects of the Internet, including e-mail, newsgroups, and FTP sites; when I use *Web* or *World Wide Web*, I mean just that, the Web.

The approach: cross-fertilization

In the past six years, everything has changed, and yet nothing has changed. The principles of good research—organizing your search, focusing your aims, tracking down facts, and evaluating the facts, material, and data you find—are the same as they were before the Web explosion of 1994.

The Internet and the World Wide Web have made more information available, faster and easier. The Web is the most democratic publishing medium in history.

Today, Internet Service Providers (ISPs) usually grant their customers five or more megabytes of disk space to create Web pages, all part of their package along with e-mail and a Web browser. So the barrier to entry, the barrier to publication, as the economists call it, is reduced to almost nothing.

That means that there is a lot more out on the Net, and more is added every day. Internauts talk of a "noise to signal ratio" in the search for information on the Internet. You have to sift and filter out the junk before you find the gold.

Even the United States National Security Agency, the famed "puzzle palace," is overwhelmed, according to a report by David Ensor of CNN. There is just too much information flowing through the matrix of world communications.

Terabytes of information already exist in hard copy, dating back to the epic of Gilgamesh, first recorded on clay tablets in ancient Sumer. Even the great ancient library at Alexandria, it is said, suffered from information overload, with 500,000 papyrus scrolls. A scholar named Callimachus compiled a bibliography called the *Pinakes*, and it totaled 120 volumes.

Information was always there; it just wasn't available instantly.

Samuel Porteous, a former intelligence analyst now working in business intelligence, noted in a 1996 article that despite the "ubiquity" of the Internet and the international satellite and cable news services like CNN, "there is still much information that is not easily or publicly available. In an age of information overload, secrets continue to exist."

That is why the time-tested principles of research are more important than ever. Research in the 21st century requires the ability to focus your aims, get what you want, and know when it is time to stop and produce the results of your research. *The Creative Guide to Research* will help you do all that.

The good news is that the Web is beginning to break down boundaries between disciplines, barriers between nations and cultures. A focused Web search, more often than not, will lead to sources (good or bad) that surprise, delight, or irritate you; sources you never imagined could exist. You will find a site in the United States listed beside one from Israel, Ireland, or Japan.

The Web is just the beginning of cross-fertilization, and that's the approach this book will take. We can all learn from the ways others do research.

I've spent most of my career as a working journalist, first in print, then radio, later for eight years in network television news, and for the past four years as an online writer and producer. I've co-written two books investigating the early history of organized crime. I've written radio plays and short stories. During my student days, I worked first in a public and later in a university library. I now teach Computer-Assisted Reporting to college seniors and graduate students.

In 1994, just as Netscape was being released, I co-wrote *Researching on the Internet*, which balanced the old ways of UNIX exploration with the exciting new opportunities opened up by the graphical user interface, first with Mosaic and then with Netscape.

In the news business, there is a term for people like me. It's "newsgeek." It implies a journalist with experience, lots of computer savvy, and a good reporter's street smarts.

In the early 1980s, my experience as a police and court reporter (plus a good sample script I had written) gave me the chance to write radio drama for a true crime series on CBC Radio called *The Scales of Justice*. After that, I took some acting classes to make me a better scriptwriter. But my training in how actors create and interpret characters also made me a better journalist. I found that during research and later in writing my biography of Royal Canadian Mounted Police undercover operative Frank Zaneth, my acting training in character development made me reach further in my quest for tantalizing clues to the life of a man who spent his life in the shadows, creating his own characters. I followed a long-cold trail that existed only in police files, sparse news accounts, and the memories of men who were rookie cops when Zaneth was a senior inspector.

That's cross-fertilization.

Here you will find interviews with and the experiences of print and broadcast journalists, librarians, academics, spin doctors, actors, directors, musicians, costume designers, former intelligence analysts, and fiction writers. All have good advice that can be shared.

This book is about research. To use a computer term, it's about input, not about output. Fiction and nonfiction, scholarship, and drama are distinct. Although you may use all the creative techniques for research I outline in this book, you should always keep in mind your final goal.

For those of you in creative fields who sometimes fear research, or believe that respect for facts can stifle a project, you will find a bit of advice repeated through this book: *Good research gives you more choices.*

Actors choose emotional experience on a stage or a set to bring a character to life. Often the greater the experience of life an actor has, the more he or she has to draw on. So it is with research: The better your research, the more choices you have when it comes time to create.

How this book is organized

The best researchers work from the general to the specific, and that's what I do in this book. I'll start by looking at what makes good research and researchers, then move to the tools you can use, and then to specific research areas. Because both online and offline research are so connected these days, in most chapters you will find information about both. Finally, we will see how some creative people use research in their jobs and projects.

Although this book has a lot of information about computers and the Internet, it is not a computer manual. It's about skills that can be applied as software and silicon change during the next few years.

Nor is this a book of Web links. Those too will change, but there are lists of related links at the end of most chapters. I have also created a resource Web site for this book to keep everything up-to-date. You will find it at *creativeresearch.on.ca.*

Part I

The Adventure of Research

Chapter 1

The Great Game

I wasn't expecting a package that day in December 1990. I was at my computer when the buzzer blasted from the speaker on the far wall of my apartment. Someone was leaning on the button downstairs. Andy, the regular postman, always buzzed three times, quick and sharp.

"Parcel Post," a man downstairs barked into the intercom.

About 10 minutes later—the elevator in the building was always slow—I was leaning against the open door of my apartment. Finally, I heard the elevator doors clunk open and a blue uniform-clad man with a narrow cardboard box under his arm walked briskly down the hall. He handed me the box and was on his way.

The return address was from the National Archives of Canada in Ottawa. For the past four years, I had worked in the archives, tracing the life and cases of Frank W. Zaneth, undercover operative and troubleshooter for the Royal Canadian Mounted Police (RCMP). During that time, postal workers had brought me boxes of documents, case files from operations and investigations that took place from 1917 to the late 1940s.

Zaneth was best known for his undercover penetration—as the radical agitator "Harry Blask"—of the Canadian labor movement during the unrest in 1919 that led to the Winnipeg General Strike. Zaneth had testified in the trials of the leaders of the strike. The official report on the riots in Winnipeg in June 1919 had been public for years. What scholars had wanted to see for more than 70 years were the files on undercover operations at that crucial time.

In 1986, Lynn McDonald, a member of Parliament, said in the House of Commons, "We know that the RCMP keeps, as confidential, files on the Winnipeg General Strike, [which occurred] a very long time ago. It is difficult to imagine that there are current security matters that could be jeopardized from files dating back to that period of time."

When we began our research, I filed Access to Information (Freedom of Information) requests for material on Zaneth with the Canadian Security Intelligence Service (CSIS), especially the western undercover operations in 1919. We did receive some information, but nothing about 1919.

CSIS, commonly described as Canada's spy agency, replied to our letters: "We conducted a review of files pertaining to subversive activities in the Prairie Provinces and could not locate any report submitted by Frank W. Zaneth."

We appealed to Canada's information commissioner. In his reply to our appeal, Commissioner John Grace wrote: "CSIS confirmed in writing...that it had made a substantial search with a view to locating Zaneth's records."

Then, the government of Prime Minister Brian Mulroney ordered CSIS to hand over to the Archives all files "not relevant to the service's mandate." So I filed new access requests to the Archives, once again requesting Zaneth material. If there were any records, they would now be part of the new Record Group 146, RCMP/CSIS Labor Files.

I opened the box. It contained 13 files, hundreds of pages of memos, reports, and lists, all about the 1919 strikes in western Canada. The files contained plans for a nationwide round up of "radical elements" at the time of the strike.

I found references to the characters I had found in other files, in trial transcripts, and in news accounts, but now there was someone new. An American named Jim Davis turned up in Calgary, claiming to be a "Wobblie," a member of the IWW, the International Workers of the World.

"I took part in a safe blowing in Chicago," Davis boasted to Zaneth, who was undercover as Harry Blask. "Half a million dollars worth of jewelry was stolen and everything turned over to the IWW." Zaneth continued to track Davis for the next few months, but it was never clear if the American visitor was actually a member of the IWW or a con man and liar.

The Archives had released without any problems files that for the past 70 years the government had refused to acknowledge even existed.

So did Canada's spies lie when they said they had found no information submitted by Zaneth? Perhaps. The files revealed that during his undercover operations in Calgary, Zaneth never formally *submitted* reports on paper. Instead he gave his reports orally to a Corporal S.R. Waugh. It was Waugh who filed the official reports.

Be careful what you ask for.

The game begins

No one will find a secret document on the World Wide Web, unless someone obtains the document, scans it, formats it for the Web, and uploads it to a server.

News Web sites, such as the one I produce for the Canadian Broadcasting Corporation (CBC), often post documents used in reports on a Web site. It is one approach that is changing the way we handle information. The Web reduces what has been called the "gatekeeper" function. A document may flash on a television screen for a few seconds. On the Web, the audience can read it for themselves.

But it was the reporter who first found that document elsewhere. Sometimes the documents are obtained from sources, usually in a brown envelope. Others are released as part of a lawsuit. The huge Web-based collections of documents on the various suits against the tobacco industry were, for the most part, evidence in lawsuits.

One site dedicated to putting documents on the Web, *The Smoking Gun*, has to obtain them first through Freedom of Information requests.

As I was doing the research for this book, one comment kept repeating—from teachers, professors, senior editors, and producers I spoke to. From the United States, Canada, and Australia, they said that many young people who have grown up with the Web seem to believe that "everything" is on the Web. I even saw a television clip of a young woman, about to go to a new wired high school, who said just that: "We'll get all we need off the Internet."

It is not only high school students who are concentrating on the Net to get information. A study reported in the journal *Nature* in July 1999 reported that more and more scientists are working online only, locating the latest research articles through the Net.

So let's use the analogy of the computer game. Popping a few words into a search engine box is simplest and just at the first level. Using the advanced features of a search engine is the second level. Combine that with e-mail listservs, e-mail newsletters, filters, and alert services, as well as Usenet newsgroups, and you're at the third level.

Beyond the third level, the degree of difficulty, the challenge, increases steadily as the researcher moves off the Net from the virtual to the real world.

A century ago, in *Kim*, Rudyard Kipling used the term "the great game" as his name for the British Secret Service, which was working on what was then the frontier between India and Afghanistan. Kipling told of the "Great Game that never ceases day and night." These words could, in a different context of course, describe the Internet and research beyond.

So as Mahbub Ali said as Kim went off to meet the teacher Lurgan Sahib: "Here begins the Great Game."

Being there

"There is nothing like going out and hunting stuff down on your own," says Todd Lewan, a national writer for the Associated Press (AP).

"There's nothing like going to a courthouse and finding documents, finding that one piece of paper in a courthouse basement. Just nothing like it.

"You can't—on the Internet—get a sense of place or scene. You just can't do it. I don't care how many pictures you see on the Net. I don't care how many multidimensional images you see, I don't care if it's 3-D.

"It is immediacy that draws in readers, a sense of scene that makes people feel like they are there. Even if you can see dozens of pictures on the Net, you can't write about the Nevada nuclear test site. You can read history and get all the figures and facts you want. There is nothing like driving in the Nevada desert and coming face to face with a moon-like crater that was made by a nuclear bomb. There is nothing like hearing the sound of a fly, a desert fly buzzing in your ear as you're looking at a steel girder bridge that was bent into a 30-foot boomerang by a bomb that was detonated a mile away. That sense of scope you can't replace just by looking at a computer screen."

The avocado field

Research is an adventure. The researcher is a tracker, a detective, a hunter, and like a hunter, the researcher is not always sitting in a comfortable office, reading documents. Sometimes he is lying in an avocado field in Cuba.

Ira Silverman, one the most respected investigative producers in the United States, worked for almost 30 years for NBC News. It was Silverman who tracked one of the most notorious fugitives from American justice, Robert Vesco. That is how Silverman ended up in an avocado field to do his research.

"We believed that he was somewhere in Central America or the Caribbean," Silverman says. "I went to several islands in the Caribbean and searched for the guy. We knew that Vesco had a kidney problem and there was a medical college in Grenada. We tried to find patient records. We went through other islands, to the Bahamas, to Costa Rica, and could not come up with him.

"We kept with it and eventually we came to believe that he had been given sanctuary by Fidel Castro in Cuba.

"It was a difficult situation, first to get into Cuba and then to get around in Cuba. We had to shake the minders that were assigned to us. And then we had to find out if Vesco indeed was there.

"We managed to put together a kind of 'treasure map' of where he might be.

"Then we organized a plan to get out of the hotel, which was watched. At that time there were 18 or 19 cars to rent. We were finally able to rent a Volkswagen.

"We headed out in the middle of the night. My chest was pounding, as if I was going to [a] bank robbery.

"We found an avocado field near a house where we thought Vesco was. We crawled out into that field, with long lenses on the camera. We were in position about four o'clock in the morning, and [we] stayed there with every conceivable species of insect life around us.

"By quarter to twelve, Vesco came out of the house and walked to a car. And we were able to tape him for about 25 seconds. That showed that indeed the denials by Castro and Cuba were wrong. He was there.

"Then we were able to get to the airport, where we had a Lear jet, and fly to Miami, and that night that 25 seconds was the lead to a two- or three-minute piece that was the lead of the NBC Nightly News.

"It is often that kind of grit that is involved in doing this work. It may or may not pay off. And if it doesn't pay off, no one knows about it except the business office."

A search for truth

The adventure of research is not limited to journalists. You will find it among scholars as well. One of my favorite research stories is by Hugh Trevor-Roper, then Regius Professor of Modern History at Oxford, and it's found in his book, *Hermit of Peking: The Hidden Life of Sir Edmund Backhouse.*

Backhouse lived much of his life in the city then known as Peking. He had presented thousands of Chinese books and volumes (stitched gatherings called *chüan*) to Oxford's Bodleian library. He also wrote what at the time—1910—was considered a definitive account of the last Dowager Empress of China.

In 1973, Trevor-Roper received a letter from Switzerland, offering him the manuscript of Backhouse's memoirs. Trevor-Roper recounts that the letter contained the opinion of two distinguished scholars who had read the memoirs and found them "of great literary and historical value" and "also somewhat obscene." The memoirs also claimed that Backhouse had worked for the British Secret Service. Trevor-Roper was in British Military Intelligence during World War II. The source, "a distinguished Swiss scientist," did not want to send the manuscript through the mail. So Trevor-Roper was handed the memoirs at Basel Airport.

Trevor-Roper read the memoirs, which he says were "of no ordinary obscenity." Backhouse claimed intimate relationships with prominent men in Victorian England and France (including Oscar Wilde and poet Paul Verlaine), as well as describing a homosexual brothel in Peking in 1899 called "The Hall of Chaste Joys." Backhouse also claimed to have been the lover of the Dowager Empress herself.

There was more intriguing information, so the distinguished professor (and former intelligence agent) began a quest to find the truth about the mysterious Sir Edmund. Like a good detective, Trevor-Roper uncovered the fact that Backhouse was a pathological liar and con man who took two major corporations to the cleaners: The American Bank Note Company and Scotland's John Brown Shipbuilding Company. Like their modern counterparts, both companies hoped to exploit the Chinese market and both were thus an easy mark for a resident of Peking and an acknowledged expert on China, a man Trevor-Roper calls "an enchanter whose spells softened the hard heads of businessmen and diplomats."

In his prologue and throughout the book, Trevor-Roper recounts his quest for Backhouse. The American Bank Note Company opened its archives to him. John Brown Shipbuilding Company, however, closed its doors.

Trevor-Roper was able to work around this problem by finding alternative sources—something a researcher should always be prepared to do—in records kept at Glasgow University. He found more intriguing information in a secret Foreign Office file called "Affairs of Sir Edmund Backhouse" and tracked down personal papers in Toronto and Sydney, Australia.

In the end, Trevor-Roper came to the conclusion that none of the manuscript was true, that the memoirs handed to him, spy-fashion, in an airport rendezvous, were largely imaginary. As for the writer of the memoirs, Trevor-Roper concludes by saying Backhouse's life was an "eccentric career of fantasy and fabrication."

So when you start research, you never know where it will lead, whether the documents you are reading are authentic, or if the person you are interviewing is telling the truth. It's all part of the adventure of research.

Links

The Smoking Gun

www.thesmokinggun.com

The Smoking Gun says it posts "exclusive documents that can't be found elsewhere on the Web." The material is obtained from government and law enforcement sources, via Freedom of Information requests and from court files.

Canadian Security Intelligence Service

www.csisscrs.gc.ca

Chapter 2

The Journey Begins

Now to research. How to begin? Joseph Campbell, in his classic book, *The Hero with a Thousand Faces*, writes of a hero who:

> *...ventures forth from the world of common day into a region of supernatural wonder; fabulous forces are there encountered and a decisive victory is won: the hero comes back from his mysterious adventure with the power to bestow boons on his fellow man.*

That's what creative research should be: a way of bestowing boons on fellow human beings.

I've been doing research for 25 years, in libraries, in archives, by snail mail, on the phone, in person, on the Internet. What I've been doing instinctively for years, librarians give a simple name. They call it the *process* of research. To a librarian, the process of research is more important than the "button pushing" of hardware and software or browsing bookshelves.

Once you know the process, once you know the basics of research, then you can keep up—as best anyone can—with the information overload of the new century. You can produce something: a thesis, a book, a television segment, a Web site, a play, a song.

The call to adventure

Any research project begins with an idea. A reporter may get a tip: Another journalist who specializes in longer narratives for newspapers, magazines, or books may become fascinated with a character or an event. A creative scholar will have an idea that becomes a thesis proposition for a dissertation or paper. A novelist or playwright has an idea for a story that is better if some background research is done.

The initial idea is the call to adventure; the outcome is the "boon" Campbell talks about. Before you start, you have to have an idea of both. Research of any sort begins, like any journey, with a first step. It ends when you reach a defined goal.

The goal

Begin by writing a goal or focus statement. The focus statement outlines your initial idea as a story. It could be, as in *Romeo and Juliet*, "a teenaged boy and girl, from feuding families, fall in love." That means the story is about Romeo and Juliet, not Mercutio, who is also caught in the middle, nor is it about the nurse or Friar Lawrence.

Steven Pressfield, author of the historical novel *Gates of Fire*, wanted to write about the 300 Spartans and their allies at the Pass of Thermopoylae when he read in Herodotus the statement of the Spartan warrior Dienekes. Told that the Persian archers were so numerous that their arrows would block out the sun, Dienekes replied, "Good. Then we'll have our battle in the shade."

I am writing this book because as a teacher, a Web producer, and a journalist, I saw a need for a book that combines and integrates both traditional and online research. I added "creative" to the mix because most research books are strictly about the factual and the scholarly, and I felt there was a need for something more.

The premise

The second step in the research process is to write down your premise. A premise is crucial to any story.

For the scholar or investigator, the premise is the thesis you are setting out to prove. It's the same for the creative artist. In 1946, Lajos Egri wrote a classic book on writing plays, *The Art of Dramatic Writing*. Egri said any work must have a premise, a driving force, a road map. He quoted the then-current edition of *Webster's International Dictionary:*

> **Premise:** a proposition antecedently supposed or proved; a basis of argument. A proposition stated or assumed as leading to a conclusion.

Egri concludes the premise of *Romeo and Juliet* is "Great love defies even death."

For one of the best-known books about the *Titanic*, Walter Lord's *A Night to Remember*, the premise is "Overriding everything else, the *Titanic* also marked the end of a general feeling of confidence....Before the *Titanic* all was quiet. Afterward, all was tumult."

It's a valid premise, even though a scholar like Steven Biel of Harvard University says it "makes academics like me squirm. In my opinion, the disaster changed nothing but the shipping regulations." But Biel himself, author of *Down with the Old Canoe: A Cultural History of the Titanic Disaster*, also has a premise, that the *Titanic* story is "one of the great mythic events of the twentieth century." His scholarly volume sets to find out why, and that is a journey in itself.

The hero of Steven Pressfield's *Gates of Fire* is Xeones, a servant (Pressfield calls him a squire) of the Spartan Dienekes. Pressfield says he wondered why many of the Spartan helots stayed to fight and die with their masters. "When I read the ancient sources about armor bearers, they would just dismiss them out of hand, and no one would say anything about them," he says. "But just using my imagination, there's no way these guys aren't going to have a huge part while their masters are fighting and dying. They're there carrying their stuff.

"I felt the relationship between a hoplite warrior and his squire (I picked the term from the Middle Ages—it's creative invention) has to be like with Tiger Woods and his caddy. They've got to be as tight as those people are; it's the officer to enlisted man type of relationship. It's also going to be a bit of a marriage.

"I know from my own experience being a caddy how you sort of identify with the very person you're serving. Even though you're being exploited, you're very loyal. I used what I knew about human nature and projected it back there.

"In the case of the Spartans, it was the idea of courage versus fear and what made these guys be sent out to die and to do it.

"After that, as I did research, everything would have to follow that theme, looking for stuff that would support that theme." Each of the characters represents a different aspect of the theme courage versus fear.

Is that the premise? Not in Egri's terms. In *Gates of Fire*, one night the characters debate courage and fear with no real conclusion. Later in the book, as a small group of Spartans are about to raid the Persian camp, Dienekes tell us the premise of the book: The opposite of fear is love.

You should articulate the premise the best you can, although sometimes the premise may be in the subconscious until you are almost finished.

Barbara Tuchman wrote The Guns of August—recounting how Europe automatically went to war in 1914—as the Cold War was at its height. It was published in 1962. Tuchman noted:

"In the month of August 1914, there was something looming, inescapable, universal that involved us all. Something in that awful gulf between perfect plans and fallible men that makes one tremble with a sense of 'There but for the Grace of God go we.' It was not until the end, until I was actually writing the epilogue, that I fully realized the implications of the story I had been writing for two years."

Finally, as you craft your premise, remember what your product will be, whether it's a term paper, a news report, an internal memo for your boss, an article in a scholarly journal, a novel, or a nonfiction book. Whatever it is, the article should be clear to the reader. When starting out on a research project, a researcher should *always* keep the reader in mind (your ultimate end-user to use computer jargon). See that reader and visualize that reader, whether it's your professor, your boss, or your mother.

The premise for this book is: *Good research gives you more choices.*

Know where you're going

Have some idea of where you're going. That will help you in the research process. For example, if you're writing a nonfiction or fictional narrative, *know your ending*. (It may change, but it's good to have an ending in mind.) If you're writing a report, write a focus statement that keeps the report as narrow as possible. That way you will be able to forgo anything that is out in left field, that doesn't pertain directly to what you're doing.

The mentor and the circle of knowledge

In the mythological round, after the hero hears the call and often before he or she crosses the threshold of adventure, a mentor appears who trains the hero for the task ahead. The best known is Merlin, who took the young Arthur and made him ready to be a king.

So what do our guides suggest as you start a research project? Like the archetypal martial arts master, the word is first slow down, be patient, observe. Look for the big picture, "the broad overview" Pressfield calls it.

Author Tracy Kidder describes how he first begins to write by "circling around an idea" before "spiraling in." Pressfield also says, "I do my research as I go along, but I start with the basics, whatever the sources, just enough to get me going, and then as I work, I continually do research, I continually read."

This approach is often called "going from the outside in."

Author, journalist, and teacher John Sawatsky refines it further. He uses the scientific analogy of "pure" and "applied" research. Sawatsky's specialty is the interview, but his views apply to all aspects of research: "There are two research stages: the pure research stage and the applied research stage. Pure research is getting information to know what to ask.

"Most journalists jump right into the applied research stage. [They] jump in far too quickly and go after specifics. At the beginning, you should really think less rather than more."

Sawatsky suggests that by using the pure research approach first, a researcher will come up with better questions and ultimately a better story. "If you start chasing after one specific theory," he notes, "you'll blind yourself to the bigger stories out there."

"In terms of doing an interview," Sawatsky continues, "you start at the bottom and you work your way up to the top. It doesn't matter what analogy you use, from the bottom to the top, or the outside to the inside, as you get to the key people who know more, you need to know what questions to ask. That is absolutely crucial."

Finding the outer circle of knowledge first and then descending to the specific works in any field. The editor of the online list Writer-L, Lynn Franklin, was trained in both academic research and as a journalist.

"I've been fascinated by the two different approaches," she says. "When faced with a particular question, a journalist will reach for the phone to consult an expert. In contrast, an academic will head for the library or, nowadays, the Internet. The most thorough research combines the two approaches.

"Take, for example, the start of a new book project. One of the first things I do is create a databank of sources. In the beginning, I might find these people from articles and books I've read. Pretty quickly, however, people I talk to will lead me to other people more appropriate to the story."

The step to the threshold

During my own journey, I discovered John Sawatsky's apt use of the terms "pure" and "applied" research as well as Tracy Kidder's approach of a circle and the spiraling in.

What does the researcher do to the research?

Always remember Werner Heisenberg's Uncertainty Principle, now applied far beyond the world of subatomic physics where it began. Oversimplified, the principle says that the act of measuring can change the event being measured. Your acts of research, reporting, writing, and publishing may bring changes in the subject you are researching. The public perception of something changes. Or, in some cases, your entry into the lives of the people you talk to will change them.

So what then does research do to the researcher?

That is the question the mentor often asks the hero to consider before he embarks on his journey.

The analogy of the circle also brings us back to the mythology of the hero. For as Campbell wrote:

> Beyond the threshold the hero journeys through a world of unfamiliar yet strangely intimate forces, some of which severely threaten him (tests), some of which give magical aid (helpers). When he arrives at the nadir of the mythological round, he undergoes a supreme ordeal and gains his reward.

To put it another way, as James Baldwin wrote in the introduction to *Notes of a Native Son*: "One writes out of one thing only—one's own experience. Everything depends on how relentlessly one forces from this experience the last drop, sweet or bitter, it can possibly give." This applies whether you are a scholar, journalist, novelist, playwright, or poet.

Links

Joseph Campbell Foundation
www.jcf.org

Chapter 3

Who, What, Where, When, and Why (Plus How)

Journalists have always used the five Ws: who, what, when, where, and why, plus how, as a way of focusing their research. Some newsgeeks, tongue in cheek, now call them (based on the programming language C++) the "5W+."

Ask yourself the six questions about your goals whenever you embark on a project.

You'll find the traditional 5W+ in any run-of-the-day newspaper, television, or online news story. For the creative researcher, the task is to go beyond the idea of putting all six in the lead, in what newspaper journalists call the inverted pyramid. The creative researcher continues to ask all six questions throughout the project.

Here we have to ask what you are researching (writing for information) and what you eventually will be writing (writing for story).

Writing (and researching) for information includes much, not all, of daily journalism, many magazine articles, some books, almost all reports written in government and business, and most academic papers.

Writing (and researching) for story includes narrative journalism found in the newspaper serials appearing now in the United States; many magazines; books of narrative nonfiction; and, of course, traditional fiction storytelling in novels and drama. In the academic world there is, as the new century dawns, a hint of the revival of (academically rigorous) narrative in fields such as anthropology, archaeology, sociology, law, and history.

You can not only use the 5W+ as you're doing your research, you can also use it in the planning process, so in this chapter we're going to go through several versions of it.

The traditional 5W+

The traditional reporter's five Ws (plus *how)* are the kind you will find in standard, run-of-the-mill newspaper, television, or online news stories:

- ❑ **Who** are you writing about? Your subject can be anyone from a traffic-accident victim to an unexpected but suddenly credible candidate for the presidency of the United States.
- ❑ **What** is the story about? What are the details and circumstances of the story?
- ❑ **When** did it happen? What time of day did the incident occur, or is it the result of events that have taken place during a period of time?
- ❑ **Where** did it happen? Does the location of the event have any underlying significance?
- ❑ **Why** did it happen? Which factors contributed to the event or motivated your subject?
- ❑ **How** did it happen? What was the sequence of occurrences that resulted in the events in your story?

The narrative 5W+

If your project involves writing for story rather than just for information, then it is time to expand the five Ws. Roy Peter Clark, senior scholar at the Poynter Institute for Media Studies in St. Petersburg, Florida, and national director of the National Writers' Workshop, recommends that you imagine:

- ❑ **who as character.**
- ❑ **what as action.**
- ❑ **where as setting.**
- ❑ **when as chronology.**

Why and **how** remain the same, expansions of the other four.

Whether you're writing a short news story, a long form narrative, or an academic paper, it is always helpful in research to think of the person you're writing about as a fully rounded character. It makes you look for more as you do your research.

I said that writing for information includes "almost all reports written in government and business." I used the term "almost all" deliberately.

Reports often reveal the **character** of the writer. Undercover cop Frank Zaneth was a "who" in my two first books. In *King of the Mob*, he was a major investigator. *Undercover* was his biographical casebook. Zaneth wrote routine police reports. Because English was not his first language, the first reports were somewhat awkward. Later, with experience, they became more expressive and more interesting. Every one of the reports, even though they were written in the formal police language of the day, was a narrative. Zaneth's aim was to write for information for his superiors. It was the essence of his character that he also wrote for story.

For **action**, no recent book brings both meanings of the word together better than Mark Bowden's *Black Hawk Down*, the minute-by-minute story of the battle in Mogadishu, Somalia, October in 1993. As an action-adventure story of U.S. Army Rangers and members of the Delta Force trapped in downtown "Mog," it is a superb read. As "action" in terms of research, of finding the "what," it is a benchmark to strive for. Bowden, a reporter for the *Philadelphia Inquirer*, was not one of the few Western reporters in Mogadishu during that time. Every event of the action is reconstructed from interviews with Americans and Somalis, from military reports, and from videotapes taken by the helicopters flying over the battle scene.

Setting is crucial in two recent articles by JoAnn Wypijewski in *Harpers*: "The Secret Sharer," which appeared in July 1998, and "A Boy's Life," which appeared in September. 1999. The main character of "The Secret Sharer" is Nushawn Williams, the man accused in 1997 of infecting at least 22 women with HIV. "A Boy's Life" profiles Aaron McKinney and Russell Henderson, the killers of Matthew Shepard. In both stories, community, setting, is also a major character.

In the Williams story, it is the poverty and hopelessness of Jamestown, New York. In the story of McKinney and Henderson, the town of Laramie, Wyoming, is a character in itself, and the setting is crucial to understanding the "who," the characters of the two killers. Wypijewski's premise: "It's just possible that Matthew Shepard didn't die because he was gay; he died because Aaron McKinney and Russell Henderson are straight." Laramie, according to the author, is a place where, if you're a straight male, "If you're telling your feelings, you're a kind of wuss."

As for **chronology**, it is so crucial to research that I've devoted an entire chapter to it later in this book.

The personal 5W+

It's also a good idea to use the five Ws and how to get an idea of yourself and your audience. That will guide your research plan.

For whom will you be writing? It is often said that academics and scholars research and write for their peers, while journalists and authors write for the public. You can break that down even further. Are you writing for *Science* or *Nature*, which serve the entire scientific community, or for a journal that serves a more narrow, specialized field? If you are in the media, your station, network, newspaper, or magazine will have a profile of the viewing and reading audience.

For a book, the publisher will want you to identify your target audience. No matter what amorphous group you are writing for, you should also visualize some human beings, whether it's your mother, your partner, your next-door neighbor, or the members of your thesis supervisory committee.

What will you be doing? Are you writing a "buck-and-a-half" (one minute, 30 seconds) segment for the evening news or your doctoral thesis? Is your book a popular title from a major publisher or a more scholarly work from a university press? Are you creating a documentary or writing a Sunday newspaper feature? The "what" will govern the time and effort you put into research.

When? What is your deadline? How much time do you have for research?

Where? Where will you be doing the research? Can you find the information sitting at home online or in a national archives? Will you be traveling to a specific location?

How? How are you going to do your research? How much will it cost? Will you get a research grant to do research where and when you want? Or will you pay for most of it out of your own pocket? Are you a full-time student with time to research? Or a part-timer who has to work for a living? If you're a journalist, will your organization pay for the research or will you have to do a substantial amount on your time and dime until you can convince the bean counters to support you?

Why? It's also a good idea to ask yourself why you are doing the project. Has your boss, teacher, or advisor told you to do it? It's something you're doing for political reasons? Has a friend or family member asked you? Is it the one thing you've wanted to do for the past 10 years? Whatever you do, it's been proven time and time again that if the project is something you are passionate about, the chances are you'll do a better job.

The researcher's sixth W

The creative researcher's sixth W is the *wish list*. Starting out you should add the wish list to your five Ws. The wish list is part of your goal and it should include all your hopes and dreams for your project.

Remember Dorothy in the *Wizard of Oz?* She wants to get home to Kansas. But as the story goes on, her wish list grows: courage for the Cowardly Lion, a heart for the Tin Man, and a brain for the Scarecrow. So keep a wish list as you work and add things to it, no matter how off the wall or outlandish they may seem. Some of those wishes may actually come true if you reach the Emerald City.

The applied 5W+

The researcher should ask a series of applied questions about the project. Nora Paul of the Poynter Institute designed this checklist as a guideline for librarians and reporters using the expensive online databases such as Lexis-Nexis. On the commercial databases, every minute costs and so does every download. Applying Paul's five Ws saves the researcher time and money. By asking the same set of questions, a researcher can save time and money.

With her permission, I have adapted Nora Paul's outline to focus on all kinds of research.

Deciding what you need

Your first step in research is to develop a guideline to the kind of information you are seeking (using your pure 5W+). Research for a term paper is different from research for a news story, an internal business memo, a nonfiction book, or a work of dramatic fiction such as a novel or a play. Asking the same questions will help you figure out where you're going on the research road map.

Who

- ❑ Whom is your project about? A politician, a Broadway star, a little-known historical figure, a criminal, a cop, a competitor, a customer?

- ❑ Whom have you already talked to (both as advisers and interview subjects)?
- ❑ Whom should you talk to (both as advisers and interview subjects)?

What

- ❑ What is the information you need about? A person, a place, a company, a report on a scientific research project?
- ❑ What kind of information do you need? Interviews from around the world, statistics or data, new sources of information, or confirmation of material from other sources?
- ❑ What type of information will be most useful?
- ❑ What information do you already have?
- ❑ What format will the material be in? Documents, books, photocopies, data from a database, a captured Web page?

When

- ❑ When is the information needed? In minutes on a breaking news story, in a hurry for an important client, or in a couple of months on a major project?
- ❑ When did the event you are researching take place? (The older it is, the less likely you will find it on the Internet.)
- ❑ When does the information change? Every few minutes for stock quotes, every few hours for weather forecast, never for an archived document.

Where

- ❑ Where did the event you are researching take place?
- ❑ Where have you already looked for information?
- ❑ Where should you look for information in the future?

Why

- ❑ Why are you looking for the information? Are you checking information you have, looking for a source, or fishing for a story or research idea?

How

- ❑ How much information do you need?
- ❑ How are you going to use the information? In a story or report, in charts or graphics, or will you input the data into some type of program for further number crunching?
- ❑ How would you prefer the information to be delivered? In the computer world, do you ask for ASCII data you will keep on a disk or material you will want to print to hard copy? Do you buy books so that you will always have them at your fingertips, or do you take them out of the library and photocopy a few relevant passages?

Finding the right source

Once you have found what you already have and what you want, the next step is to choose where you're going to find it. On the Internet? In a library? Tracking down an interview subject in Pittsburgh or Patagonia? Again that means you should ask yourself some more questions.

Who

- ❑ Who might have the kind of information you're seeking?
- ❑ Who would have the most current/most retrospective data?
- ❑ Who has done this type of research before so you can get advice? (This is good question to ask in the appropriate Internet mailing list or newsgroup if you don't know.)
- ❑ Who was responsible for collecting the information you have found? This is a question you should ask whether you're evaluating a government document slipped under your door, reading a scholarly paper, or perusing a Web site you found online.

What

- ❑ What kind of search should you use? On the World Wide Web, which search engine do you use? Do you use your local library or go online to find a rare book in an online catalog?
- ❑ What are the possible sources of error in the data? Check for bias, problems of methodology, and outdated material.
- ❑ What do you do if you don't find any information or you find too much?

When

- ❑ When do you do specific research? If a lot of letter writing, e-mail, and travel are necessary, it is a good idea to map it all out. Remember your deadline for your project. Create a to-do list and keep it updated. And then add more time, because everything will take longer than you can imagine.
- ❑ If you are going to use a commercial online service, when do you use it? If you use it individually or through a company, does it charge more for peak hours as opposed to off-peak hours? If you have access through a university library (as many students do), when do you go so there isn't a huge lineup at the limited number of terminals.

Where

- ❑ Where should you do your search? Again, name specific items in your research. Do you have go to the ends of the earth to find out a specific item? Or just around the corner? Is it commonly available information that you can get from a local source, such as a library? Or is there just one source, whether that is a rare book library, an archive, or a single person somewhere on the planet.
- ❑ If doing Web searches, which sites are most appropriate and most reliable?

Why

- ❑ Why are you doing the search? Are you looking for essential information, for material you need to know it, or is it something that would be just neat to have?
- ❑ Why was the information originally collected and posted? Is it a government database, a commercial Web site created by a marketing department, or, as is still common on the Internet, someone's labor of love, either in an academic or a private setting?

How

- ❑ How are you going to put your research strategy together for each major item?

- ❑ How much is this going to cost? How much are you willing to spend?
- ❑ If working online, how might you find the same information offline?
- ❑ If working offline, could the same information be available online?
- ❑ How can you get help if you run into trouble?
- ❑ How will you use the information in the story or report?
- ❑ How will you attribute, footnote, or reference your research?
- ❑ How consistent is this information with material from other sources, whether on or off the Net?

Expect the unexpected

Not everyone is going to make a list of 5W+ and check it twice before setting off on the research project. But it's a good idea to keep this list in the back of your mind, for it will provide the road map and the guide as you work.

Finally, expect the unexpected. And we'll discuss that in more detail in Chapter 5.

Links

The Poynter Institute
www.poynter.org

Black Hawk Down
www.blackhawkdown.com

***Harper's* Magazine**
www.harpers.org
Mostly a promotional site at time of writing. Back issues index was "under construction."

Chapter 4

The Matrix and the Nexus

In research, everything is connected to everything else. One thing leads to another. Remember *Six Degrees of Separation,* the play and the movie based on the idea that everyone on this world is just six people away from each other? It's based on fact, and "networks" of people and how they connect have been studied by anthropologists. Researchers use this connectiveness to find new sources of information.

In academic research, citations are connections, pointers to new places to research. A good bibliography is worth the weight of the book in gold.

The same goes for documents. The great American investigative reporter and researcher I. F. Stone made a career of looking for connections between documents, and the contradictions that cropped up in those connections. Documents cross reference to other documents. Documents mention names that have to be tracked down.

Connections

One document can fill in the blanks you've found. That's what happened to me when I was researching how Sam Bronfman created his bootleg empire in Canada in the 1920s and 1930s.

In 1932, the Royal Canadian Mounted Police (RCMP) assigned Frank Zaneth, then their top investigator and troubleshooter, to "get the higher ups in the bootleg trade." In other words, to target Sam Bronfman and his brothers, the men who ran Distillers Corporation-Seagrams Limited and who were supplying the thirsty United States with premium Canadian liquor.

I filed an Access to Information request with the RCMP and was eventually told that the investigative files contained more than 35,000 records. After some negotiations with the RCMP, Jim Dubro, my collaborator, and I narrowed the request to what we called "case summaries." The narrowed request meant we still had to go through some 3,000 records, many of them concentrating on a Bronfman-owned company called Atlas Shipping.

Although there was a gold mine of information in the files, material had been deleted during the Access to Information vetting process, leaving some gaps.

How was I to fill in the gaps? I thought the answer might be in Washington, D.C. The United States, of course, had a huge interest in the 1920s and 1930s in stopping the "liquor traffic" from Canada.

The material I needed was not in the stately National Archives building on Pennsylvania Avenue but in the Washington National Records Center, a stretched suburban warehouse in Suitland, Maryland, that looks as if it could be owned by a trucking company. The reading room in Suitland was crowded, claustrophobic, and institutional green, a place that compels you to go for a walk in the parking lot and its small strip of grass.

I was checking RG (Record Group) 60, records of the U. S. Department of Justice. Then came the connection—File 23-4581 Atlas Shipping. It outlined the case the United States was building against the Bronfmans at the same time as the Zaneth investigation in Canada.

There were two key documents in the box. The first concerned a secret meeting on March 2, 1935, between Zaneth and a special agent of the Internal Revenue Service, G. F. Fletcher. Also present were Zaneth's commanding officer and the U.S. Consul in Montreal. Three weeks later, probably unknown to the RCMP, there was a second meeting. The U.S. Consul, accompanied by two IRS agents, met Sam Bronfman and his lawyer. The U.S. documents filled in the blanks, left by Canadian documents.

A picture emerged that showed that Bronfman, his brothers, and his companies, in cooperation with the respectable Bank of Montreal, had created a pioneering money-laundering scheme. American gangsters had simply bought money orders at local banks with cash, usually payable to a "John Norton." When the Bank of Montreal received a money order, check, or telegraphic transfer to "John Norton," it automatically deposited the money in the account of Atlas Shipping.

Connections. Neither set of documents told the complete story. I needed both the American and Canadian files.

More connections

The matrix and the nexus

When we add the computer—the Internet—we turn the old term of the research mosaic into the matrix. It's not just a term borrowed from the recent movie about a computer-generated world that appears real. Librarians and researchers have been using the term "research matrix" and "linkage of information" for years.

A nexus is a bond, a link, and a connection.

The commercial database, Lexis-Nexis, markets itself on this idea. Its main customers are lawyers, so the first word is based on the Latin for law, *lex*, with nexus, the idea of connectiveness.

In the Common Law system used in the United States, Canada, Great Britain, and Australia, law interpreted by judges—precedents—are important. Therefore, it is crucial for lawyers to find precedents on the cases they are handling. It's faster and easier (but a lot more expensive) to do it on a computer than to plod through dusty law books.

Tree structure and hypertext

The most common way data is presented on a Web site is by using what's been known for years in the computer world as *tree structure*.

It is the same structure as the directory of files on your computer. There is an initial or *root* directory, and then branches leading to directories and subdirectories, like the trunk and branches of a tree.

It's most likely, in the beginning, that you will follow a series of tree structured menus to find what you want. On a Web page, quite often, as you go further into a site, you are actually following a tree structure defined by the site creator.

The Web adds one more advantage: *hypertext* links. Hypertext is an information retrieval system that lets you jump right away to a related subject—but you don't choose the links, the page creator does. Click on those words and you jump to a new page, perhaps half way around the world, which may or may not have the information you are seeking. That

Web page may have links yet to other another page—or you could find yourself at a dead end.

The most common acronyms you see on the Web, after www, are http and html. Http means *hypertext transfer protocol;* html means *hypertext markup language.*

Hypertext is also found in other multimedia systems and in some text-retrieval databases.

When Tim Berners-Lee was designing the nascent World Wide Web at CERN, the particle physics laboratory in Geneva, Switzerland, he was looking for a system to join the various aspects of research, people, their experiments, and machines. Hypertext was the answer. He also wanted to build in external links to other researchers. The external hypertext links, Berners-Lee says, "were the difference between imprisonment and freedom, dark and light."

Hypertext existed before Berners-Lee proposed the Web in March 1989. It can be traced all the way back to a now famous article by Vannevar Bush in the *Atlantic Monthly* in 1945. The article, "As We May Think," was about a device called memex that would increase human access to information. The article inspired many of the pioneers in the computer and information world.

Among them was a futurist named Ted Nelson who, in a 1965 article, "Literary Machines," foresaw material written in a nonlinear, nonsequential format, which he called *hypertext*. At the Stanford Research Institute in Menlo Park, California, was an engineer named Doug Englehart, the man who invented the computer mouse. In the 1960s, Englehart also did research on how computers could exchange information, how people could work together better.

Both ideas were treated as science fiction, but like all good ideas, other innovators grabbed and made them real. Hypertext, the nexus of research, was born.

On the Web today, clicking on a link is as routine as turning on your computer and bringing up your browser. Hypertext links provide connections, sometimes unexpected connections that lead to new discoveries.

The Nexus is not just limited to the Web, however. A key researcher's tool, the text retrieval or free-form database, often also allows you the user to create hypertext links within your notes, which I will discuss later in this book. So that you the researcher can make notes, and then create your own links within the database, so that you can jump from one to another.

The Internet also provides another way of creating connections, especially those essential people-to-people connections by using e-mail; e-mail mailing lists, commonly called listservs; and Usenet newsgroups.

Researchers make vital connections with e-mail and newsgroups.

Cyberspace

It's common these days to see maps of cyberspace, webs and patterns of lines crossing, crisscrossing, and recrossing this planet.

That's how it is with research. The world of research is a web, a web that reaches beyond just the Internet itself, often to places "not dreamed of in your philosophy."

As you embark on this journey, remember that there are connections between everything you do, connections among documents, among people, and, of course, the Web pages you visit and the people you meet online.

Chapter 5

Serendipity

I pulled out the map from my briefcase, a single sheet of 8½ x 14 legal-sized photocopy paper, a simple black and white lattice of squares, and placed it on the polished dining room table.

A week earlier I had highlighted one square in yellow.

"That's where Frank Zaneth's homestead was," I told my bed-and-breakfast host, Dorothy Murphy.

She shook her head and looked at the map, then pointed to three squares over from the yellow highlight. "That's where my family was," she said.

It's called *serendipity*, "the faculty of making happy and unexpected discoveries by accident," and it happens more often in research than you would expect. It's the connection you can't plan on, the happy accident that turns things around or gives you an expected gem of information.

There are actually two kinds of serendipity in research.

The first form of serendipity is pure, old-fashioned dumb luck (and your ability to recognize the opportunity, whether it knocks quietly at the back door or hits you in the face to wake you up).

The second, sometimes called *prepared browsing*, is based on the idea that fortune favors someone who is prepared. Your luck in this also may depend, as Dean Tudor has pointed out, on how well your left analytical and right creative brains work together. Intelligence analyst Sam Porteous says a good researcher has "insight and the capacity to ask the right questions."

If you have done your preliminary pure research well, if you know your stuff, you are then ready to make a leap when the opportunity presents itself. You make the connections we discussed in the last chapter, only these are surprises you like.

Serendipity and luck

In the summer of 1989, I planned a research trip to find out more about the life and character of Frank Zaneth. On a swing west, I went first to Chicago, then Winnipeg, and then Regina and Moose Jaw, Saskatchewan. Long before my trip I booked rooms at bed-and-breakfasts in each city.

Zaneth moved from Springfield, Massachusetts, to Moose Jaw in 1911 and in 1912 signed for a homestead south of the town. It was three and a half miles north of a salt lake and marsh now called Old Wives Lake. Zaneth had a quarter-section and a "preemption" on a neighboring quarter section. Just two and a half sections over was a ranch belonging to a man named Paddy Doyle, a recently retired veteran of the Royal Northwest Mounted Police.

My bed-and-breakfast host in Calgary was Paddy Doyle's granddaughter, Dorothy Murphy. Dorothy invited me to a family picnic that weekend to meet her mother, Kathleen McGinn, who was then 90 years old. Kathleen had been a teenager in the days just before World War I. And so on a hot summer afternoon, among her children and grandchildren, she told me about the land around Old Wives Lake. "We called it the Hills," she said. "The Hills are ranching country. All the homesteader had to do was build a little shack and have a couple of animals...it was mostly grassland, it wasn't fit for farming...My Dad used to say it was crazy to come up here to farm....It was damn hard, plowing, going up and down a hill..." She also told me one key thing that as a city boy I wouldn't have known, and that was not mentioned in the reference books about the time. The hill country where the Zaneth and Doyle homesteads were located was used almost exclusively for raising horses, not cattle.

Remember that I suggested that research is often like Joseph Campbell's heroic journey where "magical aid" appears. That's serendipity.

Sam Porteous tells how once a due-diligence investigation had raised red flags about a company. His investigator was in a library checking one of the executives, when someone looked over his shoulder and said, "If you're looking at that guy, you better talk to me."

"It turned out that this was the classic disgruntled employee," Porteous says, "But his information checked out." As luck would have it, the company being investigated was part of a consortium that was facing a major lawsuit—something that was not immediately apparent from the initial investigation.

Serendipity and "the right stuff"

To go beyond the obvious, the researcher has to have the "right stuff," that is, the "insight and the capacity to ask the right questions."

Sam Porteous recounts how one of his staff was working on a fraud case. The victim of the fraud, a company in Europe, wanted its money recovered. It was believed that one of the fraud artists was living somewhere in Canada.

The investigator/analyst thought the person was living in a small town, but the investigator was not sure if the man was there and if he had the money. The analyst had the idea of asking the local chamber of commerce for information on all the companies in town. The analyst then went through all the brochures sent to him by the chamber of commerce and on the back of one, the analyst recognized a phone number—that led to confirmation that the target was in the small town and was running a company worth $8 million.

Serendipity and prepared browsing

When you are using a search engine, you have to be prepared, ready for what librarians and researchers called prepared browsing, which is why the name Web browser is so appropriate.

"You start with something that a search engine, whether it be an AltaVista or something hierarchical, such as Yahoo, turns up," says Ted Anthony, a senior writer with the Associated Press. "It leads you to something that is interesting and sort of what you're looking for. But then down at the bottom you see something that is a related site. And you jump to that.

"You just keep jumping until you feel like you're getting a little bit closer to what you want. And all of a sudden you're at the exact place where you want to be.

"I am doing a story now on a town in Utah that has discovered an ancient aquifer that is 18,000 years old. They are trying to market the water. [So] I did a search for bottled water. I was just sort of following the links until up popped the International Bottled Water Association, which I didn't know existed. It certainly wasn't listed in any of the conventional sources that I initially tried. But there it was.

"It led me to this wonderful analyst who studies bottled-water marketing strategies. The interview with him really gave me a good sense as to what this town was dealing with. That was serendipity because I just did a random search for bottled water. I followed through some very amateur sites, and kept clicking, clicking toward what I felt was the direction I wanted to go. Until low and behold, up popped a source that was exactly what I needed."

"You create your own serendipity," Anthony concludes.

Links

Associated Press

wire.ap.org

Chapter 6

Rashomon

In a pouring rain, two men seek shelter in the crumbling ruins of an old temple. Both were witnesses in a murder trial and now, pausing after the verdict has been reached, they begin their own search for truth.

A third man joins them, to listen and to be the chorus or juror for that search. *Rashomon* is the name of the ruined temple in the fictional medieval Kyoto and the title of Japanese director Akira Kurosawa's film masterpiece. In the old meaning of the word, Rashomon is the work that marks the transition from apprentice and journeyman to master.

Rashomon was released in Japan in 1950 and worldwide in 1951. It won the 1951 Oscar for Best Foreign Film and the Golden Lion at the Venice Film Festival. The release of *Rashomon* is also said to mark the birth of modern Japanese film as the country recovered from World War II.

Rashomon has also entered our language as a word meaning both that uncertainty of truth and the wide spectrum of human perception. Rashomon is used in forensic science as the "Rashomon effect." References to Rashomon have appeared in works on the murder trial of O.J. Simpson, the chronicling of the Bill Clinton and Monica Lewinsky scandal, and in advanced training for business executives.

Research is a search for some sort of truth in an uncertain world. And the research should eventually be presented as some sort of truth, whether in an academic paper, a journalistic account, narrative, or, as in the case of Rashomon itself, a drama that is a search for truth. (Or is it?)

In *Rashomon,* there are a few known facts. We could create a one-paragraph news story, something like this:

> A local bandit, Tajomaru, has been convicted and executed for the murder of a samurai, Takehhiro. Testimony at the trial showed that the samurai and his wife, Masago, were traveling in the forest when the bandit attacked. The woman was sexually assaulted and her husband killed. A passing woodcutter found the body of the samurai. Police arrested the bandit riding the samurai's horse.

Like most routine news stories, this tells us very little.

Before the movie opens the bandit has been convicted of the rape and murder.

The first two men, a priest and a woodcutter, were both witnesses in the case. The third man, the commoner, listens as the two men describe four different versions of what happened.

The woodcutter says he was passing when he found first the woman's hat, some rope and amulet, then the samurai's body.

In his testimony, the bandit Tajomaru claims he saw the couple passing and was attracted to the woman. He fooled the husband so that he could be tied up. Then, the bandit claims, he had consensual sex with the woman. She then demanded the two men fight, and the bandit, in a heroic duel, killed the samurai.

Masago, the wife, also called as a witness, says that after the rape, her husband rejected her. She then fainted and awoke to find her husband dead at her side, killed with her own dagger.

A medium calls up the spirit of the samurai, who says the bandit did rape his wife. But he then says that the bandit invited the wife to leave with him. The ghostly samurai tells the court that his wife then told the bandit to kill her husband. The demand offends the honor, such as it is, of the bandit, who then rejects the wife. But the samurai then committed suicide, using the dagger, because of the shame. His ghost feels the knife being removed from the body.

The commoner knows there is something missing and challenges the woodcutter. This time, the woodcutter claims that the woman was raped, but the bandit then went on his knees to beg the woman to accompany him. She provokes the samurai and the bandit to fight. The bandit stabs the samurai with the woman's dagger.

But now the question: Is this "impartial witness," the woodcutter, telling the truth this time? Or was it he who stole the dagger?

As the story ends, the audience hears a baby crying. The commoner finds the child, steals its clothes, and leaves. The woodcutter, however, picks up the baby and decides to take it home. Raising the child will not be a burden, the woodcutter says—he already has six children.

The film is multilayered. It's not just about what happened in the forest. For example, it questions the relationship between the samurai and his wife. Was it a failing relationship or were they sacrificing themselves for each other? Both explanations could be plausible to a viewer. Is the woodcutter's second explanation the truth?

That is why *Rashomon* has fascinated audiences around the world for fifty years. If each of the characters told the truth, their truth, what then is reality?

The film is, in fact, based on a short story by author Ryunnosuke Akutagawa that has seven witnesses, with seven different versions of the events. Akutagawa gives his reader no guidance about the relative worth of each story.

Rashomon, with its theme that truth is relative, is a film every researcher should rent for an evening's enlightenment and entertainment.

On a more grounded level, any good cop or criminal lawyer will say that eyewitnesses to an event are not always reliable and that their accounts can often differ wildly.

So what then is the role of the researcher in an uncertain world?

Perhaps it is just that: to recognize the uncertainty. That brings us to the question of postmodernism.

Postmodernism

Postmodernism, which has been academic fashion for the past quarter century or so, is now facing a growing resentment, if not backlash, from the creative community, largely because too often strict postmodernism refuses to recognize the talent inherent in individual human beings. Postmodernism prefers to attribute all creativity to some sort of collective culture and sometimes views the creative artist as some kind of programmed robot.

The main reason for the backlash is postmodernism's attack on storytelling. In postmodernism, there is the belief that there should be no "grand narratives " or "master narratives." They want to knock down the author, who should not be an "authority."

I often hear graduates who work in creative fields (those not planning academic careers) say, "I am finally glad to be away from postmodern indoctrination" or "I am sick of seeing great writing dumped on by opinionated jerks who cannot write an intelligible word of English."

Postmodernism started out with good intentions, by recognizing the worth of other cultures. Anthropologists, themselves part of the Western imperial system, visited and lived with people of various cultures around the world. As their experience grew, there was recognition of the worth of these cultures. The French anthropologist Claude Lévi-Strauss was one of the earliest proponents of what is now known as *cultural relativism*. The roots of postmodernism can be seen as an early indication of globalization.

From that beginning came two more branches of postmodernism. Poststructuralism can be defined simply as saying there is no big picture, no large forces that direct human lives. Deconstruction seeks to tear down creative work of any kind to find underlying assumptions. The trouble with deconstruction is that it too often destructs instead of deconstructs.

Many postmodernists tend to believe that any narrative, any creative forming of a picture, is somehow oppressive and totalitarian. Postmodernists don't like endings. Endings are reactionary, the postmodernists say, closing off alternative possibilities and thus are, once again, somehow oppressive.

So what do the postmodernists present? Increasingly dense academic papers that are usually incomprehensible to anyone outside their subfield of endeavor. So students are taught to resist narratives in the belief that somehow, somewhere there is liberation, when the actual result is only confusion.

Postmodernism has not fared well outside the academy. It is a favorite target for conservatives (and some even say that the growth of conservatism is, in fact, a backlash against postmodernism). Many students in creative fields reject the teachings the day they graduate.

Rudyard Kipling (with any underlying assumptions he may have had at the height of the British Empire) anticipated cultural relativism in the famous lines of his poem in *The Neolithic Age:* "There are nine and sixty ways of constructing tribal lays. / And every single one of them is right!"

It could be argued then that the postmodernists say: "There are nine and sixty ways of constructing tribal lays. And every single one of them is wrong!"

That's what is wrong with postmodernism. Yet it is true that the viewpoint of our ancestors was often exclusionary.

In the past decades, hidden history has been revealed. We can now read history from the point of view of women and women of many classes, history as seen through the eyes of people of color. The long suppressed role of gay men and lesbians in all facets of humanity has been revealed.

The works of Joseph Campbell, which I refer to often in this book, show the magic and breadth and similarity of human mythology. (I would add that mythology is almost always a narrative.)

At the same time, too often some works of what is called "identity politics" are often just as exclusionary and oppressive as the grand narratives of the previous generations.

So, to borrow a phrase from the women's movement, it's time for the creative to take it all back!

Let's consider postmodernism a mutation. Like mutations in evolution, those that are harmful will eventually die off, while the more advantageous ones survive and become part of the gene pool.

So the creative researcher should embrace the idea of respect for other people (without going so far as taking over their stories, in appropriation of voice) and other cultures. That is an advantage. It will make your work richer.

The creative researcher should reject the silly notion that narrative is oppressive because it is the view of one person.

One reviewer put it this way: "Even a well-documented biography is inevitably an act of propaganda." That simply proves that there is good reason among the creative for the backlash.

Your creativity is valid. Joseph Campbell quotes the Vedas, "Truth is one, the sages speak it with many names."

I believe that as we move into the 21st century, every researcher must be aware of the variation of life on the planet. A favorite phrase at a recent narrative journalism conference at Boston University was, "It is a nuanced world." That's why *Rashomon* is considered a great motion picture.

The researcher must recognize that there are an infinite number of points of view—but do you, should you, tell them all?

Sometimes.

In *The Unredeemed Captive,* which won the National Book Award, author John Demos says there could be "an almost infinite number" of beginnings. He chooses five when writing the story of Eunice Williams, the daughter of a prominent Puritan preacher in Deerfield, Massachusetts. The family is kidnapped by the Iroquois from Deerfield in 1704 and taken to the Iroquois settlement at Kahnawake near Montreal.

Eunice, then 7, is left behind when the family is eventually freed. She becomes a member of the Iroquois First Nation.

Demos also offers three interpretations of the ending after the young girl dies, one from the Catholic point of view, one from the Protestant, and one from the Iroquoian.

So what's the solution?

Take a hike!

I believe in this new century that researchers—again, no matter what the output, nonfiction or fiction—should consider themselves as guides, marking the trail for their audience. It has been often said the Internet is so huge that it needs many guides.

I believe if anything will doom the extremes of postmodernism, it is, ironically, the Internet and the digital revolution. This is the age of information overload. There is so much information out there that the reader, even the scholar, needs coherence. In this age, the postmodernists may end up as the starship *Enterprise* did in the "Parallels" episode of *Star Trek: The Next Generation,* where the gates between universes open and the crew on the bridge was faced with 285,000 hails from 285,000 *Enterprises.*

So what kind of guide should the researcher be?

Let's go back a century. Many 19th century imperialist explorers usually never traveled light. They were often accompanied by their servants and usually traveled with tons of equipment and supplies. The explorers often shot anything in sight and cared little for the wilderness they were so set on taming. Even private pleasure trips were often grand expeditions.

After a century of hard lessons, today the ideal hiker is low-impact. The hiker is aware of how the journey can disturb an environment or a people and does his/her best to minimize that impact. You respect the world around you and at the same time try to learn as much as you can.

Every hike has a beginning and an end. Each hiker, every guide, every trip leader, is different and finds different things on the journey. A postmodernist hiker could wander forever in the wilderness and never leave, for there would be no goal, no end point to reach for. No guide.

The creative artist however, does reach for a goal, an end point. Any research project is a vision quest. The end point is the boon the hero seeks.

Practicality: preparing for the trail

So now let's get practical. How does the researcher proceed?

Your first step is to create your outer circle, to do pure research. The more wide ranging your initial general research, the greater the chance that you will find multiple points of view on a story.

An initial Web search is a good place to start, no matter what you are doing. In most cases the Web will give you a wide variety of initial sources to check out. The Web is not restricted to any one country, any one culture, any one point of view. While the information on the Web *must* be evaluated, for sites can present unreliable and one-sided information, the wide variety of information on the Net can, in most cases, ensure that you will not, at least in the beginning, be restricted to one approach, which is the one thing that postmodernists criticize our ancestors for.

That is the first circle of information. Spiral in a bit.

Then go offline and find the widest variety of published information, from newspapers to books to scholarly papers. That is the second level of our allegorical circle. From there you spiral inward again, checking out the references you find in the pages you have checked. You will find names: names of people interviewed in the news articles, academics cited in the scholarly papers, and authors of books in the bibliography.

Here you should always consider yourself an explorer. Barbara Tuchman wrote that during the research process, the historian must submit to the material, rather than imposing her own ideas on the material. If you submit, then the material will eventually supply its own answers for you.

You must always be aware that all your sources may be biased in one way or another. Memoirs can be sometimes self-serving. Interviews can be honest or they can be spin. Newspaper accounts are sometimes inaccurate and often missing key elements of the story.

So should you be objective?

That depends on what you mean by objective. Objectivity, in the journalistic sense, began when telegraphed wire stories were sent to newspapers with widely divergent political and editorial views. The straight recitation of the facts was supposed to fit into any newspaper.

In most cases, as the industry consolidated, as the party press dissolved a bit into a large urban daily serving a mass urban audience, objectivity came to mean telling all sides of the story. Quite often, however, what could be seen as objective was really what has been called "quote-counter-quote journalism," where the reporter believes quoting a number of divergent views tells the complete story.

The common answer to the impossibility of true objectivity has been to declare your biases. But then bias often exists in the eye of the reader. One person who honestly believes that he has presented an unbiased approach may be seen by others as biased and distorting the facts.

You also have to be aware of what media critics call "congenial truth," the often unspoken agreement between the reporter, the writer, the performer, and the audience, about what is reality. One group's congenial truth is another's distortion. ("They just don't get it.") Congenial truth exists everywhere, from journalism to academic papers to television drama. A true researcher tries to get beyond congenial truth.

As you work, trends, themes, and ideas will appear. If you remember that you are a guide, then you are free to take one road, knowing (and letting your reader know) that there are others.

It's never easy.

Alternate worlds

Here I have a brief word about the end product: your output.

The postmodernists forgot one thing when they attacked creativity and sought to abolish the narrative: They forgot the campfire. Our ancestors, first on the savannas of East Africa and then out of Africa in the caves that sheltered them from the ice ages, would gather around a campfire. Someone would tell a story. It might have been of the deeds of an ancestor, or of that day's hunt, or a shaman's recounting of his trip into the spirit world. Usually it was that man's story, that woman's story. On another night, someone else might tell another version of the story.

The one thing that keeps an audience gripped to the end of a good book, a hit movie, a great play, is not knowing what's going to happen. We don't know what is going to happen next in life, do we? That's why as the fire was stoked and the shadows against the cave wall danced to the flames; our ancestors were on the edge of their seats, wanting to know what happens next.

What of nonfiction, where the outcome is often known? One answer remains: traditional narrative structure.

Barbara Tuchman faced that problem when she wrote *The Guns of August*. We all know the German advance stalls at the Battle of the Marne and turns into the horrors of trench warfare. Tuchman says that if one writes nonfiction narrative in what today we would call "real time," the story builds naturally and the reader is carried along with it. Remember her premise, written with nuclear war looming, "there but for the grace of God go we." Her approach is that of a guide, a guide to the days that began World War I and changed everything.

To borrow from what Winston Churchill said about democracy, an author's point of view is not the greatest system, but just compare it with all the others.

Chapter 7

Time Factors

Time has always been the key to good research. A deadline focuses you, propels you along, keeps you working. The fact is that every project must (if it is to go beyond the research stage) be limited. That is even truer in the 21st century, as our society accelerates, as people find they have less and less time, as we all feel on the verge of burnout.

The time for a project can be measured in hours for a reporter, a television chase producer, or a business intelligence researcher. Research for a magazine article, a television documentary, and some books is often measured in weeks. Other projects—books, films, plays, and major academic research—can take years.

Jonathan Karp, an editor at Random House and a former reporter with the *Miami Herald* and *Providence Journal,* recommends, "Give yourself twice as long as you think you'll need to finish the project. This is a hard lesson for some journalists to learn, especially the ones used to writing fast and being in print regularly. But it is rare that a good book is written in only a year. You need time to pursue some blind alleys, read widely, and interview hard-to-reach sources."

On the other hand, there is increasing pressure to produce material much more quickly. This is especially true in the volatile and perishable high-tech field, where whether the subject is a technical manual or coverage of the ephemeral industry of silicon valleys, alleys, gulches, and glitches. These days work that is time-sensitive is often submitted to the publisher by e-mail, fax, or overnight delivery, chapter by chapter.

The next question to ask is: How passionate are you about the project?

The answer will also govern what you do. Your standard corporate beancounter or government bureaucrat is not going to put passion in the equation and find a cell in a spreadsheet for it. "Write the book because you want to write it," Jonathan Karp says. "Ultimately, those are the best books, and the ones that find an audience."

Money, money, money

As the old saying goes, "Time is money." Your budget often be a factor in—if not the key—to how much time you spend on research.

In a news organization, an investigative or enterprise project usually has a budget set at the project's outset. An academic research project may be governed by the amount of grant money available. For a personal project in any field, even a labor of love, the extra money available (and having to work for a living at the same time) will govern the time you spend on research.

One mistake many people make is rushing into a project without considering either the time or the money it costs. You should bean count yourself, whether you're a student, a reporter preparing to propose an enterprise project, a scholar beginning a major research project, or an author writing a novel or script that requires research. Be your own boss by asking, "Can I bring this project in on time and on budget?"

If you are figuring your research budget on a spreadsheet, or on the back of a napkin, and you are passionate about what you are doing, then you will start figuring a way to get it done. So as you create the budget, as you begin to manage the time, consider your own emotional involvement in the material you are researching. Something you feel worth doing is worth planning.

If you are passionate about a project, you will find the time—an hour here, a vacation there—to get the work done. Even for people who are paid to do research, such as journalists, writers, and librarians, it is not unusual to find that the best projects are done on their own time, and sometimes with their own money, carrying them until the project is far enough along to either present a substantial project proposal to management or to decide it is time to strike out on their own.

So how do you find the money?

- ❑ Ask your family for support. It may mean the spouse does extra work so you can take time off. It may mean your parents pay for part of a research trip. Don't forget that on a long project you will need the emotional support of family members as well.
- ❑ If the project is for your employer, you can usually get a small amount of research or seed money. A good senior editor or executive producer usually realizes that providing a small amount of money is an investment. Often it pays off. Sometimes it doesn't. (If your company doesn't do this sort of thing, and your long-term goal is working on major research projects, then it's time to update your resume.)
- ❑ If you are student, an academic, a freelance writer, and in some cases a staff writer, you should always look into the possibilities of grants, bursaries, or scholarships that are specifically aimed at the type of project you are doing. These research grants can come from government agencies, foundations, and similar organizations. Invest some time and your research skills and find out what is out there.
- ❑ People have tried to finance their research on their credit cards. Don't. If you are established in your career and can afford it, consider asking your bank for a line of credit, just as a small business would. Depending on the bank's policy, your assets, and your credit rating, you may be able to get an unsecured line of credit. Otherwise you may have to put up some form of collateral. The interest on a line of credit is usually a couple of points above prime, far lower than the interest on a credit card. You can use the line of credit for major purchases, such as equipment, airline tickets, and far-reaching travel. Less expensive research material or projects charged to your credit card should be paid off in full at the end of every month. If you can't do that, reduce the credit card debt and interest by using the line of credit to pay down the credit card. **Warning:** You should be disciplined in your approach to the line of credit, and (barring major emergencies) use the money only for the research project. Otherwise the size of the loan just grows, just with little return on it for your project.
- ❑ Set up a special savings account that is used just for your research project.

Using the calendar

Take a calendar and divide it up, working backward from your final deadline. Estimate the time you are going to spend on research. Then double it. Under most circumstances, your research will take twice as long as you estimate it will.

Set a deadline to complete the bulk of your research. Usually you will find it should be after the one-third mark of the project. Any later than halfway and you're probably in trouble and may not make your deadline. (And you will probably be doing research up until the last minute. We'll discuss details of this a little later.)

Then break down your research. Set a series of subdeadlines.

Remember you should do your outer circle, pure research, first. That prepares you for the next step. Set a deadline.

If you are going to travel, figure out where and when. You may rough out the dates but don't make a decision about specific places until after you've done your first general research, which may change your travel plans. Set a deadline.

Figure out what books you have to buy and buy them. Figure out other books you can borrow from the library. Set a deadline.

Figure out how you are going to contact people and why. Some people you may want to see in person, some you may want to telephone, and some you may want to e-mail. Set a deadline.

How you do the second phase of your research is up to you. You may want to work progressively, beginning at the start of your chronology and working through to the end. You may want to work logistically, working with what is available. Here you may be going on an outward circle and spiral, first using the resources in your local area, your local library, and local sources of information, and then expanding outward around the planet. Set a deadline.

The third phase is consolidation. By the third phase you should have an idea whether or not your thesis or premise is going to work. In the third phase you are paying more attention to your priorities. You should know what is important to the project. At this point, you start to concentrate on the essential information that you don't yet have. If finding a document, some data, or a person is a must for your project, then that is your first priority. This is the time when you drop the non-essential material or interviews that will not add anything to your research premise or thesis.

Two rules

Remember two key rules:

1. **Need/Nice.** The Need/Nice rule applies to every part of planning a research project. Ask yourself "Is it something I need to know or is it something that is nice to have?" Ask yourself a series of questions, then divide the questions into Need and Nice. That will determine how much time and money you spend on the question. If an item is high on your Need list, it is obviously worth spending more time and money tracking down. The Nice list is just what it sounds like: nice things to have. So if you can get the information on the Nice list while doing work on the Need list by all means do it, but don't waste time and effort.
2. **80/20.** Almost but not quite the same as the Need/Nice rule. In business, life, and, of course, in research you will find that 80 percent of the value comes from 20 percent of your activities. Eighty percent of the final project will be based on 20 percent of the research material you gather. You will likely spend 80 percent of your budget finding the key 20 percent of your material.

Stoking the subconscious

There is a great temptation, especially these days, to go nonstop. Our hurry-up, nonstop society is fueling this fascination with the myth of the all-night, pizza-and-Pepsi-driven computer programmer.

There's one problem with this myth: Unless you're between 18 and 20 years old, it doesn't work.

Taking a break lets your brain process what you've discovered. The subconscious is always working, finding the key connections among the material you have uncovered. It is often during long weekends, vacations, breaks, and dream time that you get your best ideas.

You should always take a break before you shift from the research to the application phase, to give the subconscious a chance to do its stuff. Coming back fresh will almost always make a better product.

Dividing and distilling

The biggest problem facing any researcher is the overwhelming amount of material that's available. The growing amount of material on the Net is adding to the problem.

Here, old-fashioned research skills are important. There's little difference between being overwhelmed by boxes of files stuffed full of papers and being overwhelmed by subdirectories stuffed with megabytes of files. You always have to keep your reader in mind as you research. As much as you might want to show off all the research you've done, your reader doesn't want to be overwhelmed any more than you do.

William Zinsser in *On Writing Well* recommends picking the two best examples out of all your research. Two, or at the most three, examples will usually tell all a reader needs to know. "Always start with too much material. Then give your reader just enough," Zinsser advises.

Business intelligence analyst Sam Porteous says that a researcher "collects a critical mass of information." Porteous notes that the business intelligence researcher has to always keep in mind that while due diligence investigation has a set format, the investigator also has to ask "what is most important to the client?" rather than throwing at the them all the data that is collected. (This applies to any audience.)

Knowing when to stop

You have to know when to stop your research. At one point it comes time to write, to let your readers know what you have discovered. There's always that extra file to look for, that last letter to the last contact to write, that last phone call to the last source. On the Net there are always new e-mail messages in your mailbox tomorrow morning.

Barbara Tuchman advises: "One must stop *before* one has finished; otherwise, one will never stop and never finish....I too feel compelled to follow every lead and learn everything about a subject, but fortunately I have an even more overwhelming compulsion to see my work in print. This is the only thing that saves me."

A deadline is the end of the road, the goal you're shooting for, so always keep it in mind. The problem for the academic, and for the author without a deadline, is that studies of any sort can go on indefinitely. One must finish, eventually, if only so one can be free to move on to the next project. Set a deadline for research long before the deadline for writing or delivery. End the bulk of research on that day no matter what. Journalists are always told that the time comes when "you go with what you've got." You can tie up loose ends, or check facts a second time, ask a few follow-up questions, or complete a long-postponed interview. Just don't do anything new. Ask yourself how much you are actually going to add to your project.

If something major happens, something that does change the focus, or the results, or your thesis, then reopen you research and ask for a deadline extension. If that's not possible, do what journalists call the "second-day story." Ask yourself if late material can be added in an appendix or afterword or published in a follow-up article or paper, rather than ripping out chapters already written and starting over.

The researcher sometimes has to make a decision to keep going. Author Martin O'Malley spent two years observing life at a major metropolitan hospital. Like many others, O'Malley used the metaphor of a circle for his research. The key was knowing when the circle was complete. So how did O'Malley know when to stop?

"You make an arbitrary decision," he says. "This came on one of the shifts in emergency when I was watching the doctor sewing up the arm of an accident victim. And while I was interviewing the emergency doctor, he asked me to reach for a number such and such suture. I walked across the room, I just opened the case and broke it and gave it to him. And I thought, 'Well I guess it's time to start writing.'"

Links

G. Wayne Miller

www.gwaynemiller.com

Wayne Miller's site with information on his books

Random House

www.randomhouse.com

www.randomhouse.com/atrandom/davidhalberstam/children.html

Jonathan Karp's profile of David Halberbstam

www.randomhouse.com/features/lastdon/profile.html

Jonathan Karp's delightful account of editing Mario Puzo

Part II
Tools

Chapter 8

Outlines and Chronologies

As you begin your research, as you cross the threshold to adventure, as you begin the outer circle or pure phase of your quest, the computer has given you some simple tools that will make your life a lot easier, help you focus, and keep track of where you are going.

For all research projects you should create an outline, and for 95 percent of research projects you should also create a chronology.

Computers have not only made these tasks easier, but today's software helps turn creating the outline and chronology into a thought and idea processing.

Outline before you start

A research project, as we have said, is like a journey, a trek, a quest. An outline, for any project, gives you a goal to shoot for, and thus helps organize your thoughts.

Teachers of dramatic writing often advise young playwrights or novelists to "know your ending." Often that ending changes as the project progresses, but that first ending provides the goal that lets you take the first step to completion of your project.

In a story, you're taking the reader on a step-by-step journey to the dramatic ending, whether that story is nonfiction or fiction. If you're writing an academic paper or an essay, you're doing the same thing—with one key exception. Your ending is in the abstract of your thesis rather than at the end. In a paper, you're often proving a case, taking the reader step by step through the evidence that supports your thesis, and, if you're honest, the evidence that's against the thesis as well.

In either case, it's a good idea to start with an outline.

Use your computer's outlining software not just to outline, but to focus your aims, as a thought processor and an organizer. Any outliner will do all that for you. From an outline you can organize your hard drive.

Remember the outline from high school? We all do and we all hated it. Jon Franklin has a whole chapter on outlines in his well-crafted book *Writing for Story*. He calls that high school outline the "English Teacher's Revenge."

If you handle it properly, an outline is really a first rough draft. How often have you had a great idea, written a few pages, and then run out of steam? Or had a great idea for a new development in your field and rushed to the word processor and then found the idea is going nowhere?

If you go to the outliner first (and almost every word processor comes with some sort of outliner) and write using it, you quickly find out where the holes are in your story, research project, or thesis. You quickly find that spot where you would stop writing.

Just let your thoughts flow. Create a few first-level categories to sketch out your project. Find out quickly where your ending is or what thesis you're trying to prove. Then fill in the blanks, using as many levels as you need (and your software permits).

Outlining software is the best answer to Franklin's English Teacher's Revenge. You don't have to write Roman numerals on a piece of foolscap. If outlining on paper is barrier to your thoughts, using the proper software enhances your creative thoughts.

If one category doesn't come immediately, leave it blank, with just the number created by the outlining software, and go on to the next. If something doesn't work, then stop (after all, you haven't invested too much effort yet) and analyze why it doesn't work. Now is the time to decide whether to go on with the project, to figure what exactly is wrong and what is right, and work to solve those problems. If it's just one of those bright ideas that goes nowhere, put this idea aside and go on to something that will work.

Each one of the steps in the outline is a step you're going to fill in with your research on the Internet, in the library, and in person.

Remember how easy it is to be overwhelmed by all those megabytes of information from around the globe on the Net. An outline will let you have some idea of the categories you're interested in. Then you can ignore (to the best of your ability) all those Web pointers that have nothing to do with your project. In the end, you'll find, as material builds up on your hard drive or home directory, that you will *have* to focus and ignore everything that doesn't match what you want.

Learn the outliner that comes with your word processor or computer. If it has keyboard commands, learn them, so that as your thoughts occur, you can write them down.

Once you've learned the outliner, get to work on your research project. If it's a story-based project, whether it's fiction or nonfiction, you have a germ of an idea: a situation, a character, a beginning. Open your outliner and enter those ideas. Now you have to know where you're going. So figure out that ending. The hero triumphs or is defeated. The nonfiction character is born, has a career, gets married, and eventually dies. Now you have a beginning and an end. Fill in the middle.

If it's an academic research project or anything else where you have to prove a case or a thesis, begin with that. A defense lawyer wants to prove that his client is not guilty, so that lawyer would then outline each of the steps in proving that case. A doctor wants to prove to colleagues that a new treatment is safe and effective. So the doctor outlines the proof, step by step, using the clinical cases that prove it. If you're a reporter and you're doing a story, you may have your lead and now you're going on the Net to get details. The outline gives you the blanks you, as a reporter, have to fill in to get the story.

Don't be afraid to change the outline. As you do your research, add the information to your outline. It's not cast in stone. If something doesn't work, drop it. If an idea works better somewhere else in the outline, move it to where it does work. That way the outline works for both those people who like to outline before they write and those people who think and build as they write. Adding material to the outline lets you see that project in a nutshell.

When all the research is done, or if you have reached your cut-off point or date, the project is half-written already. It's a dynamic, living thing, and it will change again before it's complete. An outline will keep you on the right road, or it might, as with road maps, help you find a more scenic route that helps you reach your destination in a more colorful way.

Finally, that outline is a selling tool, whether it's a book or a research (and grant) proposal. With a good outline, your project is there, in miniature. You can hand it to your agent, your publisher, your professor, or your boss, and get the go ahead.

Chronology

The chronology is an essential tool in almost all research. As with the outliner, the chronology helps the researcher focus and keep on track. The chronology raises key questions, not just the obvious when, but often the others: *who, what, where, why,* and *how*.

I used chronologies for both my books on gangster Rocco Perri and RCMP investigator Frank Zaneth. Often events overlapped. Characters were appearing in different places and in different events. The chronology helped clarify the big picture, show gaps in research, and create a timeline for a number of cases by adding historic background, and it helped me plan the writing.

I've included an excerpt from the chronology for my book *Undercover* that covers just a few months in Frank Zaneth's life in 1930. It covers seven different criminal investigations plus one key event in his personal life. Those events were, in the final book, related in four different chapters, following specific cases.

Investigative producer Harvey Cashore says that without a system of organizing, a journalist, or any researcher, is lost. He starts with the basics, the pure research, before making the first phone call.

"The heart, the backbone, of investigative journalism is the chronology," Cashore says. "Investigative journalists who don't develop a chronology are lost. It's simple, but it's incredibly effective. You put in all kinds of dates. Then I put in little headlines, 'report on Mr. X,' with notes such as 'see full report August, 1995,' with a note in my files where to get it.

"Before long not only is your story written, but you begin to see gaps in your story. That's when it begins to get exciting, because now you know what is missing from the public record. You know what doesn't add up and you have a great story."

Zaneth chronology

1930

1930 Zaneth's wife committed to Italian mental hospital. Zaneth investigating Macedonian/Bulgarian immigration racket.

Jan. 2, 1930 Veitch goes to Kingston to get Wise; Wise "talks in circles" to Zaneth and Griffith.

Jan. 4, 1930 Case postponed; Wise makes first statement to Zaneth on return to Kingston Pen (another hint Ballard was incompetent see notes).

Jan. 6, 1930 Zaneth makes a buy in Hamilton.

Jan. 7, 1930 Webster confirms Ballard did not call right witnesses; Zaneth analyses Wise and finds him wanting.

Jan. 8, 1930 Q Curwood shows up at O division HQ; while Zaneth is chasing the red herrings that Wise left him.

Jan. 16, 1930 Zaneth explains to Ballard, simply, why Bassi is innocent.

Feb. 7, 1930 Zaneth has another fruitless meeting with Ballard.

Feb. 12, 1930 Spectator reporter talks to RCMP about Perri using planes to drop drugs.

Feb. 15, 1930 Zaneth arrives in Meridian, N.Y.

Feb. Zaneth in New York (Roma).

Feb. Zaneth in Newark (Roma).

Feb. 17, 1930 U.S. Customs seize narcotics from *SS Majestic*: see list in Jacob Bloom intelligence file

Feb. 18, 1930 Key shipment of heroin arrives in New York on *SS Majestic* (Brecher).

Feb. 19, 1930 Zaneth back in New York.

Feb. 21, 1930 Zaneth in Maspeth, N.Y. and NYC.

Feb. 22, 1930 Zaneth goes on a NY patrol.

Feb. 23, 1930 Zaneth returns to Toronto.

Feb. 27, 1930 Zaneth meets Mrs. Frada.

Feb. 28, 1930 Zaneth in Oakville, interviews Blackhurst about drug smuggling from Middle East to Canada.

March 1930 Castellamare war begins. RCMP begins Bobcaygen bootlegger operation. Charles Feigenbaum first meets Pincus Brecher.

March 4, 1930 McKenzie King introduces Canada Export Act prohibiting export of booze to countries with Prohibition; U.S. Customs seize drugs from Ile de France: see list in Jacob Bloom intelligence file.

March 12, 1930 Zaneth is tipped that Perri uses coal bunkers at Stelco for smuggling drugs; while in Hamilton he meets with Ballard re witnesses for the Masi case.

March 14, 1930 Jacob Bloom arrested in Southampton.

❑❑❑

You can create a chronology in several ways:

- ❑ You can create a simple chronology in a word processor and manually enter each date. That is how I created the chronology for Frank Zaneth.
- ❑ You can use an outliner and use outline levels for year, month, and day.
- ❑ You can enter a chronology in a spreadsheet, using a program such as **Microsoft Excel**. The spreadsheet will allow you to enter the dates in any order and then you can automatically sort the date column and the spreadsheet will put everything in chronological order.

Completing an initial outline and starting a chronology is the first step in your initial research.

Chapter 9

Tracking Characters

In journalism, biography, and narrative history, finding the essence of a character, chronicling the character, is often the difference between success and failure. In fiction and drama (for both the writer and the actor), creating a believable, living character is what it's all about.

This is a chapter about the tools you can use to create that character, whether nonfiction or fiction. The computer can help you ask a series of questions, questions to yourself about the character as well as questions for an interview both with and about a character in academic, journalistic or narrative nonfiction.

For fiction and dramatic writers, the same questions and ideas can help you create the background research that produces more believable, richer characters. As the actors say, "There are no small roles, only small actors." A good nonfiction researcher tracks every character for one simple reason: You'll never know when or where they're going to show up.

Character tracking is one area where a free-form database will help you. If you create a database of characters, then you should include the character sketch or outline in the database and then search for a name.

If you prefer, you can use one of a number of story structure creation software aids, marketed mainly for fiction and drama but which can also be useful as a guide for nonfiction, real-life characters.

The essence of character

Often the public face of a character is very different from the private life, which is one reason we are all fascinated by the tell-all biography, the discoveries in private papers, or that suddenly revealing television interview.

The first person I wrote about successfully was Kathleen Blake "Kit" Watkins (later know as "Kit" Coleman after her third marriage in 1899). In 1898, Kit became the first woman in history officially accredited as a war correspondent, when she received a war pass from the U.S. War Department to cover the Spanish American War.

For 20 years, Kit wrote a column for the *Toronto Mail* (later *The Mail and Empire*). Kit was a single parent—a challenge for a woman in the 1890s. Although Kit often wrote about her life and her two children, there was much that remained a mystery.

Kit's relatives gave me access to the few remaining private papers, which provided clues. Other elements came from what could be called old-fashioned detective work. For example, I found the year her marriage broke up by checking old city directories and discovering when Kit and her second husband, Edward Watkins, began living apart.

In those precomputer days, I recorded every column and news story she wrote on a white file card. I recorded on a pink file card the addresses of major characters.

I went to Ireland to search for Kit's roots. In Galway, I was able to find out more about her family, through her uncle, Father Thomas Burke, who was a famous Catholic orator in the mid-nineteenth century. Two priests at St. Mary's Priory in Tallaght had researched Burke's family. With that information, I revised a genealogical request I had previously filed with the Genealogical Office in Dublin.

The result was a surprise. Kit always claimed she had been born in 1864. The research showed she was born in 1856, and that she had a previously unknown and possibly arranged marriage to an older man that had lasted from 1876 to 1883. When Kathleen Willis (born Ferguson) arrived in Canada, she cut eight years off her age.

Paper and people

Jerome Loving of the Department of English at Texas A&M grapples with the essence of character in long, scholarly biographies, such as his recent book *Walt Whitman: The Song of Himself.*

"How did I get to the essence of the character?" Loving says. "I think a biographer lives with his subject in a kind of relationship of a doppelganger....you choose someone that you really think a lot of. You think you know the person.

"I don't know of a more thorough exposure to another personality. And I don't think you could have this in a living person, because you wouldn't have access to all these private papers and things, and letters and so on, and private diaries. I don't know how you could be more intimate with another living breathing thing even though he's not now living or breathing.

"What I came to discover about Whitman's character...was that he really felt life was like nature itself. He was a part of nature and flowing with it. So death was just part of the game, the game of life. He decided he was stoic near the end, but it didn't start out that way. And I hadn't quite realized that when I taught him for years.

As for narrowing the focus of a biography, Loving notes that "you have to know what to leave out...because two-volume or multivolume biographies don't sell."

Time constraints are also critical. "You have to put limits on what you're going to do...you can't read every book from cover to cover."

But Loving doesn't see a wealth of material as a problem. "There is not enough material as far as [the researcher] is concerned...if it's a labor of love...you want all the material you can [find]."

For other stories, there is not the vast amount of paper that there would be for famous poets and authors. For journalist Martin O'Malley, being there was key for his biography of troubled hockey player Brian "Spinner" Spencer.

O'Malley had first written about Brian Spencer when Spencer was a rookie called up for a game at Toronto's Maple Leaf Gardens. Spencer's father, living near Prince George, in the interior of British Columbia, wanted to watch the game. But the television network switched coverage to another game and the older Spencer got in a truck with a gun and went down to Prince George. There he held the television station hostage and ordered them to put his son's game on. The RCMP responded. Spencer's father shot at the RCMP. The police shot back; they killed him. "Brian was informed of this between the second and third period," O'Malleyrecalls. The following September, O'Malley wrote a magazine profile of the Maple Leaf rookie. Years later in the mid-1980s, O'Malley picked up the newspaper one day and saw a new story about Spencer, long gone from hockey and living in Florida. He had been charged with murder.

"I just thought I was going to do another magazine piece, but it very quickly became a full-fledged book," O'Malley says. "I commuted to Florida over the course of six to nine months. I attended the trial. I also went to his hometown. I talked to his friends, lived with his friends, covered the murder trial, and wrote the book."

According to O'Malley, trials are a writer's delight: "You have lawyers for both sides presenting arguments....It unfolds right in front of you." Having firsthand access to his subject's friends and acquaintances was also invaluable. "The leads from the people attending the trial are especially good...the access provides intimate stuff."

Spencer was found not guilty of murder and planned to go on a publicity tour for the book, which was called *Gross Misconduct*.

But just after O'Malley finished his book, Brian Spencer was gunned down in West Palm Beach, the victim of a random shooting. "I chose to just do an epilogue. I didn't rewrite the whole book," says O'Malley. "The last chapter deals with Brian's own murder."

Character, content, and contact tracking

O'Malley began his reporting career in the 1960s, the age of smoke-filled newsrooms and clacking typewriters. For his books, including *Gross Misconduct*, O'Malley says he used alphabetically ordered manila folders.

"A - B - C, I'll just keep dropping it in," he says. "There could be interviews. There could be clippings. I can make it easy. It's all geared to making it as easy as possible at the writing stage. So I can just pull out exactly what I need. Sometimes it's just awful when you're trying to write and you just can't find a vital piece of information stuck under the yellow pages or something. So it's really important to organize."

As I said, the computer can make finding that vital piece of information a lot easier.

For character tracking, a good database is a key tool, one that can help you find information in seconds.

Investigative producer Harvey Cashore makes a distinction between information and character. "You have to focus on getting that information, knowing you're going to get that great story in the end and the characters are going to fall into place."

Cashore still uses an old DOS database called **Q & A** for all his investigative projects. He enters every contact in a database he designed himself. Every source goes into the database, in structured fields for name, phone number, comments, and questions. Cashore says he deliberately added one mandatory field.

"I can't enter a source," he says, "without putting in a proper story assignment. It might be John Smith but I can't put him in without putting in the story. Otherwise sources get lost. Then I can call up all the sources for that story." If a source is involved in two unrelated stories, both stories are entered.

"Every name I ever come across on a story I am researching goes into the database, in its own special file," Cashore says. "It will always be there. I now have 5,000 names in the database I've built up over the years. I don't know if a name is going to be important. Then I have a field that I call comments and it could be 'see reference to him in court document, August '99.' Then I enter questions, such as 'Ask him about the psychiatric report.'"

For every bit of information Cashore also creates a to-do list. "By the time I've finished reading a document I have about 25 sources listed, about 25 to-dos, and then I develop a chronology and...file it in the database."

Where Cashore uses Q & A, I use a free-form database called **askSam**, which I'll talk about in detail a little later. My database of story contacts going back 15 years contains more than 1,000 entries, with standard address fields, plus keywords, a story entry, and a large field for notes (what Cashore calls comments).

The beauty of the free-form database is its flexibility, the combination of structured fields and extensive unstructured notes. You can use a preformatted address template for a contact file, or create fields for characters, most of whom are long dead.

Mark Kramer, writer-in-residence and professor of journalism at Boston University, uses the academic word processor **Nota Bene**. Kramer, who teaches literary journalism and who "immerses" himself in his subject's world takes "elaborate notes" as he works. Then he says, "I read the notes and come up with 100 topics [for example in his book *Invasive Procedures: A Year in the World of Two Surgeons*]: surgeons, drugs, love of tools, hidden emotions, outside scenes. I start filling them in and pretty soon the material will tell me what will fit in my topic list.'"

The character sketch or outline

You probably remember the character sketch from high school. As with the outline, the computer has made the character sketch or character outline a much easier tool that helps you as you do your research.

Lagos Egri, author of *The Art of Dramatic Writing*, created the character outline in 1946, and it has been a favorite of dramatic writers for 50 years.

The character outline, or "bone structure" as Egri called it, has also been adopted by nonfiction writers as a way of asking the same questions about the character of living people as it has to spark the imagination of dramatic writers.

Egri noted that all characters are a mass of contradictions. For the dramatist, it is the conflicts caused by internal and external contradictions that make a character real. The bone structure helps focus the writer on those contradictions.

Egri divided the outline or bone structure into three general areas: physiology, or a physical description of a character; sociology, or the community and social background to the character; and psychology.

Physiology includes such things as height, weight, and appearance; sociology includes class, occupation, education, religion, and reading; psychology includes ambitions, temperaments, attitudes, complexes, sex life, and imagination.

You can create your own outline or adopt Ergi's with as many or as few categories as you want, using either your word processor or a free-form database. The advantage of the free-form database is that you can create a template and if every one of the character categories becomes a field, then you have a ready-made, fill-in-the-blanks form that helps you know more about your character. What you are doing when you fill in those blanks is a sort of interview with both yourself and the character, asking what is important to your story.

If you're a journalist, a nonfiction author, or a scholar, you use the categories in the character outline or bone structure to ask more questions. If you're a dramatic or fiction writer, the character outline or bone structure gives you questions to ask in your background research and allows you to use it in the way Egri originally intended: to stimulate the creative imagination and add more to the core of a character. For an actor or director, filling in the blank spots in the outline helps create back-story and make a more rounded character.

Story structure software

A recent innovation is story structure software. Originally aimed at screenwriters, story structure software again asks questions the writer should answer. For the dramatic writer, once again it is the imagination that answers the question. For the narrative nonfiction writer, the same software can stimulate research.

The best known is the expensive (it's created for Hollywood, after all) **Dramatica Pro** from Screenplay Systems. Screenplay offers a second, stripped-down version, **Dramatica Writer's DreamKit**. A less-expensive alternative to Dramatica Pro is **Storybuilder** from Seven Valleys software.

Both Dramatica Pro and Storybuilder present character files. But Storybuilder's is closer to Egri's bone structure, asks many questions, and is certainly a better value than Dramatica. Storybuilder offers a series of categories and questions within those categories, while Dramatica's character sketching ability is limited and the light version, Writer's DreamKit, is limited to one catch-all "motivation."

Conclusion

To wrap up this chapter, let me emphasize once again that this is a book about research. The computer gives the researcher new tools to organize and to remind the researcher that it is all about asking questions. As all the researchers quoted in this chapter (all of whom are writing nonfiction) point out, the more you research, the more questions you will have. Software, whatever kind, simply makes the real questions easier to recognize.

Finally, once again, respect your reader. Even if you are using software built originally for dramatic purposes, if your project is nonfiction, do not make anything up and do not add anything you cannot verify.

Links

Texas A&M University
www.tamu.edu
Boston University
www.bu.edu
Nota Bene
www.notabene.com
Screenplay Systems
www.screenplay.com
Seven Valleys Software
www.svsoft.com

Chapter 10

Online or Offline? Use Both

Someone who knows the bush—a guide, hiker, or explorer—has the tools and experience to get where he wants to go, safely and in one piece, no matter where he is. He has fun doing it, even if he does not know the specific area he is exploring.

The Internet

The Internet is a sophisticated and challenging tool, but for a researcher, it is just one tool among many. You cannot ignore traditional libraries and archives, but you will find that those libraries and archives are now online. Depending on how well-organized and well-designed their Web sites are, you can save time, money, postage, and headaches by doing preliminary research from "the comfort of your own home," as an old commercial once said.

You cannot—yet—read their hard-copy holdings from the comfort of your home. You cannot ignore the advice of experts or the testimony of witnesses—but you may find some of their statements on the Internet.

At this still early stage, the Internet seems to be the best medium for volatile information and fast-changing data. E-mail is a great tool for the researcher. The e-mail explosion has created a new form of communication. The Net makes contact around the world cheap and easy, saving long distance and travel costs.

The starting line

Every year I give my journalism students an assignment. Find a starting point on the Internet (a Web site, an e-mail message) and then write a story, as if you had received the information from a person, a phone call, or a snail-mailed news release. The conclusion every year after this exercise is that the Internet is a good starting point, but only a starting point.

That's also the opinion of a highly experienced television producers. Sig Gerber says the Net gives a researcher the ability to check out an idea.

"It can't be pure speculation because someone has to approve it," he says. "You have to come with some fairly substantial facts, so where do you find those facts? The Internet has made it much easier; in the past, you had to put shoe leather into finding people to talk to.

"If you know how to put the question to the Internet, you can actually come up with fairly interesting and diversified information....Especially if it is a contentious story, you are bound to have people out there who want to tell their story, to voice their opinions.

"Once you're into your area of research, you can see if your premise holds with fairly concrete information. It is important to substantiate your premise.

"Once your premise is solid and you have enough to persuade whoever is going to make a decision, then comes the real hard work of finding the facts that substantiate the premise or [discovering] your premise is flawed and [won't] stand up to scrutiny."

Where does the Internet work for research?

- ❑ The Net keeps you current. You find out which topics people are discussing.
- ❑ You can identify experts or interesting angles in your field and find conferences about your subject.
- ❑ You are alerted to new developments, breaking news, and recent information in your field.
- ❑ You have easy and inexpensive access to some news archives (usually from the mid-1990s and later).
- ❑ You can narrow down a broad topic or expand a limited one.
- ❑ The Net is international. It broadens your horizons and exposes you to a wide range of voices on all topics.

- Your access to Web sites is almost limitless. You'll find personal Web sites for specific people, and topic Web sites created by hobbyists and enthusiasts. You can visit Web sites that offer divergent views on controversial issues or open the door to obscure subjects. There are also Web sits created by companies for e-commerce, public relations, and investor relations.
- You can use e-mail to verify information, as well as to pre-interview or follow up with sources.
- You can find links to paper sources in libraries and archives, or to hard copy of illustrations and graphics.
- The Internet is open 24 hours a day, 365 days a year, despite rain, sleet, snow, and sometimes earthquakes (depending on your service provider and the server at the location you're seeking).

Where does the Internet *not* work for research?

- You may have difficulty evaluating the material on the Net. The old adage, "garbage in, garbage out" still applies, although on the Net this problem is called the "noise to signal ratio."
- Confirming information obtained on the Net can be difficult because there is no paper trail.
- Books and magazines are still the best method for storing, most information in an easily accessible form. It is often difficult to collect, store, and collate all the material on one topic from many Web sites.
- Some of the information on the Internet comes to you in e-mail and newsgroups. It's easy to be swamped, and sorting out what is relevant takes time.
- The Internet is growing so quickly that it's almost impossible to keep up with the changes. The whole spectrum of available information by e-mail, newsgroups, and the World Wide Web can overwhelm the researcher. Search engines are often weeks, and sometimes months, behind in finding and cataloging sites.
- The older the information, the less likely it will be on the Web or on computer. Remember that the first Web sites began appearing in 1991 and 1992. In January 1993, there were 50 Web servers. By late 1994, with the release of Netscape, the number

of sites increased into the thousands. The first newspaper databases, run or hosted by commercial services such as Lexis-Nexis, were created in the late 1970s through the mid-1980s. Before that, everything exists only in hard copy.

In coming chapters you will see how researchers of all kinds have used the Internet, and when they can't have turned instead to more traditional sources of information.

Hard copy or electronic?

Some material may not be on the Web or the Internet, but may be available on the relatively expensive proprietary databases such as Lexis-Nexis, Dialog, or Dow Jones. You should look in proprietary databases for:

- ❑ Summaries and full-text articles from newspapers and magazines around the world since that organization went online (rare in the 1970s, more common in the late 1980s and into the 1990s).
- ❑ Summaries and full-details of recent legal cases (depending when online collection of that specific legal information began).
- ❑ Certain specialized technical and academic journals.
- ❑ Certain medical and scientific information.
- ❑ Certain government information and data, including patents.
- ❑ Detailed information on companies from Fortune 500 corporations to small businesses.

Finding material in proprietary databases takes skill and practice. If you are a student, it is quite likely that you can receive basic training and get some free access through a university library or through dedicated class or library terminals in certain professions such as journalism, law, and medicine.

Libraries in news organizations, law firms, and major corporations also have access to proprietory databases, but using them is often so expensive that searches are almost always restricted to company business and usually require a specific project or departmental budget number. To save time and money, the search is always done for you by a trained specialist researcher or librarian.

Public libraries also have access to information databases, some extensive, some limited. For free or for a fee, depending on what you are looking for and the library, a librarian will do a search for the information for you.

Once you have a lot of practice in deep Net searching or are trained at a university in a journalism, law, or library school, you have the option of doing your own search on a Web-linked proprietary database such as Lexis-Nexis. You can access Lexis-Nexis and search its news archives via the Web using a major credit card at the business home page. Nonsubscribers can search for one day or a week with prices (as of February 2000) starting at $24.

In late February 2000, Dow Jones announced a new partnership with Excite search engine to "develop a business portal designed primarily for the needs of small and midsize business Internet users" on a site will be called **work.com**. The other major commercial service, Dialog, is available at **dialogweb.com** but doesn't offer a Web-based search service to the small business or individual researcher at this time.

The current Web-based alternative to the proprietary database is the Northern Light search engine, which also has a pay-for-view service called *Special Collections*.

Citation searching

It is often cheaper to have the librarian run a *citation search*, which gives you a list of titles or abstracts. You can then get the hard copy of the article from the library you are in or through an interlibrary photocopy service. In certain cases, you can order a printout or disk copy of what you are looking for, but this is more expensive.

Libraries also have access to extensive collections of CD-ROMs that include bibliographies and indexes, such as newspapers, magazines, biographies, and academic dissertations, as well as extensive business and investment analyses.

The librarian is usually the person who searches the material for you—again, a trained professional is quicker at this in most cases—and it's the librarians job to help you out.

Some news organizations are also putting citation searches up on their Web sites. You can enter keywords and then get a list of stories on your chosen subject. Then it is up to you to decide to open an account, pay with credit card and get instant access to the article, or print out the citation list (or highlight, copy, and paste if the Web site won't let you print), then go to the library and look up the original.

One good site for citation searching is the Associated Press, which, at this writing, allows you to search its database for the past two years.

Hitting the books

Books and magazines are still the most efficient storage medium known. They are also a darned good retrieval system. As anyone who has looked at a computer screen for hours, knows it is hard on your eyes, your shoulders, and your back (no matter how old you are). You begin to miss things. Books are still the best medium for putting a lot of good information in one place with ease of retrieval (you open the book; you don't have to wait for it boot up). It's an open question whether or not the much-touted electronic e-book will ever succeed in the market place. So look for hard copy for:

- ❑ Extensive information in books and reports.
- ❑ Today's and this week's information in newspapers.
- ❑ Personal information in letters and diaries.

For years to come, researchers are going to be spending most of their time working with paper. Why should anyone spend time, effort, and money transferring to electronic format material that already exists in an easy storage-and-retrieval format that has worked well for centuries? Many books written in the pre-computer era were created by typewriter and hot-lead linotype, so no electronic copy ever existed. Under international copyright law, the author and heirs generally retain the rights until 50 years after the author's death, so there can be legal problems involved as well.

Well-known works, such as Shakespeare's plays and the King James Version of the Bible, have been converted to computer format and are available on inexpensive CD-ROMs. Other famous works from the past, now in public domain, are available on the Web through Project Gutenberg.

(Micro)film at 11

As paper becomes fragile (especially among documents), or too bulky to store (such as newspapers and magazines), or starts to fall apart (as in the case of books and magazines printed on acidic woodpulp-based paper), then some way has to be found to preserve the material.

Usually it is transferred to *microform*—either microfilm (long rolls of film) or microfiche (single sheets of film the size of a file card). Even newspapers that are available online and in databases such as Lexis-Nexis are still preserved on microfilm. A retrieval system will give you the text of the news article. Microfilm gives you a glance at everything: the layout, the pictures, the headline, the stories on either side of it, and the ads that surround it. Checking the microfilm will give you some sense of context for a story. So look for microform copies of:

- ❑ Newspapers.
- ❑ Magazines.
- ❑ Newsletters.
- ❑ Government and corporate documents.
- ❑ Rare and fragile books.
- ❑ Personal papers.
- ❑ Theses and dissertations.

The main drawback with any form of microform research is that it can be even more mind-numbing and give you more eye strain than staring at a computer screen. Most microforms are still printed on a film-sensitive paper and, depending on the library and its budget, it can sometimes be a messy and smelly business.

An alternative—if you have your own microform or can borrow one—is to use a commercial document processing company that scans microforms and turns that old film into computer data.

Only human

Human sources are often your best source of information. Although some scholars swear by the literature and look askance at journalists and writers who work the phones, it must always be remembered that academic literature is written by humans, not robots.

You may find human sources by finding Web sites, or catching a name in an e-mail message or newsgroup posting. That network of contacts will be invaluable to you once you contact them on a person-to-person basis. The scholarly community is a network of friends, colleagues, and contacts who often advise and point people in the right direction.

The personal interview is often your best source of information. See Chapter 21 for a discussion on the in-person and telephone interview and Chapter 22 for information on the e-mail interview.

The answer is both

Remember what I said at the beginning of this book. If you consider the adventure of research the equivalent of a computer game, then the Web, at the moment, covers just the first couple of levels. A lot of the real stuff is most often in the higher levels, off the Web.

That may be changing. As years pass, you will find the Web becoming a factor in higher and higher levels of the research adventure. A few years ago, the Web still largely restricted to "geekdom" and experiments. But now, cost-conscious governments are distributing more and more information on the Web. And some of it may soon be only available on the Web. In the academic world, the cost of printed and bound paper journals is skyrocketing, and so "the literature" is going on the Web, where it will stay.

Links

Lexis-Nexis
www.lexisnexis.com

Dow Jones
work.com
www.dowjones.com
www.djnar.com

Dialog
dialogweb.com

Northern Light
wwww.northernlight.com

Project Gutenberg
www.promo.net/pg/

Part III
Mostly Online

Chapter 11

Almost All You Need to Know About Internet Research

It is worth repeating that the Internet is not the same as it was when I started doing Net research in the days of UNIX and using command line instructions. Ten years from now the Net will be much different from today's Internet, but in some ways it will be the same. It may be that you won't be sitting at a desktop computer, but using a personal digital assistant, generations evolved from today's popular Palm, which has merged with your mobile phone and has more memory capacity than the computer you have now. Intelligent agents could scour the Net for you as you sleep and present you with updated data each morning over breakfast. But you'll still be using the Net for research.

Use everything

Use all the resources of the Internet:

- The World Wide Web.
- E-mail, including your own e-mail contacts and mailing lists.
- Newsgroups and Web forums.
- Live chats and instant messages where appropriate.
- Telnet—porting into another computer.
- FTP sites (some are not Web connected).
- Live streaming events using video and audio where appropriate.

Search engines

Search engines will remain the main gateways to information on the Internet, although not the only ones. Get to know a few search engines and choose the ones that work best for you. You should also keep up with how the search engine world is changing and try out new ones that come highly recommended.

You should choose four favorite search engines—one meta-search engine (that searches other search engines) and three regular search engines—that return good results for you. Learn them well. In most cases, that is all you will need.

That means going beyond just typing a few words in the dialog box on the opening screen:

- ❑ Use your meta-search engine first. I believe that a meta-search engine based on your personal computer is best for most researchers. It is likely that some of what you are seeking will show up in an initial run by a meta-search engine.
- ❑ *Always* learn how to use the search engine's advanced features. It will make your quest for information so much easier.
- ❑ Print out the help and FAQ (Frequently Asked Questions) pages for the four search engines you have chosen and learn all the tips and tricks for those engines. Keep those pages close to your desk as a manual. If the search engine changes its look, its user interface, and its search methods, as it will, perhaps frequently, then update your manual.
- ❑ Learn how to narrow your initial search if the search engine allows you to do that.
- ❑ Make sure each of the three regular search engines you use has different strengths that will enhance your search.
- ❑ Use specialized search engines that may help for specific projects.

Learn Boolean searching

For any kind of searching using a computer, you must understand the basis of the *Boolean search,* using *Boolean operators.*

"Learn Boolean and learn to do it at well," advises award-winning science fiction writer Robert J. Sawyer. "The Internet is teeming with material and you can find it really quickly with a proper Boolean search. It stuns me that people don't know how to do one."

The two basic Boolean operators are "AND," which helps you narrow a search, and "OR," which helps you widen a search. How to do a more detailed Boolean search is explained in Chapter 14.

Indexes and guide sites

As well as choosing four search engines that work best for you, you should also work with the best index site on the web, Yahoo!, and also look for sites that index your field of interest.

There are many guide sites for journalists; some are set up by working reporters and editors, others by journalism professors. You will also find general guide sites for academics, lawyer, doctors, and other professionals. If you are working in those fields, it is wise to find and bookmark the guide sites as starting points.

The second level of guide sites is aimed at one specific topic. Often enthusiasts and hobbyists create these sites. Many sites are great gateways to information and are kept up-to-date; others are created, posted, and then seldom updated. Personal guide sites are often reliable, because the enthusiast knows the subject, but I caution the researcher to evaluate each site carefully. *Find and bookmark guide sites for your project.*

E-mail: the killer application

It's not glamorous, and it's not the darling of Wall Street. It's neglected by Silicon Valley and every Silicon gulch on this planet, but e-mail is still the killer application on that keeps the Net alive. It was e-mail that made the Net what it was long before the Web came along.

E-mail is the researcher's best friend. E-mail lets you reach contacts, check information, and keep in touch with the world of your research.

Despite the glamour and attraction of the Web, e-mail services can only grow. One proof is that e-mail newsletters, alerts, and filters are valuable to people. Subscribers are willing to pay for valuable information, delivered in a timely way, by e-mail. So far, most people are not willing to pay for access to Web sites.

Find and subscribe to the most valuable e-mail lists, newsletters, and alert or filter services that will enhance your research.

Newsgroups and Web forums

Newsgroups (also sometimes called Usenet, based on the network that distributes the newsgroups) have also been around since the early days of the Net. While e-mail, like snail mail, comes directly to your mailbox, your Internet Service Provider (ISP) controls which newsgroups you receive, so a client of one ISP may receive more than the clients of another. Access to newsgroups is usually wide open on most ISPs, but may be restricted in some universities and corporate settings. Estimates of the number of actual active newsgroups range from 30,000 to 45,000, although some have little or no traffic or are inactive.

A recent survey and talks to my own students show that few people are aware of the value of newsgroups, because most are concentrating on the seemingly more glamorous Web. But newsgroups can be valuable for the researcher. Anyone can "drop in" at any moment and then drop out if the group isn't what he wants or if her question has been answered. Many of the smaller newsgroups are not overwhelmed with junk, and it is there a researcher can also find good sources of information.

A growing alternative to the traditional newsgroup is the Web forum, which is a similar-style discussion thread but based on a Web site and not sent out to the world as part of Usenet. Some e-mail lists and newsgroups are archived on Web sites as Web forums.

You should find and evaluate newsgroups and Web forums, and then join any that may be relevant to your research.

Chat, messages, FTP, Telnet, and more

Other resources on the Net are not used often for research, but can come in handy with some projects:

- **Chat** is a wide-open way of talking to other people, but usually isn't too useful for research. Chat, of course, is most popular in chat rooms where people want to meet other people for various reasons. It is useful in two ways: You could perhaps do a live interview with someone in the private corner of a chat room, or you might visit news and other sites that often sponsor live chat sessions with politicians, celebrities, and others in the news. You can join in the discussion or, in many cases, read an archived chat session later. There are two ways to chat:

- **IRC chat** is the traditional way of chatting on the Web. IRC stands for Internet Relay Chat and you need IRC software, which can be obtained for free or a low cost to participate in a channel.
- **Web chat** occurs on a Web site and you do not need an IRC client.

- **Instant Messaging** is relatively new to the Internet, but some people have used it as an alternative to live chat to send messages and questions. In addition, corporations are using sophisticated forms of instant communication for online meetings.
- **FTP** (File Transfer Protocol) was one of the earliest features of the Net. Today your Web browser does FTP for you whenever you download a file, and there are a number of shareware FTP clients available.
- **Telnet**, or logging into a remote computer, was once the only thing you could do on the Internet. Today, telnet is rare (unless you are managing a Web site when telnetting in is sometimes needed), but it still exists. While many libraries these days have Web front-ends for people who want to log in, some libraries still require that you telnet in. To do that you need telnet client software. Windows 95 came with a simple telnet client, so if you use a PC there is likely one called **telnet.exe** on your hard drive in the Windows subdirectory. You can also find more sophisticated telnet clients on the Web.
- **Streaming video and audio** is also useful to researchers. (It's called streaming because of the way the packets are sent over the net to give you the audio or video in real time rather than having to wait while it downloads to your hard drive and then plays). Many television and radio stations and networks stream both live and recorded video and audio on the Web. Depending on the site, the video and audio may be archived indefinitely. You can watch old newscasts for items that may be valuable for research. Radio is making a comeback on the Net. You can listen to live programming from around the world, in almost any language, using software such as Real Player. Recently, some companies have offered live audio or video Webcasts of key news conferences, annual meetings, and speeches by senior executives, any of which could be sources of information. The use of audio is not limited to big business. In September

1997, the science journal *Nature* published a paper on the discovery in Jiahu, Henan Province, China, of six 9,000-year-old flutes made from the hollow leg bone of a red-crowned crane. Included on *Nature's* Web site was an audio track of the one still-working flutes playing a Chinese folk song.

As for the future, who knows? Someone in Silicon Valley or in a small office somewhere else may even now, as you read this, be creating a new application that will spin the Internet into yet another direction.

Chapter 12

Taming a Search Engine

Search engines are like medieval barons, creating alliances (long term or temporary), trying to enhance their wealth by adding more territory, and eyeing their neighbors with some envy.

As I said a little earlier, your best approach is to find your favorite search engines and work with them, while being aware that things could change in a year. In 1997, AltaVista was the hottest search engine on the Net block; this year, 2000, it's Google, and next year, who knows?

Keep it simple

There is so much information out there that the best advice, as it has been for years, is *KISS: Keep It Simple Stupid*.

That means for a majority of your searches, a simple search will work and work quickly. I'll discuss all kinds of advanced searches in Chapter 13.

Personal favorites

Currently, I use the following search engines:

- **Copernic** is the meta-search engine that I use on a daily basis. In my opinion, it is the best of several meta-search engines that you download and use from your hard drive. It is not only

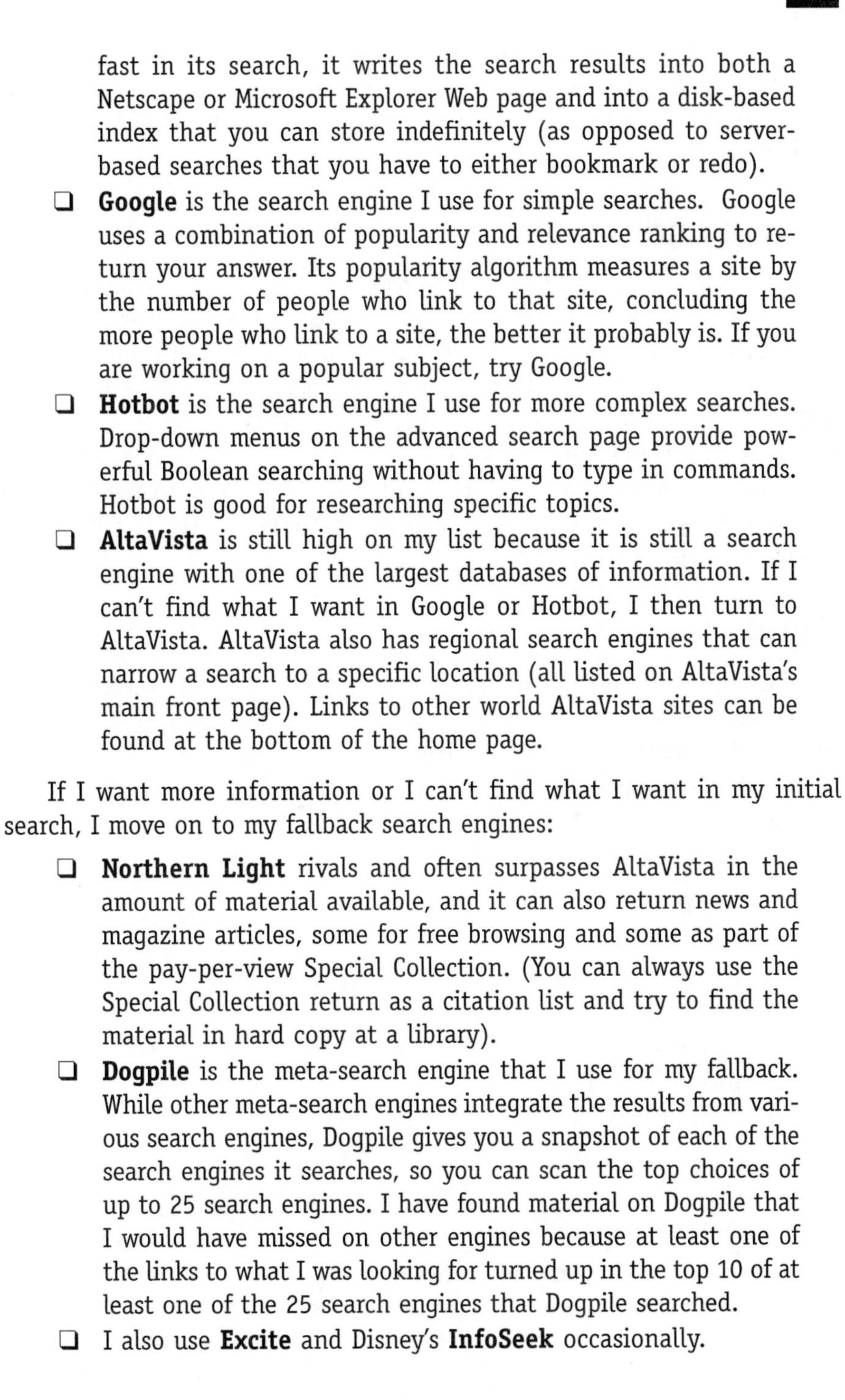

fast in its search, it writes the search results into both a Netscape or Microsoft Explorer Web page and into a disk-based index that you can store indefinitely (as opposed to server-based searches that you have to either bookmark or redo).

- **Google** is the search engine I use for simple searches. Google uses a combination of popularity and relevance ranking to return your answer. Its popularity algorithm measures a site by the number of people who link to that site, concluding the more people who link to a site, the better it probably is. If you are working on a popular subject, try Google.
- **Hotbot** is the search engine I use for more complex searches. Drop-down menus on the advanced search page provide powerful Boolean searching without having to type in commands. Hotbot is good for researching specific topics.
- **AltaVista** is still high on my list because it is still a search engine with one of the largest databases of information. If I can't find what I want in Google or Hotbot, I then turn to AltaVista. AltaVista also has regional search engines that can narrow a search to a specific location (all listed on AltaVista's main front page). Links to other world AltaVista sites can be found at the bottom of the home page.

If I want more information or I can't find what I want in my initial search, I move on to my fallback search engines:

- **Northern Light** rivals and often surpasses AltaVista in the amount of material available, and it can also return news and magazine articles, some for free browsing and some as part of the pay-per-view Special Collection. (You can always use the Special Collection return as a citation list and try to find the material in hard copy at a library).
- **Dogpile** is the meta-search engine that I use for my fallback. While other meta-search engines integrate the results from various search engines, Dogpile gives you a snapshot of each of the search engines it searches, so you can scan the top choices of up to 25 search engines. I have found material on Dogpile that I would have missed on other engines because at least one of the links to what I was looking for turned up in the top 10 of at least one of the 25 search engines that Dogpile searched.
- I also use **Excite** and Disney's **InfoSeek** occasionally.

Choose the search engines that work well for you and with which you are most comfortable. The more you practice with your chosen search engines, the better you become at searching, and the faster you will find most of what you are looking for.

Simple and popular

Simplicity. That's why, as I write this, Google is so successful. Google has a clean front page and often returns a good answer to a simple search query. If you put in one or more words, Google assumes the Boolean operator "AND" between the words. But you should note, that at this time Google is one of the few search engines that does not support the "OR" operator and that means you cannot widen your search.

Google's "I'm feeling lucky" button takes you directly to the first Web page it returns. For very simple searches and for specific sites, that usually works.

Drop!

Your next choice is those search engines that allow you to use a drop-down menu to be more specific. Hotbot is best, because it gives you a wider variety of choices on your initial search.

On the left-hand side of the Hotbot page, you are given choices the include:

- all the words ("AND" search).
- any of the words ("OR" search).
- exact phrase.
- the page title (in the bar at the top of the page, not the first headline).
- the person.
- links to this URL.
- Boolean search (design your own).

I've always found that Hotbot's choice for finding "the person" works. If the person is mentioned on the Web (and a lot of people are these days), Hotbot will find him or her.

Hotbot also allows you to narrow your initial search with a series of date and language choices. Using the date choice is never a good idea, because it is hard for the spider that does the real searching to discover

Figure 12-1. Simple search in Hotbot.

when the page was actually created. As for language, most Web sites are in English, but narrowing the search to English alone may actually eliminate some useful sites (many have multilingual pages and a link to a promising page may also link to a companion page in English).

If you want to narrow your search even further, Hotbot's advanced search page gives you not only the three initial drop-down menus, but up to four "word filters" that allow you to narrow the search even further by including or excluding words, a person, or a phrase.

Hotbot also allows you to use a drop-down menu to limit your search by region of the world or narrow your search to a specific domain.

Hotbot's corporate partner Lycos offers what Hotbot calls a simple search on its advanced search page, a drop-down menu that allows some Boolean choices.

Disney InfoSeek's advanced search page is so hidden, it's easy to miss. It's called "Search Options." Once you're there, it allows you a similar choice to Hotbot, by including or excluding a phrase, name, or word, as well as other menus that allow you to narrow the search by region or generic domain name.

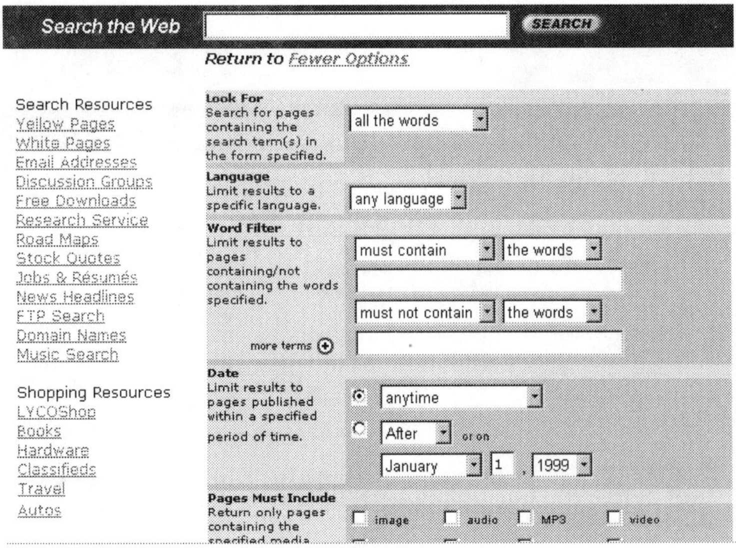

Figure 12-2. Advanced search engine in Hotbot.

Specialize

If you can't find what you want or if you find just too much on one of the popular portal search engines, try something specialized. There are about 2,000 specialized search engines on the Web, restricted by geographical location, subject matter, or language.

There are a number of easily accessible gateways to specialized search engines. **Beaucoup**, *www.beaucoup.com,* one of the most popular, is an example of how one person can produce a good site, since Beaucoup is a one-person band. Beaucoup was originally a good guide site to specialized search engines, indexes, and other guide sites. It has recently had some meta-search capability and will soon add a shopping page. Beaucoup has a number of categories, so it is worth checking to see if your topic is covered.

Guide sites

Choose the search engines that work well for you and with which you are the most comfortable. The more you practice with your chosen search engines, the better you become at searching and faster you will find most of what you are looking for. Here are some good ones to check:

- **Yahoo!** Yahoo! combines a multitude of subject indexes, researched and posted by human editors. Yahoo! is a good place to start to get a sense if there is easily accessible material on your research subject on the Net. Check Yahoo! to see if anything stands out in the subject index that the meta-search engine missed. Some critics say that Yahoo! is slower to add material because it uses human editors rather than robot spider/crawlers. But one area where Yahoo! excels is its **Full Coverage**, which responds well to breaking news, with its editors quickly putting up a list of appropriate sites. Yahoo! also has strong regional operations, so for some projects with international content or for links on news stories in countries outside the United States, don't just stick with Yahoo!'s main site, but try the others as well.
- **Direct Search.** This is a comprehensive and powerful library site, created and maintained by Gary Price of George Washington University. The site is "a growing compilation" of search interfaces of resources that Price says are not easily searchable from general search tools such as AltaVista, Hotbot, and Infoseek. While general search tools are essential for information retrieval of Internet materials, many users do not realize that large amounts of information are not searchable via these tools. Direct Search is a U.S.-based site, but it has strong Canadian and international content as well.
- **JournalismNet.** This Web page is a prime source of information for journalists who use the Internet to assist their reporting. This excellent index and link resource is created by Julian Sher, investigative producer for the CBC's *the fifth estate*. It's described by Sher as "a working journalist's guide to the Net": 80 different Web pages with more than 3,000 links designed to help journalists (and anyone else) find useful information fast. Journalists from around the world visit it more than 80,000 times a month.

News media sites are often good guide sites and provide links from a story to related sites. Daily news is quite often buried in the site after 24 hours but sections of a site labeled "In-Depth," "Special," or documentary site are likely both to provide the best links and stay visible on the site. Try **CNN.com, ABCNews.com., CBC.ca,** and **BBC.co.uk** first because broadcast sites with an international focus are likely to have a regularly updated overview of many issues. Newspaper sites are a good second choice, but unfortunately, many newspaper sites tend to bury their best in-depth coverage (like yesterday's newspaper). One exception is the *Chicago Tribune*, but even there it is sometimes hard to find (you have to go to the drop-down menu and click on "Web specials").

Ask your friends

Finally, you can tame search engines and find information by checking with people, friends, co-workers, and contacts. A recent poll by Angus Reid says that while most people reach sites from search engines or related links, a third found sites by word of mouth, followed then by reviews or mentions on TV or radio.

Links

Copernic
www.copernic.com

Google
www.google.com

Hotbot
www.hotbot.com

AltaVista
altavista.com
altavista.ca

Northern Light
www.northernlight.com

Dogpile
www.dogpile.com

Excite
www.excite.com

Infoseek
www.infoseek.go.com

Excite
wwww.excite.com

Beaucoup!
www.beaucoup.com
2,000+ search engines, indices, and directories.

Argos
argos.evansville.edu
A moderated and peer reviewed search engine specializing in the classics.

Evaluating Search Engine Models for Scholarly Purposes
www.dlib.org/dlib/december98/12beavers.html

Noesis: Philosophical Research Online
noesis.evansville.edu/bin/index.cgi_noesis
An experimental philosophical search engine.

Yahoo
www.yahoo.com
wwww.yahoo.ca

Yahoo Full Coverage
fullcoverage.yahoo.com/fc

Direct Search
gwis2.circ.gwu.edu/~gprice/direct.htm

Journalism Net
www.journalismnet.com

Search Engine Watch
wwww.searchenginewatch.com

Media sites

CNN
cnn.com

ABC News
wwww.abcnews.com

CBC
cbc.ca

BBC
bbc.co.uk

Chicago Tribune
www.chicagotribune.com

Chapter 13

The State of the Search Engine

As recently as 1994, the original search engines did nothing but search. Yahoo! came from students at Stanford, Lycos came from Carnegie-Mellon University; both aimed at helping researchers find material on the Internet.

Now the leading search engines are portals and leaders in the dotcom investment frenzy. Deals are made almost every day. Always remember that search engines are commercial operations, in business to make money, and thus the demands of the stockholders and the executives will have a direct effect on how the search engines serve you and answer your questions. As part of that commercial operation, there are also search engines and directories that exist behind the search engines researchers use, and you should know something about them and how they operate.

There are now questions about how much of the Web the search engines actually cover. A study of 11 search engines by Steve Lawrence and C. Lee Giles of the NEC Research Institute in Princeton, N.J, published in *Nature* in July 1999, indicated that the search engine the authors ranked the best, Northern Light, covered just 16 percent of the total Web, while Hotbot covered 11.3 percent and Yahoo just 7.4 percent.

If the overlapping coverage of the 11 search engines is combined, Lawrence and Giles estimate that the search engines cover about 42 percent of the Web. (Lawrence and Giles estimated the size of the Web, at the time of the study in February 1999, at about 800 million pages, with six terabytes of text data on about three million servers.)

How search engines work

That's why I suggested earlier that you pick one meta-search engine, three search engines, plus Yahoo! and any specialty sites to try and get as complete a picture as you can for your research efforts.

To use your four search engines well, you have to know how the search engines work and to be aware of new developments that could be skewing your results. Like old Julius Caesar's Gaul, a search engine is divided into three parts, the spider/crawler, the index, and the searching and ranking algorithm. The only thing you, the user, actually see is the last of the three, which determines what you actually see in answer to your search query.

The spider/crawler

The spider or crawler (sometimes called a trawler in Europe) is the computer that actually goes out and searches the Web. The spider goes to a Web site, reads all or part of the page (depending on how it's programmed), then follows all the internal and external links to find other pages. So it goes, onward and everywhere, 24 hours a day, seven days a week, until it has reached a good proportion of the now close to one billion pages on the Web. Then it starts all over again, revisiting the sites, to see what, if anything, has changed.

Another way that spiders find out about sites is through submission of the URL, usually from the creator of a site. Usually this is done through a "submit URL" button somewhere on the search engine site. The submitted site then goes into a job queue for the spider to check, sometimes in a few minutes or sometimes in a few days.

The index/catalog

The spider finds what it wants on a Web page, then writes to the second part of the system, an index or catalog that contains information on every site it has visited.

The searching and ranking algorithm

When you put a question to a search engine, the searching and ranking algorithm is the part of the software that you actually see in operation. You put in your questions, and this part of the system then goes to the index, finds the words you have entered, and then ranks the pages in accordance with its programming in an attempt to fulfill your answer.

So when you put in a question, you never get a "live" update. The search engine goes to that part of the index that answers your question, an answer that may be several months old.

What search engines look for

- **Page title** on a Web page appears in the bar at the top of the browser. The crawler looks at the title, assuming that it's important. Often the title is just that, a title, but sometimes it is a junk word put there by a Web site creator who is more techy than designer. Other titles are overly long, and these usually come from consultants who tell designers that the more words in a title, the better search crawlers like them. That, however, isn't necessarily so.
- **Meta-tags** are keywords and descriptive tags that appear at the top of the code that creates a Web page. The user doesn't see the meta-tags unless they use their browser to see the "document source." There are often three and sometimes more meta-tags on a page. For example, the tags could include:

  <META NAME="keywords" CONTENT=" keywords" >
  <META NAME="description" CONTENT="describe the site">
  <META NAME="PROGRAM" CONTENT="used to describe TV programs">

  When Lawrence and Giles did their study on accessing the Net, they found 123 distinct types of meta-tags that they note suggested "a lack of standardization in usage." Different search engines treat meta-tags differently. Hotbot and Infoseek place a high priority on meta-tags; Lycos ignores the tags.
- **Content.** Search engines also treat content differently. Most search engines give higher priority to words appearing high in the Web page, in headlines, and the first few paragraphs. So if, for instance, you were looking for Julius Caesar and there was a reference to Caesar low in one Web page, that site would rank low in the returns of most search engines.
- **Rejects.** Search engines are also programmed to reject certain pages. The spammers, mostly from porn sites, try to manipulate the crawlers. They spam in a number of ways, by repeating

words over and over in the meta-tags, by putting more words on the page in the same color as the background color so the viewer can't see them but the crawler can. The people who run search engines are wise to the racket and program the crawlers to reject those pages.

What search engines don't see

Search engines are best at tracking what are called "static Web pages," pages that don't change. There are several kinds of pages that search engines can't see, although you may find there are links to those pages from others:

- **Dynamic Web pages.** These pages are created automatically when you access the page, either from a CGI (Common Gateway Interface) script or dynamic database through a SQL (Structured Query Language) server. Many news sites use either CGI or SQL to create text pages. Most e-commerce sites use a form of SQL server to retrieve catalog copy and are not crawled by the spider. Databases with numerical or other data that require input from the user will also not be crawled by the spider.
- **PDF.** These pages, created in Adobe Portable Document Format, are not crawled by search engines. PDF files are most common on many government sites around the world (the United States and Canadian federal governments frequently use PDF files). You can read most PDF files directly from the Web if your browser has the proper plug-in, but spiders just pass them by.
- **Registration and password protected sites.** Spiders have no access to sites that require a password, such as the *New York Times* site, although I have seen links from other sites to internal *New York Times* pages, which show up on search engines. Clicking brings you to the front page if you are not registered. I have also found that the front pages of password protected sites, which should show up, rank low on a search engine's ranking and usually have to be found manually.
- **Excluded pages.** Sites can exclude themselves by using a "robots.txt" file in a tag line telling spiders to back off.

The hidden factors

There are two hidden factors that also affect how you see the results from a Web search: popularity ranking and paid placements. Search engine companies want people to come to their sites and use their services. They believe that by putting popular sites up top, they will get more customers. There are two types of popularity ranking:

- **Link popularity** is the system pioneered by Google that looks at the number of links to a given site.
- **Click popularity** is measured by the number of users who click on a link returned by a search engine. The more people who click on the link (whether or not they stay on it or are satisfied with the result), the higher that link ranks in a search engine return.

While popularity ranking may help the casual user, it can be a headache for a researcher who has to delve deeper.

Paid placements are controversial. They are another revenue steam for a search engine company, and so far the paid placement results appear in a separate box on a page. However, there are fears that eventually paid placements will appear in the general return from a search engine and not be identified as paid.

The powers behind the throne

The casual user may believe that the various popular search engines are in fierce competition with each other. But when it comes down to the silicon and software behind the search engine, there are a number of search engines that serve many others:

- **Inktomi** started out as a search engine based at the University of California at Berkeley. When it was spun off, Inktomi became the search engine computer that serves Hotbot, Excite@home, AOL search, Iwon, and Snap. The spider and indexing components of Inktomi are common to all its clients, but the ranking and return approach of each of the sites is a bit different, which is why you may get different results. On Inktomi's corporate site (*www.inktomi.com,* but you can't search there) the company says its search service powers 80 Web portals, including communications giants Ameritech, Bell South, British Telecom, and NTT (Nippon Telegraph and Telephone).

- **Direct Hit** is the company that provides click popularity rankings to Hotbot, Lycos, Looksmart, and Microsoft MSN. Its corporate site and search engine is at *www.directhit.com*. On the Web site, the company says "By analyzing the activity of millions of previous Internet searchers, Direct Hit provides dramatically more relevant results for your search request."
- **LookSmart** uses human editors to compile its directory of Web sites for its own search site and provides that data to search engines and other companies. It's at *www.looksmart.com*. On the site, LookSmart says it "currently provides its navigation products to leading Internet portals, ISPs, and Web sites including The Microsoft Network, Netscape Netcenter, Time Warner Inc., Excite@Home, Sony, British Telecom, US West, AltaVista, NetZero, and more than 370 ISPs."
- **Open Directory** uses volunteer human editors to compile results and catalog sites. It supplies data to Netscape Search, AltaVista, Hotbot, Lycos, and AOL search as well as the metasearch engines Dogpile and Savvy Search. It's at *dmoz.org*, where there is also a long list of the company's clients.
- **Real Names** works with AltaVista, Go, Google, MSN, Dogpile, and Looksmart, as well as the search function in Microsoft Internet Explorer 5.0. Real Names works by selling companies and even individuals (for $100 a year) a "subscription" to a keyword. Then, if a user on a search engine enters a keyword, either a generic word or a brand name, the subscriber's site comes up first in the Real Names search return. Real Names is at *www.realnames.com*. Both Microsoft and Network Solutions own shares in Real Name.

In addition to the main partnerships, there are secondary or backup partnerships between different search engines. AltaVista is in partnership with AskJeeves for its Ask AltaVista service; the MP3 search on Lycos is provided by FAST; secondary results on Netscape Search come from Google. MSN gets its prime results from LookSmart, backed up by AltaVista.

Alliances and corporate partnerships shift. AOL currently works with Inktomi and Open Directory; it used to be in partnership with Excite. GoTo, which primarily uses paid placements, once used WWWWorm. Now it uses Inktomi as backup to return nonpaid listings. In late June 2000, Yahoo! dropped Inktomi as its search engine and signed on with Google.

Fig 13-1. Real Names result in Google.

The Portals (Show me the money!)

Users get to search the Net for free, but someone has to pay for the computer hardware, the buildings, the programmers, the software, and the electricity bill. That's why most of the search engines are becoming portals, or gateways to the Net. The business focus of the search engine/portal is to sell "eyeballs" (the common Net media measurement slang) to advertisers. If your portal becomes the most popular gateway to the Internet, and users and their eyeballs keep coming back, then you can charge more money to advertisers and, unlike many Internet dotcoms, actually make a profit. Portals not only offer search services, but news wires, shopping, horoscopes, and free Web-based e-mail.

Convergence, the melding and merger of electronic media, is escalating the portal wars as media companies and telcos (telecommunications [formerly telephone] companies) join in. Disney, which owns ABC, also owns the Go.com portal site (which includes what used to be the InfoSeek search engine). NBC, part of General Electric, owns Snap. The merger deal between AOL and Time Warner is aimed at creating a major portal, although details have not been released. Even the august *Encyclopedia Britannica* has become a portal.

It's a strategy that is succeeding, at least so far. You only have to look at the ratings compiled by Media Metrix to see that the portals are the top sites on the Net. For the month of December 1999, Yahoo! was the most-visited site in their survey with 36,400,000 unique visitors. That's a lot of eyeballs and the reason behind Yahoo!'s financial success. In the same survey, the top sites by corporate ownership were:

1. AOL Network (ISP, network, some content, search engine)
2. Yahoo! Sites (Portal, index and search engine)

3. Microsoft Sites (software, MSN, search engine)
4. Lycos (2 search engines, portal)
5. Excite@Home (cable ISP, portal, search engine)

The actual search engine, the original draw to a portal site, is becoming a lower priority among some portals. That's why the search engine world changes so rapidly, and that's why there are more messages on research mailing lists about "stinky search engines." That's why in this book, I am talking about the basic principles of search engines, so you, the researcher, can adapt to changes in corporate ownership, the corporate mission, and search engine partnerships as they come along.

What search engines actually do

"The search engines don't index everything. If you think they do, well they don't," says Steve Lawrence of the NEC Research Institute. "Search engines tend to index different parts of the Web. Search engines don't necessarily update at consistent intervals, and it's hard to tell which one is updated most recently...If you're looking for some particular information, it's good to use several search engines."

The study by Lawrence and Giles showed that the average age of new documents on Northern Light was 141 days; the median (or middle rank) was 84 days. On AltaVista, the average age of a new document was 166 days and the median was 33 days; on Hotbot the average was 192 days and the median 51 days. For all documents in the survey, the average new document was 186 days old and the median was 57 days.

In the *Nature* paper, Lawrence and Giles expressed the fear that with growing use of popularity ranking, it might be increasingly difficult to find less popular high-quality pages.

"For a lot of inquiries the search engine gets, they match many, many pages. Nobody is going to look through a million pages or whatever. So it's probably a good idea to rank the pages by quality," Lawrence says, "The number of links to a site is one of the better ways of doing that."

The two researchers also note that "There may be a point beyond which [it] is not economical for [search engines] to improve their coverage or timeliness."

According to Lawrence and Giles, limited resources are a significant factor for search engines. "[Search engines] haven't that much money. There are competing things that search engines would like to spend money on...some applications [for example, portals, finance centers, and calendars] may be better advertising, and portals get a lot of their revenue from advertising...there is less economic incentive for search engines to satisfy less-popular queries."

Lawrence sees improvement in search engines' efficiency coming from two sources: computers' increased production rate to index original text and improved algorithms.

Meta-search engines also have some drawbacks, Lawrence says, including contractual agreements that may place limits on how they use the big search engines.

"There are limitations in their resources and meta search engines take up more band width resources. On the other hand, there are the client-based search engines, like Copernic and Bullseye, [that] can crawl all over the search engines...so they can be comprehensive and they can get as many hits as the user wants."

Another area where a researcher has to evaluate a meta-search engine is relevance ranking, Lawrence says. "There is the possibility that meta-search engines have better relevance tracking or worse relevance tracking. It could be better because, for example, in combining the best results in several searches. Or it could be worse because the meta-search engine doesn't know all of the details about the results of the original search engines.

"For example, there could be an inquiry to five search engines. Four of them return [helpful] results and one of them returns a whole bunch of irrelevant results. It's not necessarily easy for a meta-search engine to identify that, because they don't have the full text of all the pages in general. They're just going on the titles and the short summaries that the search engines provide. They can have problems in merging results of search engines."

Links

Media Metrix

www.mediametrix.com

Media Metrix is a ratings company for Web sites.

Top Ten ranking

www.mediametrix.com/TopRankings/TopRankings.html

NEC Research Institute

www.neci.nj.nec.com/neciwebsite/indexpage.html

Inktomi Corporation

www.inktomi.com

Direct

directhit.com

LookSmart

www.looksmart.com

ODP—Open Directory Project

dmoz.org

RealNames Corporation

web.realnames.com

GO Network

www.go.com

Chapter 14

Advanced Search Toolbox

The computer is nothing more than a hunk of silicon, wires, plastic, and metal, hardware that plays or runs software created by programmers who may or may not actually care about how you, the customer, use the millions of lines of code they have created.

This is just a way of saying again that the computer is a tool. Once research notes were scribbled on papyrus scraps. Now they are stored on a high-speed rotating disk also called a hard drive.

In this chapter, I'm going to give you a briefing on the computer tools for searching the World Wide Web, commercial databases, some library and archive retrieval systems, and your own notes in a free-form database.

Search basics

To find something on the World Wide Web, in commercial and proprietary databases, and in databases you create yourself, you have to understand the basics of word searching.

In these silicon days, everyone loosely uses the term *keywords*. That's why so many searches fail. To do a successful search you have to understand the basics of search words. Search words you should know include:

Controlled vocabulary (sometimes called "fixed vocabulary") words are the words you will find in a library catalog, whether the catalog is online or old-fashioned file cards. Professional librarians choose the categories and the words. Another form of controlled vocabulary is found in various indexes and bibliographies for various academic disciplines.

Keywords are often chosen by an author, editor, or publisher to describe an article or dissertation. They are usually listed either at the beginning or end of an article. Keywords can be entirely random and arbitrary if chosen by an author, or they can be a subset of controlled/fixed vocabulary. Some software can only search keywords, not full text, which again means a researcher could miss something. As I noted earler, on the Web, meta-tags act as keywords.

Full text means just that: A computer has searched and indexed every word in an article on a Web site or computer database. Commercial services include the huge proprietary databases such as Lexis-Nexis, Dialog, Dow Jones, and Westlaw for legal information, and news transcript services such as Burrelle's Information Services in the United States and Bowden's in Canada. The Northern Light search engine, often called the poor person's Lexis-Nexis, offers full text services through its Special Collections pages.

Stop words are words that a computer is programmed to ignore. Common stop words are "the," "of," or "in." A trick sometimes used by instructors teaching Web searching is to ask the student to do a search on the phrase from *Hamlet*, "To be or not to be." Depending on the search engine, the words by themselves usually come up with no hits.

Truncated words are shortened so there is a common spelling. For example, if you were searching for anything using the word *research* and, again depending on the search engine or database, typed in *research** (with the asterisk [*] as a wild card), the search engine would also look for words like *researcher* or *researching* and the plural *researchers* and *researches.* Some search engines automatically truncate specially indexed words. This is called stemming.

Boolean Operators include the words *and, or,* and *not*, and provide the basic syntax for any searching, whether on the Web, in a commercial database, or in a free-form or relational database on your own hard drive. **Boolean logic** lies at the heart of any computer. It is what makes the silicon chip work, so I will discuss it in detail.

One weird word

So how do you choose which word to ask?

Because each search on Dialog or Lexis-Nexis costs money, librarians, over the years, have found ways to make the most efficient word searches.

Ruth Von Fuchs, who taught me online search techniques at the University of Toronto's Faculty of Information Science in the early 1990s, calls it the "one weird word" approach.

She recommends starting off with the rarest word or phrase in a search. One example she uses in her course is "ozone layer." "Ozone" is a better choice than "layer." Layer could bring up recipes for three-layer cakes.

If you can't find the word or phrase you want, begin by writing a question to yourself. Von Fuchs advises a researcher to imagine writing an old-fashioned telegram, where every word costs extra.

One suggestion is to write the search terms underneath each other—and then eliminate the unnecessary words. The academic term for this is *concept analysis,* but most librarians say they are "listifying" it.

Types of searches

Just as there are different words you have to know, there are different types of searches:

Field searches are found in structured databases, such as flat file (the kind that is used for simple mailing lists) or relational databases; in databases that mix structured header fields ("author," "title," "subject," "source") with full text; and in free-form text retrieval databases that allow you to create fields, perhaps for names and addresses in a contact file.

If you have a multiple choice of fields, such as "author," "title," or "subject," choose the field best suited to your search. If you're doing a search on Ernest Hemingway, do you want books by Hemingway? The obvious choice is in the author field. Books about Hemingway? The obvious choice is the subject field.

Many Internet search engines allow you to do a field search, for example searching the Title field on a Web page.

Full text searches are just that. Your research source allows you to search almost every word (except the stop words).

Search methods

You will find in the world of research that most of your sources have various combinations of field and full text searches, using a variety of search methods.

Natural language searches

Natural language searches are hot in the Web world these days. Search engines purport to ease your searching by inviting you to type in a sentence: "Why do dogs bark?" "Why are computer chips made of silicon?" or "Who won the 1919 World Series?"—and then giving you an answer. Natural language searches are part of the marketing push, trying, not always successfully, to make it easy for the public to search the Web.

In reality, programmers are still hard at work on natural language algorithms. Those algorithms are similar to the icing on the cake; underneath, a natural language query is always translated by the computer into a more structured Boolean search.

The first natural language computer was actually designed way back in 1961 at the Massachusetts Institute of Technology and created so you could ask questions about baseball in plain English. What the computer did was first throw out the stop words and then turn the question into an equation. "Who won on the first of July?" became an order to list teams in the win column that played on July 1 of that year.

My advice with natural language searches is to try a couple and see if you get lucky. It is likely you will have to use one of the more traditional methods of searching.

Meet George Boole

To understand Boolean search, we must go back in time almost two centuries to England. A schoolteacher, mathematician, and logician named George Boole, a mathematical genius, lived from 1815 to 1864. As a teenager, Boole went to work as a schoolteacher to support his family. After writing a series of brilliant papers, he was appointed professor of mathematics at Queen's College, in Cork, Ireland, even though he had no university degree. Later he was rewarded with honorary degrees and medals.

One of the things Boole was interested in was looking for a way to use mathematical algebra to describe how logic might be applied to everyday events. Boole believed that the relationship between ideas or concepts could be described mathematically, but in plain English (or any other language). He proposed that questions that needed answers could be described in the terms of an equation, but written in English, using the word **AND** to narrow the concept and the word **OR** to widen the concept.

The words *OR, AND,* and *NOT* are the most common Boolean operators. Other Boolean operators are *LIKE, EXACTLY LIKE, EQUAL TO, LESS THAN,* and *GREATER THAN.*

Tip: It's a good idea to always put your Boolean operators in ALL CAPS. Some Web search engines actually want you to use all capitals. For the rest it doesn't matter, but putting your Boolean operators also helps your eye look at your "equation" and make changes more easily.

Boolean operators can also be traditional mathematical symbols **(+, -, =, <, >).** Almost every Web search engines uses + (*AND*) or – (*NOT*) as a common search standard.

You should note that on the Web, in many search engines the plus sign **(+)** has a dual role. It can be the symbolic equivalent of *AND*, but it is also a signal to the search engine that the word preceded by it must be retrieved.

Boolean searches can be used to ferret out numbers and dates as well as text on commercial information databases such as Dialog or Lexis-Nexis. Boolean searches are also used in relational and flat file databases and in free-form or text retrieval databases such as askSam.

So, for example, let's say you are looking for information on laws affecting the Internet. It's a huge topic. So you could do a Boolean search for **Internet AND law.** If you wanted to look at all the laws except those on pornography you could do **Internet AND law NOT pornography.** Note for this example, I am using Lexis-Nexis syntax. Search engines may be a bit different.

Let's take it a little narrower, by confining ourselves to the United States and Canada. So you could narrow it to:

Internet AND law NOT pornography
United States OR Canada

Because things are moving so fast, let's narrow the dates, so we would have something like this:

Internet AND law NOT pornography
United States OR Canada
GREATER THAN 1998

This means the computer is looking for information about the Internet and the law in the United States and Canada, excluding pornography, that was posted after the end of 1998.

You shouldn't make the search too narrow, because too many conditions could eliminate vital information. If a search comes up with nothing, delete your conditions one by one.

Many Web search teachers warn against using the **NOT** operator. In the example above, valuable information could be lost in an article that happens to use the word "pornography." On the other hand, sometimes the NOT operator is necessary. One of my students was once doing a search on "twins" and was overwhelmed with links. Then we decided to use the NOT operator and did a query on **twins NOT Minnesota**. That query, of course, eliminates the Minnesota Twins baseball team as well as any twins living in Minnesota, but it did narrow the search considerably and was more useful to the student.

You should note that these are simple examples and each software application, such as a free-form database, or search engine would have its own syntax for actually writing out a Boolean search or for using drop-down menus to make it easier.

Proximity searches

Proximity searches look for two words within a certain distance of each other. Proximity searches are most common on commercial full-text information databases, the kind that include newspaper, magazine, or journal articles. It's worth noting again that every one of these databases has its own software and search syntax.

To go back to our previous example, this is the way you would ask for information about law on the Internet using the Lexis-Nexis syntax: **Internet w/5 law**.

That means you're instructing the computer to look for the word *law* within five words of the word *Internet*.

AltaVista is one search engine that allows proximity searches by using the word **NEAR** or its symbolic equivalent, the tilde **(~)**.

Date searches

Date searches allow you to narrow your search by looking for material within a certain date. It's best to use date searches with commercial databases, where the date is likely to be the date of the article, paper, or decision you are looking for. On the Web, unfortunately, a date can mean anything, depending on the search engine. It can be the file date of the Web page (if the search spider can find it), the last updated note, or other dates found by the search spider.

Structured Query Language

One other approach for searches is called *Structured Query Language,* or *SQL*. SQL is most often used with relational databases, where data is stored in a number of different tables. Common relational databases are Access and FoxPro.

The SQL language is a way of using simple English (or any other real language) to ask questions and get information from one or more tables in a database using Boolean operators and then, in addition, sorting the information with commands such as **order by** and **group by**. SQL is most useful in databases with distinct fields and a number of separate tables.

A detailed explanation of SQL is beyond the scope of this book, but you use SQL often on the Web without seeing it or knowing it. If you go to an e-commerce site and ask to buy a book, a CD, or a live lobster, the page you see, listing the book's title, for example, is not a single Web page. Rather, it is created on the fly when a SQL-Server (called a See-quel Server) queries the underlying database and retrieves the information, which is then automatically converted into a Web page.

Priority plus+

If search engines have one thing in common, one standard, it is the use of mathematical or algebraic symbols for Boolean searching. All the major search engines allow the use of the + and – signs for basic searches. However, not all search engines support the use of the word *and,* and fewer support the *or* and *not*.

As I mentioned, a plus sign (+) is the equivalent of the Boolean AND. So if you were searching for the Minnesota Twins you would use the following:

Minnesota +twins

Or if you want to know something about the pitchers on the team you could use:

Minnesota +twins +pitcher

Note that the + is just before the words I want in the search. This leads to the second role that the plus sign has in many search engines.

A plus sign (+) also establishes priority. It tells the search engine it *must* include the word in the search and the closer the word is to the front of the line, the higher priority for you the user. That's the reason the + goes right before the word. For example, if we go back to our initial example of Internet and law, the two words alone would get many thousands of hits. So first you choose the most important word. In this case it would be law, which would narrow the search considerably. Your search query could look like this:

+law +internet

That tells the search engine that the pages it retrieves must have the word *law* in it and secondly also have the word *Internet*. But that's still a bit wide, so we will narrow the options further.

The minus sign (-) is the same as the Boolean operator NOT. You can narrow the search by excluding pornography. To go back to our example of someone searching for sites on twins who wants to exclude the baseball team you would use:

+twins - Minnesota

To exclude pornography from your search, you would use:

+law +internet -pornography

If you wanted also to exclude libel from the equation, you could enter:

+law +internet -pornography -libel

Remember to always check the FAQ for the search engine you want to use to see exactly how it uses the syntax.

Phrase searching

Most search engines allow you to do a *phrase search,* which is one of your best friends if you are not using a drop-down menu. You can use it to find people, company names, titles, and phrases by putting the phrase you want in quotation marks:

"Bill Clinton"
"Career Press"
"Gettysburg Address"
"identical twins"

You can also add a phrase to a wider search. To return to our legal example, if you are looking for Supreme Court decisions on the Internet, you could enter:

+"supreme court" + internet -pornography

This would give you decisions, but it could also include decisions by any court that calls itself "supreme." Two choices could be:

+"United States Supreme Court" +internet -pornography

or

+"Supreme Court of Canada" +internet -pornography

You should note that both AltaVista and Google also use what is called "automatic phrase matching." If you enter a series of words, but not in quotation marks, those search engines compare your phrase with a list in their indexes and provide any matches they find.

The results

You have found the best words for your search, joined them using the proper Boolean operators, and now you have a result.

Whether it's a commercial database or the Web, you will be given a listing of the results generated by the computer. But have you ever wondered just how the computer comes up with the list and why it sometimes looks so different from what you expected?

Every search engine uses an algorithm designed by programmers to generate the list of results. That list is usually the result of what is known as *relevance ranking*. You have put in the question and run the program, and now the software decides which of the sites or articles or pages it finds is most relevant to your request.

In the early days of the World Wide Web, the search engines automatically displayed the relevance ranking for each query. Now most of them don't; the engine just presents you with a list. Northern Light still gives you its estimate of how each link stacked up to your query. If the computer gives you a ranking of 99 percent, the search site has given you the best answer it feels matches your query. If it's 40 percent, then the software is less certain that there is a perfect match.

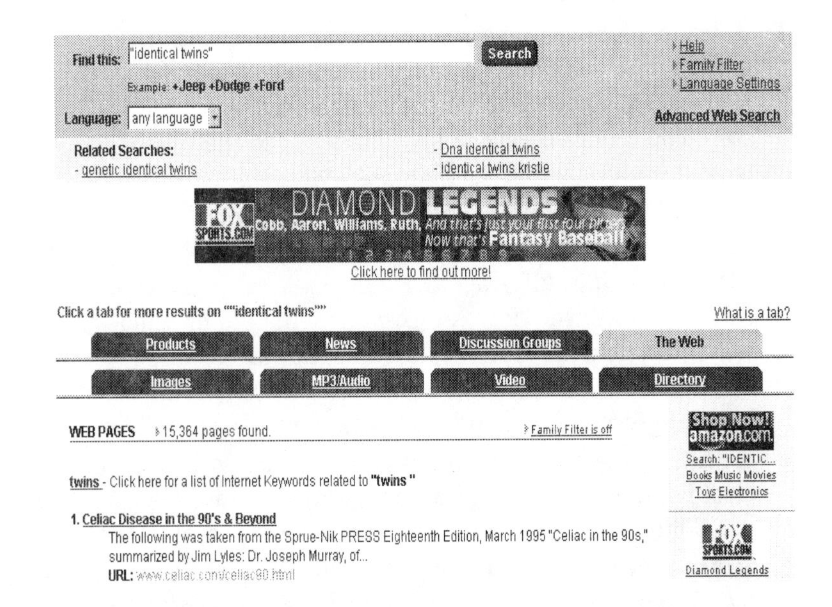

Figure 14-1. Relevance ranking in Northern Light.

Some search engines then take your search a step further with *relevance feedback*. Once you have your initial list of responses to a search, you narrow the list down by telling the search engine which ones you like. The computer then conducts the search again.

There are other factors beyond simple relevance that can also affect your results on the web search engines (but not commercial databases). Popularity rankings and paid placements can also affect your results.

Chronological ranking is more common on commercial databases where date searching is more reliable.

One last word before we move on. Remember the old computer phrase "garbage in, garbage out." The list you get is only as good as your query, and the answer is only as good as the material on the Web or the database you are searching. The human factor, the researcher's "right stuff," the ability to make connections, that feeling in your gut, is just as important as what George Boole's literate algebra has turned up for you.

Relationships

Once you put in the words you want to search and push the **Search** button on your chosen search engine, you may be presented with a number of choices. Some search engines allow to you narrow your search further:

- ❑ **Related searches.** The search engine looks for words that relate to your search. In AltaVista they are displayed under the search box, expanding on the search you have chosen. So for *jeep*, you have a choice of types of jeeps or the role of the jeep in history.
- ❑ **Related search types.** These allow you to narrow the search by choosing the type of search you want to do. Recently AltaVista began offering click tabs that can take your search in a different direction; for example, clicking on the News tab will bring up news stories related to the search words you have entered. If you are looking to buy something rather than doing pure research, the products tab may a better choice.
- ❑ **Similar pages.** Some search engines, such as Google and Excite, believe that if you find a page that comes close to what you want, then you may want to narrow the search that way.
- ❑ **Subsearching.** Subsearching lets you narrow your search terms by adding new words, often by using a dialog box that asks "Search within these results."

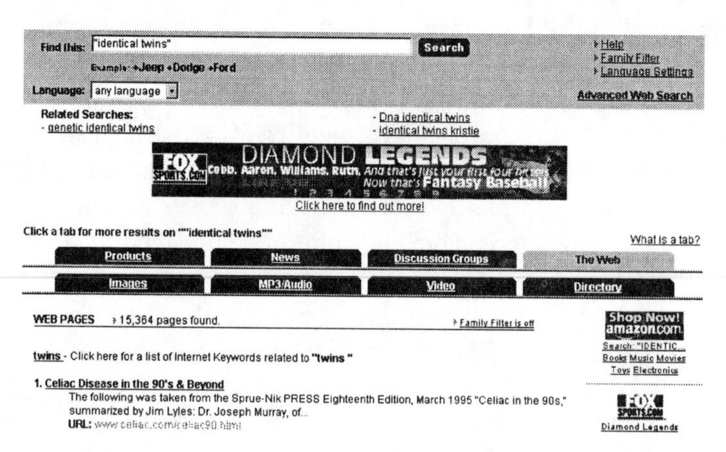

Figure 14-2. AltaVista offers related search folders, including products.

Now you have the basics for all the major search engines. This should help you get a handle on searching, as long as you also work with the help pages of your chosen search engines. The industry is highly competitive and moving at warp speed, which is why I have chosen not to be too specific. Otherwise, the material may quickly become dated.

Links

Supreme Court of the United States

www.supremecourtus.gov

Launched April 2000.

FLITE—Supreme Court Decisions, 1937-1975

www.fedworld.gov/supcourt/index.htm

Database of historic decisions by the United States Supreme Court.

Oyez Oyez Oyez

oyez.nwu.edu

Northwestern University U.S. Supreme Court Multimedia database.

LII: Supreme Court Collection

supct.law.cornell.edu/supct/

Cornell University Supreme Court site.

The Federal Judiciary Homepage

www.uscourts.gov

Home page for the judicial branch of the US government.

The Supreme Court of Canada

www.droit.umontreal.ca/doc/csc-scc/en/

Supreme Court of Canada site at the Université de Montréal law school.

Chapter 15
E-mail

Few experts foresaw the "e-mail explosion," although it is obvious that e-mail was the "killer application" that made going online successful in the first place.

Twenty years ago, when the first commercial online services were being planned, few mentioned e-mail. The engineers planning the first "new media"—teletext and videotex—were talking about hardware, and the executives were prematurely talking about profits from advertising dollars. The information was to come from "on high," so to speak, and the public would passively accept it. The analogy, of course, was television, and it was the wrong analogy.

Even on the Internet, back in the days when it was Arpanet and a research tool, it was first thought that it would be used for "official" government business. Scientists and researchers soon found other uses for the Net, and e-mail blossomed.

There are a couple of great advantages to electronic mail: time and money. One technical term for e-mail is *asynchronous communications*. It means something that happens at different times. Thus if you are writing a message to someone at 9:31 p.m. in eastern North America, it's 6:31 p.m. on the West Coast, and you might be able to phone someone in California. If the phone's busy, you're out of luck, at least for now. It's also 3:31 a.m. the next morning in Berlin. If you phoned, you'd probably get someone out of bed. It's 12:31 p.m., just past noon, in Australia, and you'd probably be able to reach the person you want, if you wanted to pay for a long distance call Down Under.

Asynchronous communication solves that problem. You can post your e-mail message and the person you sent it to will receive it when it's most convenient for them. Your answer (if there is one) will appear in your mailbox, at your convenience, when you log on. You're not playing expensive telephone tag either locally, nationally, or internationally.

In one way, e-mail is just a modern return to an old way of communicating: the letter. For centuries, the only method of long distance communication was by letter. Ancient Mesopotamia used clay tablets encased in clay envelopes. The Greeks and Romans used both wax tablets and parchment. From the 16th to the 19th centuries, Europeans and North Americans were superb letter writers.

The next step in communication, the telegraph, added the speed of early electronics, and cost shortened the verbiage. Letters and telegrams fill the archives, and scholars have written long, sometimes fascinating, sometimes boring, works on the collected letters and telegrams of many famous men and women.

Now e-mail can combine speed with the intimacy of a letter.

A few years from now, a scholar will write a dissertation on the *Collected E-mail of the President* and a tabloid will publish some star's naughty e-mail messages. E-mail has already been key evidence in criminal and civil trials, including the U.S. anti-trust case against Microsoft, in which the Justice Department subpoenaed Microsoft CEO Bill Gates's e-mail.

Once, five years ago, using e-mail was like living in a small town; you knew everyone in town (whether the community was a real one or a virtual one with a specific interest) plus a few people in other towns. There were the same problems as in any town; there were the fights between neighbors, and those who thought they were big fish in the small pond, the wise elders, and the up-and-coming whiz kids.

Everything changed, at least according to old Net hands, when America Online (AOL) opened the gate from its proprietary service to the Internet and thousands of AOL customers flooded onto the Net, without any knowledge of the Net's customs.

Now e-mail is like living in a megalopolis, and people are often overwhelmed. The idea of waking up and having thousands of e-mails is almost a cliché and is used to create humor in television commercials. Spammers shove junk e-mail through your electronic doorway every day.

Five years ago, researchers could use e-mail and often get a reply, if not always a speedy response. While e-mail remains one of the best and most reliable sources of information for a researcher, it is also likely that, unless the recipient knows you, your e-mail will be lost in the shuffle, routed to a low priority folder, or deleted. So don't count on it.

E-mail programs

You are probably already using an e-mail program, most likely the one you were first introduced to. If you like it, keep using it. For most e-mail users, there are two choices

- **E-mail client software** are either stand-alone programs such as **Eudora, Pegasus Mail, Forte Agent,** or **Microsoft Outlook Express;** come with a browser, such as the mail component of **Netscape**; or they are a combination of the two, as **Microsoft Outlook Express** works with **Microsoft Internet Explorer.**
- **Web-based e-mail** is provided by an increasing number of sites, including **Microsoft Hotmail**, **Yahoo!**, and many others. The advantage of Web-based e-mail is that it has allowed thousands of people who don't have a home account and Internet Service Provider (ISP) access to e-mail.

For the serious researcher, the best idea is to have both. E-mail client software means you can manage your e-mail on your hard disk. Having a Web-based e-mail account means you can use it anywhere when you travel, at a friend's, in a cybercafe, or in a library or other public-access Net terminal.

Tip: If you are traveling, you can usually configure Hotmail and many other Web-based e-mail programs to check as many as four other ISP or business e-mail accounts using the POP (Post Office Protocol). That means you can check the e-mail accounts you use at home, at school, or at work. Click on the **Pop Mail** and fill in the information required. It's the same information you used to set up the original account. One drawback is that some corporate firewalls won't let you through to check your e-mail. Hotmail POP gives you the option of leaving the original messages on the mail server, so you have them when you return.

If you are going to be doing serious long-term research and you have a choice (if you work in an office, your company will choose your software for you), you should find the software that works best for you. Because most of the e-mail clients come bundled with other programs, or have freeware versions or trial versions, you can try some out and see which works best.

The main choices are Eudora, in both free and paid versions; Forte Agent, which you have to pay for; and Pegasus Mail, which is free.

E-mail filters

Once you've chosen your e-mail system, the next step is to create folders and filters, whether you are using disk-based e-mail client software or a Web-based e-mail system.

It's a lot easier if the software presorts your mail for you. That way you can choose which material to read first and which to put aside to another day if you're busy.

First you set up a series of **mailboxes** or **folders,** depending on the software, to expand your inbox. You should always create folders for any mailing lists you belong to, so that separate lists go to different folders. You should also create folders for projects, key contacts, and friends.

Then you create the filters, which may be called just that: **Filter, Message Filter,** or **Rules.** You then fill in the dialog box to fit the filter and folder you want.

If it's a **"Subject,"** that's an easy choice, but note that message headers can change over time, so you may have to have several rules all pointing to one folder.

If you're filtering all the mail from one mailing list to a folder, it's often best to use the **"To:"** address, which is usually the address for the mailing list. The mailing list uses the actual poster as the return address. However, on some mailing lists, you have to you the **"From:"** address, since all the messages usually come through one address. Similarly, if you want all the mail from one colleague sent to one filter, then use the **"From:"** function.

Most e-mail programs also allow you to use a **Kill** function filter, which helps you get rid of spam, although the spammers are wise to this ability and change addresses often.

The advantages of using e-mail

"The advantages, obviously, are quick communication, and the ability to manipulate and translate information. Even something as quick as a fax can get lost in transition," says Ted Anthony of the Associated Press. "E-mail is a very good way to approach...to get things in the background. Something that arrives in your e-mail is a lot more likely to get read and responded to because that's the one place where you look for things to arrive. If somebody puts a fax on your desk...you [might] put three folders down on it. And then eat your lunch on top of it.

"E-mail imposes a structure of organization on loose information because...the e-mail will be in the place where the person who you want to read it needs it to be."

Networking on the Net

The Net is one of the best and easiest places for researchers to network and track down potential sources:

- **E-mail one-on-one.** The best thing about e-mail is *asynchronous communication*. You can send a message halfway around the world, go to sleep, and if you're lucky, have a reply by the time you get up the next morning. You can reach out and ask questions, ask for advice, and set up appointments, all by e-mail. You can follow up with new questions as your research progresses.
- **E-mail lists (listservs).** There were, as of February 2000, more than 91,000 publicly accessible mailing lists on the Net in English, the main language of the Net, plus thousands more private e-mail lists. (For example, the professional psychiatric community has several private lists that are open only to members of the profession). E-mail lists are often called listservs after one of the most popular list-management software, but there are others, so what you call a listserv could actually be managed differently. E-mail lists are the best source of ongoing information and discussion for the researcher. Find an e-mail list that concentrates on the topic of your research and subscribe to it. You will find the latest information, discussions about the controversial issues in the field, and opportunities to make contacts and ask questions. One popular and informative e-mail list is the Computer-Assisted Reporting and Research list.
- **Newsletters.** E-mail newsletters are another source of information, providing news in your field of research, once a day, once a week, once a month, or whenever the newsletter editor gets around to sending it. These can be a valuable source of information provided to you by an expert. Some are free; others come in two versions, a basic free newsletter and an enhanced, more

detailed letter that charges a subscription. Other newsletters, often in specialty fields, can cost hundreds or thousands of dollars for a subscription.

- **Alerts and filters.** Alerts and filters are a bit different from edited e-mail newsletters. As the names suggest, these e-mail messages alert you to some development in your field. Alerts can come from government agencies, environmental and other advocacy groups, public relations agencies, and news services. Filters allow you to enter keywords and the service then returns any news story or alert fitting that keyword.

The Net is people, not hardware and software, and people are almost always ready to point you to a good source or the right mailing list or newsgroup:

- Find the proper newsgroup or mailing list. You can do that by checking directories and lists of mailing lists, and keeping the file that lists all newsgroups current.
- Lurk for a while. (More about that a little later.)
- Post a general question outlining your research, and ask for contacts via e-mail. Contact potential sources you've already identified on the mailing list or newsgroup privately.
- If you're answering a similar query and recommending that the poster contact someone you know, cc (carbon copy) a copy of the message to your contact or, if necessary, ask permission to pass on the name before answering the query.
- Sometimes (not always) your message will be passed on to other people on other groups, and your network of sources will grow.
- Never spam your query by posting the same message to a large number of newsgroups and mailing lists. Net culture frowns on spamming. If you've done your homework, checked the mailing list or newsgroup, and lurked, then you will know how to focus your question to that group. Take the time to write individual queries.
- The Net is also often a great place to avoid gatekeepers and public relations people. I once tried several times, with conventional methods, to contact one source for a story. During research for a book, the source's e-mail address popped up unexpectedly in a list provided by someone else. I sent a focused

e-mail query and an interview was quickly arranged. Don't assume busy or famous people won't answer your query; they just might.

- Direct contact doesn't always work. Some executives still have secretaries or assistants screen their e-mail. Other people will use a filter to prioritize their e-mail and your query may end up in a low-priority mailbox.
- Some people will reply by saying they're too busy. Some will reply, agreeing to the interview, and then never answer the follow-up questions. Others won't reply at all. The more people on the Net, the more spamming, the more the e-mail box is filled with messages, and the more this problem will grow.
- Don't ignore old-fashioned paper in searching for people online. More directories these days are listing e-mail addresses along with street address and phone number. Put your e-mail address on business cards so sources can contact you. If someone gives you a business card with an e-mail address on it, make sure that e-mail address goes into your address book.
- Check with associations and organizations, either by phone or e-mail, as part of your homework. More and more are going online and certainly some of their members will handle e-mail queries.
- When you're finishing up a conventional phone or personal interview, *always* ask for an e-mail address. If the source isn't online, they sometimes will say they can be contacted through a spouse, parent, or child who does have an e-mail address.

Mailing lists

Finding e-mail lists

There are specialized search engines and directories that work with e-mail and newsgroups:

- **Topica** is a meta-search site for mailing lists and e-newsletters. It ranks the lists and has good descriptions.
- **Lizst** is a resource for finding more than 90,000 e-mail lists and 30,000 newsgroups. **Note:** Lizst gives you only the name of the list or newsgroup and instructions on how to subscribe.

- **Publicly Accessible Mailing Lists** is another good resource with descriptions of the lists and background information.
- **Directory of Scholarly and Professional E-Conferences** evaluates lists that would be of interest to scholars and academics. Not all the lists on the site are purely academic, although the topics may be of interest to scholars. For example, it lists a history list that is primarily of interest to veterans.
- **Internet Mailing Lists in History** is a directory site maintained by the Department of History at Tennessee Technical University. It has good links to other mailing list guides and directories (not just limited to history).

The list sites don't always overlap and they add new material at different times, so it's a good idea to try a couple of them to find the list you're looking for.

Joining a mailing list

There are three key addresses for a mailing list:

1. **Administrative address.** In most cases, this is the address of the computer that manages the list, and usually has an address that includes listserv, listproc, or majodromo. This is the address you send messages to subscribe, unsubscribe, check who is a member of the list, and so forth. Never send discussion messages to this address; you're usually talking to a computer, not a human being
2. **Discussion address**. This is the address you send the messages to when you want to post.
3. **List owner.** This is the e-mail address of the person who runs the list, and any questions about list culture or notes about list problems should be sent to that address. For some private or moderated lists, you cannot join automatically but have to write to the list owner to get approval. That person controls the subscriptions and decides who gets on.

Lurk and research

If you subscribe to an appropriate mailing list or join a newsgroup, lurk first—that is, just read the mail for a few days or even weeks to get a sense of the culture of the list. Lurking is crucial to contacting potential sources. It's more than "Netiquette." Lurking gives the researcher a sense of the total volume of messages on a mailing list or newsgroup. Personalities emerge quickly.

Nothing destroys the credibility of a researcher more than making a glaring error online. Not only will it dry up most sources of information, but if you are on a mailing list, you're likely to get criticized ("flamed") for your error.

Approaching sources online

You should establish yourself in the mailing list by contributing your knowledge and information. Post messages answering questions when you can help. If you can intelligently add to an ongoing discussion, do so. You'll become part of the neighborhood, and your personality will come through to the often thousands of people who are reading the list or newsgroup.

Now you're ready to go online and approach the sources you've picked out by lurking.

Posting questions to a mailing list

If you've lurked for a few days or weeks, you should have a sense of the group of people you'll be working with. You should know by now which questions are and are not welcome.

Students, for example, will often get flamed if they post a question that is obviously a "help me with my homework because I haven't done it" type of question. On the other hand, if you've done your homework, a tightly focused question will often get the answer you want.

Some people have called the Internet, especially e-mail, "the gift economy." The saying comes from the custom among many aboriginal people who have an economy that works through the exchange of gifts and favors rather than money for goods and services. It's the same on the Net; you ask, receive an answer, and then either give back or give forward when you're able to help the person who helped you or others.

When you post a general question, you should:

- ❑ **Identify yourself.** State whether you're a student, a staff reporter, a producer, a freelance writer, a professor, or a businessperson.

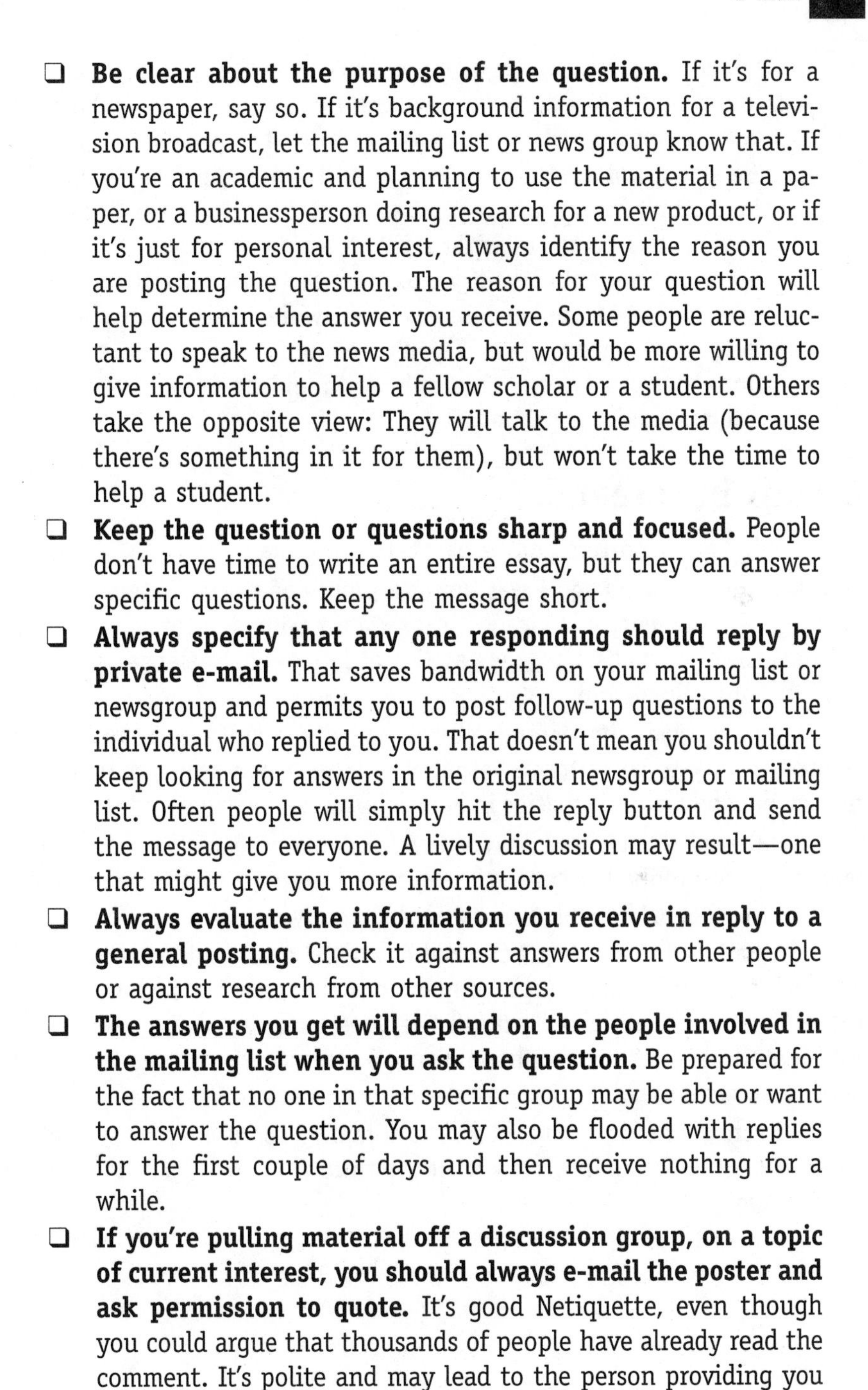

- **Be clear about the purpose of the question.** If it's for a newspaper, say so. If it's background information for a television broadcast, let the mailing list or news group know that. If you're an academic and planning to use the material in a paper, or a businessperson doing research for a new product, or if it's just for personal interest, always identify the reason you are posting the question. The reason for your question will help determine the answer you receive. Some people are reluctant to speak to the news media, but would be more willing to give information to help a fellow scholar or a student. Others take the opposite view: They will talk to the media (because there's something in it for them), but won't take the time to help a student.
- **Keep the question or questions sharp and focused.** People don't have time to write an entire essay, but they can answer specific questions. Keep the message short.
- **Always specify that any one responding should reply by private e-mail.** That saves bandwidth on your mailing list or newsgroup and permits you to post follow-up questions to the individual who replied to you. That doesn't mean you shouldn't keep looking for answers in the original newsgroup or mailing list. Often people will simply hit the reply button and send the message to everyone. A lively discussion may result—one that might give you more information.
- **Always evaluate the information you receive in reply to a general posting.** Check it against answers from other people or against research from other sources.
- **The answers you get will depend on the people involved in the mailing list when you ask the question.** Be prepared for the fact that no one in that specific group may be able or want to answer the question. You may also be flooded with replies for the first couple of days and then receive nothing for a while.
- **If you're pulling material off a discussion group, on a topic of current interest, you should always e-mail the poster and ask permission to quote.** It's good Netiquette, even though you could argue that thousands of people have already read the comment. It's polite and may lead to the person providing you with more information. If the person says no, and you feel the

comment is still worth using, consider whether it can be used anonymously ("One poster on the newsgroup") You will find that the poster will usually say yes to that request.

- **Be prepared to be shot down in flames.** Sometimes your idea won't work, you've missed something, or your boss or adviser has come up with a silly idea and told you to do it anyway. The replies you get to a general posting will tell you whether what you're doing is worthwhile and if you should keep working on it, or if you've enough ammunition to tell your boss or adviser, "This isn't working, let's drop it" or "This angle seems more promising."

E-mail in research

All kinds of reporters and researchers use e-mail.

"A couple of years ago I was doing a profile of a developmental economist at the University of Chicago," says Walter Collins, a former newspaper editor, now a journalism teacher at Notre Dame and freelance writer who lives in South Bend, Indiana.

"I interviewed him extensively along with faculty colleagues, but I wanted to talk to some former students. He gave him a list that included faculty members at universities in Massachusetts, Montana, and Hong Kong.

"Snail mail would have taken days...telephoning in this age of voice mail is increasingly frustrating....Because I wanted limited information from these people, I decided to contact them by e-mail.

"In half an hour or less I tracked down the e-mail addresses I needed, sent off messages with a couple of questions about my profile, and gave the recipients the option of replying to the questions by e-mail or sending me a time and date for me to phone them. I stressed that I was looking for anecdotal responses.

"Within 36 hours I had excellent e-mail responses from two of the three and a telephone interview with the third (fortunately, not the one in Hong Kong)."

Links

Forte

www.forteinc.com

Home page for Forte, creators of Agent and Free Agent.

Eudora Email by Qualcomm

www.eudora.com

Pegasus Mail by David Harris

www.pegasus.usa.com

PAML (The Directory of Publicly Accessible Mailing Lists)

paml.alastra.com

PAML Links page

paml.alastra.com/sources.html

Internet Mailing Lists in History

www.tntech.edu/www/acad/hist/lists.html

Tile.Net

www.tile.net

Guide site that lists e-mail lists, newsgroups and FTP sites.

Topica

www.topica.com

Topica a meta-search engine for lists.

Directory of Scholarly and Professional E-Conferences

www.n2h2.com/KOVACS/

A directory of scholarly and professional lists and conferences.

Subject index

www.n2h2.com/KOVACS/Sindex.html

Chapter 16

Newsgroups and Discussions

Newsgroups don't get enough respect. The 1998 survey of journalists by Steve Ross of Columbia University and Don Middleburg of the consulting firm Middleberg & Associates, showed that few journalists got ideas from newsgroups, and that the younger Web-weaned generation of journalists knew little or nothing about that information resource on the Net. Even the name seems to be changing, with more and more sites calling the newsgroups "discussions."

In some ways, it's not surprising. Newsgroups often do deserve their bad reputation, especially ones such as **alt.conspiracy** where, as the name suggests, conspiracy theorists hang out and describe the latest theories on a dozen subjects. Another problem is that spammers like to pick e-mail addresses off newsgroups, so people who post on one can expect junk e-mail.

But getting to know newsgroups is well worth the risk. With estimates of the number of newsgroups, in all languages, ranging from 35,000 to 80,000, it is quite likely you will find valuable information, contacts, and leads in newsgroups, as long as you look for the right ones, lurk to find out the level of discussion, and carefully evaluate all the information you receive on the newsgroup.

Newsgroups were at the heart of Net culture in the early days, where Netiquette was born, where FAQs (Frequently Asked Questions) and RFCs (Request for Comments) spread around the world, creating a community.

Communities do thrive on the Internet, from *Star Trek* fans to electronic support groups, to newsgroups that will probably give you more help on computer problems than overworked or overpriced tech-support lines.

Dan Bjarnason, a correspondent with the Canadian Broadcasting Corporation's *National Magazine*, is a believer in newsgroups.

"I like using the Internet to find out historical things," he says, "Who did what when, or who was where to see how things link up historically. I use newsgroups far more than searching the Net for this type of thing. I think you can find out far more obscure detail data through newsgroups.

"There was a deal between Churchill and Roosevelt where Britain was in its darkest hour, needed help." Churchill needed destroyers and asked President Roosevelt for some obsolete U.S. ships. But Roosevelt couldn't give them away; it was against the law. "He said, 'We will trade for them.' Churchill said, 'We will give you some bases—Newfoundland was one, Bermuda was another—if you will give us those destroyers....'

"I wanted to know the names of those destroyers and where they actually ended up," he states. "I can't think of a more obscure question. I asked that on two or three World War II newsgroups, and a couple of military history ones. Within half an hour I was getting answers back from people somewhere who knew that information."

Bjarnason says that the people who participate in newsgroups are usually generous with their unique, and sometimes esoteric, knowledge. He also notes that newsgroups are "self-correcting." Members usually respond to inaccurate statements with correct information.

What are newsgroups?

Newsgroups, sometimes called Usenet or discussion groups, are similar to e-mail with one key exception: Usenet is a network of Internet Service Providers (ISPs), so the messages go to your ISP and not directly to a mailbox, the way e-mail messages do.

Newsgroups are divided into hierarchies. The original eight came first from universities:

- **comp**—groups covering computers and computer science.
- **humanities**—groups covering mostly literature and music.
- **misc**—miscellaneous topics.
- **news**—news of the Usenet.

- **rec**—recreation and entertainment.
- **sci**—science.
- **soc**—society, culture and social issues.
- **talk**—discussion and debates.

The early "Netizens" soon felt they were restricted by the original hierarchy and created the **alt** or alternative, which is perhaps the most notorious of the newsgroup hierarchy because it is so wide ranging that it includes almost anything.

Other subject hierarchies include:

- **biz**—business topics.
- **bionet**—biological science.
- **k12**—kindergarten through high school.
- **hiv**—HIV- and AIDS-related topics.
- **microsoft**—for Microsoft-related topics.

Others are geographical, related to countries (**can**—Canada; **uk—**United Kingdom), cities (**tor**—Toronto), regions (**ba—**the San Francisco Bay area), or are tied to organizations and universities.

Reading newsgroups

To read newsgroups, you need a newsreader and the most likely way to do that is through your Web browser. Netscape has a newsreader built into to its **Netscape Messenger**; **Microsoft Internet Explorer** and **Windows 98** have a newsreader built in to **Outlook Express.**

A more powerful alternative to both is Forte's popular **Free Agent** newsreader (the newsreader is the freeware version of Agent, Forte's combined e-mail and newsreader).

To use these newsreaders, you first download a long list of newsgroups available from your ISP. Subscribing to one is a simple as clicking your mouse. The first time you will receive all the messages or message headers (depending on your software) stored on your ISP's hard drive (there could be a couple of thousand for heavy traffic groups). Subsequent downloads will be any messages that have come in since your last download. You can unsubscribe just as easily, by clicking your mouse.

Finding newsgroups and Web forums

Newsgroups were an early innovation on the Net and they have a long history. The term FAQ (Frequently Asked Question) is almost synonymous with newsgroups. Many groups define themselves through their FAQs, and in those days before the World Wide Web, they were stored at an FTP site at the Massachusetts Institute of Technology (MIT). Today they are at MIT and at the **faqs.org**, a mirror site for the RTFM site that is organized for easier retrieval of information than the site at MIT.

Both sites are a treasure house of FAQs and other files related to many of the thousands of newsgroups. It's also a good place to get the latest information on a group's subject. The volunteers or staffers who write the FAQs update them frequently.

There are specialized search engines and directories that work with newsgroups and Web forums:

- **Lizst** is a resource for finding more than 90,000 e-mail lists and 30,000 newsgroups. Lizst gives you only the name of the list or newsgroup and instructions on how to subscribe.
- **Deja**, formerly **Dejanews**, is a search engine that actually searches the messages on 80,000 newsgroups and Web forums dating back to 1995. Deja also lets you search through newsgroups' names to find appropriate topics.
- **Forum One** searches 310,000 Web forums, some of which are open and some which are closed to search engines because the site requires registration. You can also search for topics.
- **AltaVista** also searches the newsgroups. Enter your words in the dialog box and then click on **Discussions.**
- **Usenet Archive Directory** is a site that has links to those few newsgroups that archive all or part of their discussion threads.

Working in newsgroups

The same rules apply to working in newsgroups as in e-mail, although the availability of FAQs makes it easier to check out a newsgroup before subscribing. Once you've subscribed, lurk for a while, get to understand the group's culture, and if you are going to post a question, identify yourself and give the reason why you are posting the question.

Links

Main depository for newsgroup FAQs at MIT

ftp://rtfm.mit.edu/pub/usenet-by-group/

FAQs.org

www.faqs.org

Mirror site to MIT, easier navigation.

Index: Archives of newsgroup postings

starbase.neosoft.com/~claird/news.lists/newsgroup_archives.html

A directory site that lists sites that archive certain newsgroups.

Free Agent

www.forteinc.com

Lizst

www.lizst.com

Deja

wwww.deja.com/usenet

Forum One

www.forumone.com

Chapter 17
Evaluation, Evaluation, Evaluation

There's an old saying that applies both to real estate and to retail: Success depends on location, location, and location.

In any research, but especially on the Internet, success depends on one thing: evaluation, evaluation, and evaluation.

In this chapter, I'll give you the basics of evaluation by considering traditional methods. Then, we'll look specifically at Net evaluation and verification, and how to evaluate search engines.

Beware of geeks...

It was the ancient Greeks who first recorded their evaluation of data. Hacataeus of Miletus (part of Ionia, a city whose ruins are found in what is today Turkey) is considered one of the founders of both history and geography. Hacataeus wrote two books: *A Map of the World,* probably the first geography or travel book, and an epic history called *Genealogies*.

His opening sentences in *Genealogies* are significant: "What I write here is the account I considered to be true. For the stories of the Greeks are numerous, and my opinion, ridiculous." Hacataeus was perhaps the first person we know of who evaluated his data and then stood by that evaluation. He had gone to Egypt and realized that the time line of history was longer than his fellows Greeks had assumed. Egypt, he discovered, was ruled by men when Greece was supposedly still ruled by the gods.

Herodotus of Halicarnassus (another Ionian city, also in modern Turkey) lived about a century later and is called the "Father of History." Herodotus is best known for his account of how the Greeks defeated the Persian invasion. His nine-volume history contains many more accounts of his travels to the Black Sea region the Greeks called Euxine, Babylon, Phoenicia, and Egypt. Herodotus was a man of his time; he stood between the time of epic poetry and factual history. His stories contain a mixture of myth, tall stories, and fact. Herodotus evaluated the stories he was told. Not all modern scholars agree with his methods—but he took the first steps. Herodotus would often qualify his stories with "as I am informed." In one famous passage, he said, "I am bound to state what is said, but I am not bound to believe."

You should always be evaluating the information you find in traditional sources, newspapers, books, and even official documents as you browse, troll, and plumb the Net. Check the little things that journalists watch for. A misspelled name, for example, could be a warning sign, even in an academic paper, that the author was careless in other areas as well. Do any statements seem exaggerated? If so, why has the author exaggerated? Is it a spur of the moment statement by e-mail, or is that exaggeration more deliberate? Are you reading instant, quick-off-the-mark analysis, the results of a carefully crafted study, or a meta-analysis (a study of all previous studies on a subject)?

What do you think has been left out of the report? What an author omits may be just as important to a researcher as what he includes. What's ommitted could reveal much about the bias of the information you are reading.

Don't ignore bias as a valuable source of information. Even an untrustworthy source is valuable for what it reveals about the personality of an author, especially if he or she is an actor in the events. Barbara Tuchman wrote, "Bias in a primary source is to be expected. One allows for it and corrects it by reading another version....

"Even if an event is not controversial, it will have been seen and remembered from different angles of view by different observers. If the event *is* in dispute, one has an extra obligation to examine both sides."

Tuchman also says the researcher should be on the look out for *corroborative detail*. Tuchman notes that whenever an author makes a generalization, she was "instantly on guard," and her immediate reaction is "Show me."

What is the proof offered for any statement? In one way corroborative detail is proof of what the writer is stating. In another, it is the anecdote that enlarges and enlightens. Corroborative detail adds the human dimension to a story.

Working backward

If you are suspicious about anything in a book, magazine, or document, look for internal corroborative detail. Then verify everything—names, dates, places, and details—through as many authoritative sources as possible. Work backward to the original source, and then confirm that the original source is authentic and reliable.

For example, I was researching the life of Rocco Perri, a tough little gangster who ran many of the Prohibition rackets in Ontario during the 1920s, supplying both Ontario and its thirsty American neighbors with booze. Many of the later stories of Perri's life were based on *one* 1940s newspaper article that appeared sometime after his disappearance and presumed death (ending up in a barrel of cement at the bottom of Hamilton harbor).

A year of research, looking through official documents and reading reel after reel of microfilm, proved that the article was wrong. The article did, however, come at a key point in history, when newspapers began a more systematic collection of clippings. The 1940s article was based on hearsay, from people who thought they knew the story. Earlier, more accurate, newspaper articles had not been clipped, and were not easily accessible to reporters at the time of Perri's disappearance.

As Barbara Tuchman said, "Show me." Create a step-by-step case, almost as if you were in court in front of a jury. Can you prove your theory or statement? Check. If you can't prove what you've set out to prove, you have two choices: Leave it out or communicate your doubts with qualifications.

Evaluation checklists

One way of evaluating any data you find on or off the Internet is to use the 12-point checklist created by my colleague Dean Tudor for evaluating both offline and online information:

1. **Recency.** Do the data appear to be the most current on the subject or the most appropriate for a historical time period?
2. **Relevancy.** Is there a direct correlation to the subject? Is the tone of the source popular, scholarly, or technical?

3. **Authority** What is the reputation of the data? What is the reliability of the source (history, context, viewpoint)?
4. **Completeness.** At what point has the researcher gathered sufficient data to produce a relatively unslanted report? Can the subject be understood by the researcher and the intended audience?
5. **Accuracy.** Does the source furnish background data and/or in-depth data? Are complex issues oversimplified? Are terms adequately defined?
6. **Clarity.** Can bias be recognized? Are there any logical fallacies? Are all assumptions (hidden or otherwise) identified?
7. **Verifiability**. Can subjective materials be verified? If not, why not?
8. **Statistical validity.** Can the conclusive data be supported by standard statistical testing? Was statistical inference needed? Are there clear explanations for using "averages" or "percentages"?
9. **Internal consistency.** Do the data contain internal contradictions?
10. **External consistency**. Do the data reflect any contradictions among the source documents?
11. **Context.** Do the data reflect some sort of common sense or experience of the world within the context of information demand? Can fact be distinguished from opinion? Are sources taken out of context? Can the document be placed with the era circumstances that produced it?
12. **Comparative quality.** Are some data clearly inferior to other data? Which are the "best" data in context of the above 11 tests (that is, most recent, most relevant, the most authoritative, the most complete, the most accurate, and so forth).

From *Finding Answers: The Essential guide to Gathering Information in Canada* by Dean Tudor, McClelland & Stewart, 1993. Reprinted with permission of the author.

There are a number of similar checklists created by librarians and scholars, and you will find links for them at the end of this chapter.

What the beancounters do

It is not just librarians who professionally evaluate Web sites. Accountants and others in the financial industry, including securities regulators, do it now as well. How do you evaluate other business and financial sites, whether you are an investor, a journalist, an investigator, or a librarian? What can all researchers learn from the beancounters?

In late 1999, the Canadian Institute of Chartered Accountants released an international study, *The Impact of Technology on Financial and Business Reporting*, by Gerald Trites of St. Francis Xavier University and two colleagues. The study is mostly concerned with how the Web can present business data that is in line with securities regulations and with Generally Accepted Accounting Principles (GAAP).

According to the study, one key factor to understanding the evaluation of financial and business sites is the rule in the stock markets that all information must be given to all users or potential investors at the same time, in the same way. So to the 12 points in the scholar's list, we can add:

- ❑ **Understandability.** Do you understand the information in such a way that it can help you to make a decision?
- ❑ **Relevance.** Is it timely? Does it have *predictive* and *feedback value* (that is, does the information improve your ability to make decisions by confirming or correcting your expectations)?
- ❑ **Reliability.** Is the information reliable? Does the information have *representational faithfulness*? Does it actually represent what it says it does? Is the information *verifiable*? Can it be duplicated by independent, outside sources?
- ❑ **Comparability.** How useful is the information compared to information from other companies or on other sites?

The accountants also raise a number of issues about the information on the Web that are worth exploring:

- ❑ **What are the boundaries of information?** For some in the financial community, the very existence of hyperlinks on the Web is a problem. An annual report follows certain agreed conventions; a Web site usually does not. So the accountants and regulators ask: When does a viewer know that the financial information follows U.S. Securities and Exchange Commission (SEC) or other regulations and when does it not? If the information on a site follows regulations and accepted accounting practices, what about the links that go offsite? The SEC has said that a site is responsible for hyperlinks from disclosure and filing documents. In news sites, you quite often see the disclaimer that the news site is "not responsible for the content of linked sites." That allows the news site to link to controversial sites while warning the users that they must make their own judgment on the content of the material.

- ❑ **How secure is the site?** The concern here is not with the denial of service attacks on Web sites such as Yahoo! that made headlines in February 2000, but the security of information on any site, financial or otherwise. If a site has poor security and can be hacked, then the information on it can be suspect.

So do the accountants' worries apply to the rest of the world?

Consider the boundary issue beyond the financial markets. The famed *Britannica Encyclopedia* is now online at **www.britannica.com**. It's now a Web portal supported by advertising.

I did a Britannica search on a favorite subject, Robin Hood. Not only did I get links to the Britannica's article on Robin Hood, but I was provided with a variety of other sites, some created by popular magazines, some by universities and some by enthusiasts. Although there is a short description of the site by Britannica editors, the question remains: how much of the Britannica's cachet is transferred to those sites beyond the boundary of the encyclopedia?

Security is also a concern. Producer Sig Gerber is worried about authenticating material on the Net when there is no face-to-face interaction, as in a personal interview or meeting. "You cannot trust anything that's on the Internet that deals with conflicting opinions, that deals with scientific data," he says. "How do I know that a reprint of a scientific paper that sits on the Internet has not been changed by someone? I want to see it in a learned journal, in *JAMA* (the *Journal of the American Medical Association*), the way it has come. You must be vigilant."

The problem for researchers is that there soon may be no paper. As the cost of printing and distribution goes up, more scholarly and scientific journals are migrating to the Net and there may not be paper versions. So how then does a researcher know a site is secure and the data authentic?

Figure 17-1. Robin Hood search on Britannica.com.

Peer review

Peer review provides a check-and-balance on the scientific and academic community. In more than 95 percent of cases, peer review is a strong indication of reliability.

Even with a peer-reviewed study, it is best to follow the advice that former President Ronald Reagan used in his negotiations with the old Soviet Union: "Trust but verify."

John Polyani, who won the Nobel Prize for chemistry, recently called peer review "a police force that is hard to dupe." He noted, "My research program is regularly scrutinized by anonymous international juries of experts, picked by third parties from among the leaders in my field....In the universities it is excellence, as judged by those who have demonstrated that they know it when they see it."

But Polyani's analogy of a police force is perhaps more apt than he knows. Despite bad publicity, and although the majority of police officers are good cops who do a hard job well, there are cops who make mistakes, there are a few cops who have one track minds and work to convict the wrong people, and there are just plain bad cops. Scientists and peer review are no different.

A strong public challenge to peer review began with the rise of the AIDS crisis, when peer review was affected by prejudice and blinkered thinking. In early 1981, Dr. Michael Gottlieb of UCLA identified cases of pneumocyctis carnii pneumonia and cytomedgalovirus in gay men. Gottlieb's discovery was one of the first warning signs of the AIDS epidemic. He approached the *New England Journal of Medicine*, but he was told that peer review would take three months at a minimum. Gottlieb then called the Centers for Disease Control and the report was published in the *Morbidity and Mortality Weekly Report*, which had a faster turnaround time; the now-famous report was published on June 5, 1981. It took six months for the *New England Journal of Medicine* to publish Gottlieb's complete paper.

The following year, Dr. Ayre Rubenstein at the Albert Einstein College of Medicine found what is now known as AIDS in babies in New York City. The *New England Journal of Medicine* rejected the paper in July 1982, after six months delay. The reviewers believed that AIDS was confined to gay men.

First with AIDS, and then with the parallel movement among women with breast cancer, then with growing patients' rights movements in other branches of medicine, public trust of peer review has been damaged. Fortunately, most of the scientific and medical community has, during the past 20 years, responded with more respect for patients and a realization that faster turnaround may be necessary in some cases.

There are also problems of conflict of interest. On February 22, 2000, the *New England Journal of Medicine* admitted it violated its own financial conflict of interest policy 19 times in the previous three years by selecting doctors who had financial ties to drug makers to write review articles about drugs.

Dr. Marcia Angell, the journal's editor-in-chief, told the Associated Press (AP) the review was prompted by a news report about one violation. It then found 18 additional instances. Angell told the AP that the stricter policy for review articles is difficult to maintain because "there's so much connection between academia and the private sector now."

Always ask who paid for the study. Then ask whether or not that would indicate bias in a study. Sometimes it does, sometimes it doesn't. A recent example is a study published in *JAMA*, "Oral Androstenedione Administration and Serum Testosterone Concentrations in Young Men," which notes that the "work was supported by an unrestricted grant from Major League Baseball and the Major League Baseball Players Association, New York, NY, and National Institutes of Health." The major leagues funded the study after the controversy that erupted when the press reported that Mark

McGwire was using "andro" as part of his quest to surpass Roger Maris's home run record.

To return to Polyani's analogy of the police force, those who are old enough will remember the sergeant in the TV series *Hill Street Blues*, who always said, "Be careful out there."

Who should evaluate the Web?

The anarchic nature of the Web has brought with it questions of regulation. In sensitive areas, governments have tried and, so far, failed to regulate what goes on the Net.

Attempts to control what some call "indecency"—information ranging from erotica to hardcore pornography—have failed. So have attempts to control what could be called "hate propaganda." The international nature of the Net makes it difficult to enforce regulations.

A number of software companies, some serving families with young children and others serving corporations, act to either monitor or filter access to specified sites. The question always is, who decides which sites should be blocked? No one wants kids straying into pornographic or dangerous sites, but often the nannyware (as it has been called after one of the first packages NetNanny) blocks breast cancer sites that unfortunately have wrong key words or block gay rights sites that some consider politically incorrect. (Countries such as the People's Republic of China are use similar software to block access to information from the West.)

There have been proposals that some authority evaluate sites and give them some sort of seal of approval. **Webtrust** is offered by the Canadian Institute of Chartered Accountants and the American Institute of Certified Public Accountants. With Webtrust, the accountants offer assurance that the site is complying with the appropriate regulations. If you click on the seal, the site is linked to the accountants' report on the site.

As a journalist, I want access to all kinds of sites, good or bad. News sites are generally exempt from the filtering software, as on any given day a news site can have information that may be violent, use expletives, or be sexually explicit (consider, for example, the Starr Report on President Clinton's activities).

I believe the accountants are on the right track, and Webtrust is a better model for the researcher than a filter that may block access to a key site. A verifiable button saying a site has been peer reviewed, for example, would rate it higher in an evaluation scale. But in the end, it is up to the researcher to make the final determination of how valuable it is.

The gatekeepers

Always consider the gatekeepers. Gatekeepers are the checkers, the ones who evaluate the information before it is published either in paper or on the Internet.

Peer review is a strong gatekeeper, which is why, with very few exceptions, a peer-reviewed article is considered reliable. News organizations have editors who act as gatekeepers and try to ensure that information presented to the public is accurate, fair, and reliable. Magazines and book publishing houses have editors.

The Internet also has gatekeepers. If an Internet site has a reliable gatekeeper, such as a news site affiliated with a major news organization, it can be considered reliable, as can government sites, university sites, and sites run by nongovernmental organizations (NGOs).

Remember that gatekeepers are not infallible. One of the problems that many people fail to realize is how much the media has changed in the past decade; it isn't always safe to assume that print (or television) is more reliable than the Net.

Beginning with the first corporate mergers in the mid-1980s, then with the recession of the early 1990s, and now with new mergers, the beancounters in all media are less concerned with gatekeeping than in the past. The number of editors in all media organizations have been cut back. Magazines once had staff members called fact checkers who did nothing but check every sentence in an article. There are a lot fewer fact checkers these days. In many book publishing houses, rigorous editing is a thing of the past. There have been a number of scandals in recent years in both the magazine and book fields where writers, unfortunately, made up material and passed it off as fact, and it survived a penny-pinching and sloppy editing process. It could be that a well-edited Internet site is more reliable than a poorly edited magazine article.

The Chinese wall

The "Chinese Wall" used by the media describes the ideal barrier between the editorial and advertising departments. Even small town newspapers and some trade magazines, where the advertising department has considerable influence, advertising material is always labeled as "advertising," including advertorial copy that is laid out to look like editorial copy.

There is often no Chinese Wall on the Net. Many purely commercial sites offer value-added material to enhance their products. If the site is well managed, the value-added material could be a valuable source of information, but just as often the site is designed to enhance sales.

The solution: Attribute and cite

Always attribute any material, whether you find it on the Internet or a more traditional source. If you are in an academic environment, you are obliged to cite all sources of information. A journalist and author should always attribute information whenever possible. Citation and attribution shows respect for your reader and lets them do their own evaluation of the research you have done.

Links

Evaluation

Alexander and Tate Evaluation at the Wolfram Library

www2.widener.edu/Wolfgram Memorial Library/webeval.htm

One of the best evaluation sites with five-point checklists for evaluating five different kinds of sites.

Smith, Alastair G. "Testing the Surf: Criteria for Evaluating Internet Information Resources." The Public Access Computer Systems Review 8, no. 3 (1997)

info.lib.uh.edu/pr/v8/n3/smit8n3.html

Evaluation hints by Alastair Smith, Senior Lecturer, School of Communications and Information Management, Victoria University of Wellington From the University of Houston site.

Evaluating Information Found on the Internet

milton.mse.jhu.edu/research/education/net.html

Site from Johns Hopkins University Library.

Evaluating Internet Research Sources

www.vanguard.edu/rharris/evalu8it.htm

From Robert Harris at Vanguard University.

Striking It Rich or Finding Fool's Gold? Thinking Critically about Web Information

www.ala.org/rusa/mars/etsproj.html

Training site from the American Library Association with links to site with hints on evaluation.

Britannica

www.britannica.com

CICA The Canadian Institute of Chartered Accountants

www.cica.ca/cica/cicawebsite.nsf/public/homepage

Home page for the Canadian Institute of Chartered Accountants.

About WebTrust

www.cica.ca/cica/cicawebsite.nsf/public/SPASWebTrust

The CICA Web trust information page.

AICPA

www.aicpa.org/index.htm

Home page for the American Institute of Certified Public Accountants.

AICPA Webtrust page

www.aicpa.org/webtrust/index.htm

JAMA home

www.jama.amaassn.org

Oral Androstenedione Administration and Serum Testosterone Concentrations in Young Men

www.jama.amaassn.org/issues/v283n6/abs/jci00000.html

The *JAMA* study on andro that was supported by Major League Baseball.

New England Journal of Medicine

www.nejm.org

Chapter 18

Evaluation, Evaluation, Evaluation: Site Verification

When you are evaluating any Web site, always check to see who created the site. Sometimes you can evaluate the e-mail address of someone posting an e-mail or a newsgroup message the same way.

Honest corporate, educational, and institutional Web sites usually have an **About** page that lists who owns the site and includes an address and a phone number for a live human being. Be wary of sites that purport to represent companies, schools, or institutions but have only an e-mail address.

You should always check the domain name to get an idea of who created the site. Even with the domain name, it is best to go further and verify the information about who owns the site.

Domain names

When you go to an Internet address you always see a suffix at the end, such as **.com**, which is known as the domain name. That usually gives you a clue about the site, and why it was created.

A few years ago, it was easier to evaluate a site by its top level domain. However, since the U.S. government opened up the domain registry of some names, the old rules and guidelines are no longer followed, especially with the current frenzy for dotcom companies, so the researcher has to be careful. In addition, with the growing international aspect of the Net, a researcher should know the domain name rules in other major Net-using countries.

Here are some key definitions:

- **A top level domain (TLD)** is the two- or three-letter suffix code, preceded by a dot or period. There are two types of top level domains: *generic,* such as **.com** (a commercial site); and *country codes,* such as **.ca** (Canada) or **.hk** (Hong Kong).
- **A second level domain** consists of the letters preceding a suffix code. Examples are **co.uk**, for a British commercial site; **bu.edu** for Boston University in the United States; and **amazon.com** for a commercial organization.
- **Third level domains** precede the second level domain and are found in areas where geography determines the domain. For example, the BBC's address is **bbc.co.uk,** while the government of the Canadian province of Alberta's is **gov.ab.ca.**
- **Fourth level domains** are also usually geographical. In the Alberta provincial government, for example, the Resource Development ministry is found at **resdev.gov.ab.ca.**
- **www.** is, of course, the standard prefix that normally would precede a Web site. Most sites still use www., but many are now dropping it (technically it isn't always necessary) to get a shorter address people can remember. Examples are **CNN.com** and **CBC.ca.**

The world of dotcom

In its earliest days, the Internet was confined largely to the United States. There were seven original top level generic domains: **.com, .edu, .gov, .int, .mil, .net,** and **.org**. Each had its own role. For Americans, there was also the **.us** country domain, which was little used in the beginning but is now growing as the number of people using the Net expands.

By early 2001, the Internet Corporation for Assigned Names and Numbers (ICANN) will have approved additions to existing top level domains by adding new suffices, perhaps *.store* for businesses or *.arts* for artistic endeavors. The private companies that register domains have been invited to submit proposals for the new TLD suffixes. ICANN will then chose the winners. Meanwhile, the original generic names now must be divided into two parts: those that are truly international, and those that are available only in the United States.

International generic domains

- **.com:** This is the commercial domain and can mean companies or even individuals. It can represent a major corporation such as **ibm.com**, or the restaurant around the corner. Individuals are also registering dotcom addresses either for current businesses or future considerations.
- **.net:** Originally this domain was intended for computer networks such as administrative computers and network node computers. It was later used (and still is) by some Internet Service Providers. However, since the U.S. government opened up the registration process, .net has become an alternative to .com. Often companies will buy the .net address to protect themselves from cybersquatters who register names in hopes of cashing in later.
- **.org:** Within the original Net community, .org came to be used for nonprofit and nongovernment organizations (NGOs). One well-known example is the Associated Press, which uses **ap.org**. The AP is a commercial organization, but as an international newsgathering cooperative, it is officially not for profit. The .org domain has been opened up to anyone who wants to use it.
- **.int:** This domain is for organizations established by international treaties or international databases. It is not open to public registration and thus information on an .int site is probably reliable.

U.S. domains (.us)

- **.edu**: This was originally intended for all education institutions. In the mid-1990s, the United States decide to limit .edu registrations to four-year colleges and universities. Other U.S. schools and two-year colleges are registered under the **.us** domain. Since most .edu sites are universities, information can usually be considered reliable, but the researcher should check whether or not the information comes from a faculty member or a student. The .edu university sites also include university phone and e-mail directories and a news release site that keeps up-to-date on research and other activities in the university community.

- **.gov:** The .gov domain was originally intended for any kind of government, but in the mid-1990s, the U.S. government restricted it to federal agencies. State and local agencies are registered by country, state, and local code. Outside the United States, .gov can be a second or third level domain name. Most government information can be considered reliable (at least from the government's point of view).
- **.mil:** This domain is used by the U.S. Department of Defense, with each branch of the service as a second level domain, such as **navy.mil**.
- **.us:** This is the country domain or country code for the United States domain. Geographical registration would use **name.state.us**. U.S. subdomain codes are:
  - **.ci:** This subdomain is used for city government agencies and is a subdomain under the "locality" name (such as Los Angeles).
  - **.co:** This subdomain is used for county government agencies. For example: **.co.SanDiego.ca.us.**
  - **.state:** This subdomain is used for state government agencies.
  - **.k12:** This subdomain is used for public school districts. A lower domain designation, **.pvt**, can be used in the place of a school district name for private schools.
  - **.cc:** This subdomain is used for statewide community colleges.
  - **.tec:** This subdomain is used for technical and vocational schools and colleges.
  - **.lib:** This subdomain is used mainly by state, regional, city, and county public libraries. It is sometimes also used as a subdomain for other top level domains. For example, a university library may use the .lib subdomain in an .edu domain.
  - **.mus:** This subdomain is used for museums.
  - **.gen:** This is a little-used subdomain for sites that don't fit into the structural level. But so far most U.S.-based sites prefer the top level .com, .org, and .net.

Canadian domains (.ca)

Canada was one the first nations to follow the United States onto the Net. You will find that many Canadian organizations use the three international generic domains. Registration for the **.ca** domain began in 1987, long before the Internet explosion. The committee working on domain names and registration invented a purely geographical approach.

There are currently three levels of Canadian domain names using the designation .ca:

1. **National level** (**.ca**): The organization must be:
   - ❑ **gc.ca:** The designation for the Canadian federal government (GC stands for government of Canada and is used for both English and French sites).
   - ❑ federally incorporated.
   - ❑ have offices in more than one province or territory.
   - ❑ own a registered trademark.
2. **Provincial level** (**.on.ca**, **bc.ca**): The organization must be:
   - ❑ a provincial government, using the .gov subdomain (Note: Quebec uses the French .gouv for both English and French information).
   - ❑ provincially or territorially incorporated.
   - ❑ a registered partnership or registered proprietorship.
   - ❑ a school district, referral hospital, university, or college.
3. **Municipal level** (**toronto.on.ca):** This is for organizations like:
   - ❑ municipal governments.
   - ❑ schools.
   - ❑ hospitals.
   - ❑ libraries.
   - ❑ museums.
   - ❑ local organizations.

Canadian individuals currently cannot register themselves as domain, so those who want to do so (like the author) use a dot-com address.

For researchers looking for Canadian university sites, the domain hierarchy can be misleading. Many Canadian universities actually use the top level, .ca domain; for example, I teach at Ryerson Polytechnic University, which uses **ryerson.ca,** while my alma mater, York University, uses **yorku.ca.**

British domains (.uk)

The United Kingdom has organized its domain structure by adding a second level domain that defines what the site does:

- **.co.uk:** commercial enterprises.
- **.org.uk:** organizations.
- **.ltd.uk:** UK limited companies.
- **.plc.uk:** UK public limited companies.
- **.net.uk:** Internet Service Providers.
- **.sch.uk:** UK schools.
- **.ac.uk:** "academic establishments," including universities.
- **.gov.uk:** government.
- **.nhs.uk:** Britain's National Health Service.
- **.police.uk:** UK police forces
- **.mod.uk:** Ministry of Defense, including branches of the armed forces.

If you are looking for university sites outside the United States, in any country, as well as looking for an .edu subdomain (for example, the City University of Hong Kong is **cityu.edu.hk**), you may find a clue with the second level subdomains .ac (academic), and sometimes .acs (academic computing services), .cc (campus computing) or .ccs (campus computing services). For example Israel's Tel Aviv University is found at **tau.ac.il.**

~ Tilde=Personal

A site with the tilde, or as some call it, "the squiggle" **(~)**, is usually the sign for a personal or small business site. It is most often found on a site maintained by an Internet Service Provider; sometimes it is also found on a university site. The ~ is actually a shortcut, a signal to the computer hosting the site to go immediately to the subdirectory with the name following the tilde.

Who owns the site?

If you want to check the site even more, you can check to see who has registered the name by checking the appropriate **whois** site for the country where the site is. In the United States, the prime site for registering the three generic top level domains is Network Solutions, found at **www.networksolutions.com**. A list of whois sites can be found in this chapter's Links.

You type in the name, and if it is registered, most whois databases tell you who runs the site. (Some will tell you only whether or not the name is available.

In most whois databases, you will find two names and addresses. The first, the administrative address, gives the contact person for administering the site. It can be the name of the person who actually created the site, or in a corporation, educational, institutional, or government site, the name of the employee who is, on paper, in charge. The technical contact is the name of the person in charge of the actual computer where the site resides. This could be the person who runs the site, if he or she has his own server; an employee from the MIS, IT, or computer department; or, if the site resides on computers run by one of many Web hosting companies around the world, an employee of the company.

The whois databases are a place to start if you want to track down a site and find the person who runs it, because the information includes actual street addresses and phone numbers.

Links

U.S. and International

Network Solutions

www.networksolutions.com

Domain Name Registration Services

www.networksolutions.com/cgi-bin/whois/whois

Whois look up for domain names .com, .net, and .org.

Register.com

www.register.com

Commercial rival to Network Solutions with an easier search engine for checking .com, .net, and .org.

The U.S. Domain

www.nic.us

U.S. top level domain rules.

www.isi.edu/in-notes/rfc1480.txt

Text of rules for U.S. domain.

Dotcom rules

www.isi.edu/in-notes/rfc1591.txt

Rules for generic TLD.

Canada

CA Domain

www.cdnnet.ca

Canadian domain registration and whois site.

Australia

www.aunic.net

Australian top level domain services and whois.

Europe

European whois

www.ripe.net/cgi-bin/whois

Nominet UK Network Information Centre

www.nic.uk/

British top-level domain whois service

www.nic.uk/domains/index.html

Explanation of rules.

Asia Pacific

APNIC (Asia Pacific Network Information Center)

www.apnic.net

Interactive TLD Map.

Top Level Domain links for Asia Pacific region (including Pacific Rim countries Canada and the United States

www.apnic.net/maps/tld-list.html

Hong Kong

HKNIC

www.hknic.net.hk/hknic

Hong Kong TLD registration and whois.

Part IV

Mostly Offline

Chapter 19

File It

How are you going to organize all of your research material so you can find it quickly?

There are many ways of doing it, and quite often the way researchers organize their material reflects their personality and their project. If you are working for an employer, often you will have to use the software that comes with the job.

Barbara Tuchman recounted how she used 4 x 6 cards for her notes and a loose-leaf notebook with pages about the same size for interviews. The material was then filed together in a binder or shoebox, in the proper order, so that when she started to write, the chapter was already roughed out. She also said she used the small cards to "extract the strictly relevant" in the days when "copying was a chore." Now that the computer has eased the chore of copying, the danger for the researcher is still to extract the relevant and to pare it down in this age of information overload.

Even if you have a computer, do not ignore the practicality of paper. I keep a thick notepad by my desk where I scribble notes during phone calls, especially the unexpected incoming calls. I also use the notepad for jotting down ideas, names, phone numbers, and anything else that is relevant. Most of the notes are then transferred to a computer file, but the notebook remains on my desk. It's not a good idea to tear pages out of the notebook; you may inadvertently destroy something on a back page.

Even if they do have a computer, some researchers and reporters also keep and use a tab-divided notebook, the kind still sold for high school and college students. That way specific notes for a project can be entered in the notebook and, if necessary, later transferred to a computer file.

In the corporate environment, you may be using group information software, such as Novell's **GroupWise**, **Lotus Notes**, or **Microsoft Outlook**. The advantage of this type of software is that you can join notes with contact lists, to-do lists, and calendars. The disadvantage is that the ability to search your notes is limited.

Ted Anthony of the AP uses Microsoft Outlook to organize his material. He creates "a story board" in his computer using the **Notes** function in Outlook.

"I keep loose notes. Each note represents a story idea," he says. "Then when the story idea goes from idea to something I am working on, it becomes an entire folder."

In that folder Anthony creates as series of notes.

"One of the notes I use as a list of people to call. I am continually adding to that list. I put in parenthesis after I interview them or leave a phone message for them to show what the status is of that interview....Other notes can be anything. They can be just free-form ideas.

"When I find something on the Internet, whether it is text from a Web site or an old clip that I got from Dow Jones news retrieval, I cut and paste that into another sticky note. [Notes in Microsoft Outlook look like 3M's Post-It Notes.]

"Those things are all organized in one folder, so that all loose, free-form information relating to a topic goes into that folder.

"Then when I am going on the road, all I have to do is copy that folder onto a floppy disk and take it along and load it into Outlook on my laptop.

"I have all of the stuff dealing with that story, without carrying a great deal of a paperwork along. Now, that's not to say that I don't use paperwork. I mean, I have a thick folder for everything I do."

Freedom with free-form

If you want to try something with more powerful search abilities, an alternative is the free-form database, also called a text retrieval database, an electronic filing cabinet, or a free-form PIM (personal information manager). A free-form database is largely unstructured and handles any information that may come from a variety of sources. Thus, it doesn't fit into a traditional flat file or relational database, but at the same the user needs the retrieval power of a database to find key elements in that unstructured information.

Because research is often anarchic (especially information you find on the Internet), a free-form database is more than helpful in storing the information you find on the Net.

The structured personal information manager such as Microsoft Outlook often limits your ability to search for key words or concepts, whereas the free-form database searches across the entire file.

For example, in the free-form database, the search engine looks both in the semi-structured part of the database, such as a name field, and throughout any unstructured notes you may make.

AskSam and **Info Select** are favorites among journalists (including me), professional investigators such as police officers, and lawyers, as well as some academic researchers. A new and interesting addition to the group is the more academic Scholar's Aid shareware program, which has some free-form elements.

The power of free-form databases solves one of the problems in the age of information overload: storing and handling the vast amount of information out there. They are electronic filing cabinets, and whether you're using one large file or a number of smaller ones, they will make your research life a lot easier.

askSam

AskSam is one of the original free-form or text retrieval database software. Its powerful DOS version was used by many professional researchers and investigators and first came to the attention of the media when it was used by the Congressional Iran Contra Committee. Many users, however, also found the askSam command language daunting and a barrier to their research.

That changed with Windows, when askSam solved the problem by using standard Windows commands and lots of drop-down menus to make your information storage and retrieval simple. The software combines a word processor with database retrieval and reporting; information can be totally unstructured.

An askSam file can contain pure text or it can be structured, as in a database for research sources and contacts.

AskSam has also designed special import templates for researchers, which include a general Internet template and templates for Eudora files, Lexis-Nexis, and generic e-mail.

For this project, I used askSam to:

- Store e-mail, including e-mail interviews and notes from mailing lists that I found interesting or relevant.
- Maintain a list of contacts with extensive notes on the contacts.
- Create a template for an e-mail questionnaire.
- Store transcribed interview notes.

If you take the time to preplan how you set up your askSam files, it will make your research life a lot easier in the long run. An askSam file can, of course, hold multiple documents and you can search those documents within that single file. You will find, however, that as your project progresses, that single file may become too large to be manageable.

Review your outline and decide how you are going to divide up the information. You can have as many or as few askSam files as you need. If you go to your outline, you can decide that, for example, that for all your first level categories, you will also create an askSam file.

You can also "divide and distill" further, if you wish, by creating files at the second or third levels of your outline, but that may in turn create too many files.

AskSam also lets you create bookmarks on documents so you can quickly find important material. Then you can add hyperlinks to documents within a file, in another askSam file, or even to an external Web page.

AskSam comes with a number of ready-made templates that can be used to store the information that you are researching, although you may have to modify the template to fit your needs and your software. For e-mail, for example, you can use templates for generic e-mail, **Eudora** and **Microsoft Outlook**.

Once the file is created, askSam presents an opening screen that lists the importing, storing, and reporting features of the template.

The power of askSam for research is in its variety of search methods, including text, field, Boolean, proximity, date, and numeric searches. AskSam also allows you to do a more sophisticated Boolean search by joining several words or concepts. You also can combine field, numeric, proximity, and date searching in askSam's Advanced Search feature.

AskSam has the formal reporting functions of a flat file or relational database. There are a couple of ways of using the reporting functions to make information retrieval much easier. For example, the Internet and e-mail templates come with some pre-configured reports. One works with the subject field of the e-mail or Usenet message. Because an askSam search creates a new file, you can then use the searching tools we discussed above to narrow the search.

With askSam's hypertext ability all you have to do when you find what you want is double click on the subject line you've found and askSam takes you back the original page.

You can enhance your report, of course, with other features such as footers, page numbers, and page counts, etc. You'll find instructions for that in the askSam manual.

Info Select

Info Select, another popular free-form database, evolved from a DOS note-taking software called Tornado, which was first released in the 1980s. It's still based on note taking, or as the company, MicroLogic, says in its publicity, "lots of miscellaneous or unstructured information."

Info Select offers an alternative for more structured information, but like askSam, it can search across all fields, structured or unstructured. It is also a cheaper alternative to askSam.

Info Select divides the monitor screen into two large areas. MicroLogic calls the large area on the left side "the Selector." The Selector works like an outline, with notes contained on the right side of the screen in an area called the Workspace. You can vary the size of the Selector and Workspace by dragging this dividing line to the left or right with your mouse.

The top level of the outline structure is called a Topic. You can then create a large amount of free-form text in notes. The Topic appears in the left-hand Selector, the notes on the right-hand Workspace. Every Note, Topic, or other item you create can have a caption of a single line of text describing the item.

If you prefer structured information, perhaps for a contact list, or a simple bibliography, you can do that in Info Select and combine with unstructured notes.

The one weakness in Info Select is that it doesn't have a hypertext function, although it can work with standard Web addresses by activating your default browser.

You can even make Info Select your e-mail client by integrating it with Windows 95 or 98's Internet Mail function. You can also use its calendar and tickler functions to manage your time.

As with askSam, the advantage a researcher gets with Info Select is the ability to search across all the possible places for a word or phrase that may appear either in your notes or in a more structured contact file. You enter the word, phrase, or number that you want to find. As you type the word, the dialog box actually tracks the success of your search in a block of colored squares representing the notes, leaving only those notes with the word you want highlighted.

Info Select then changes the Selector so it displays the result of your search. The matching words or numbers will be highlighted inside the Note items.

What Info Select calls a **Neural search** finds items containing as many occurrences of several words as possible.

As I was writing this book, Info Select released Info Select for the Palm Organizer. Essentially it is a Palm plug in for Info Select.

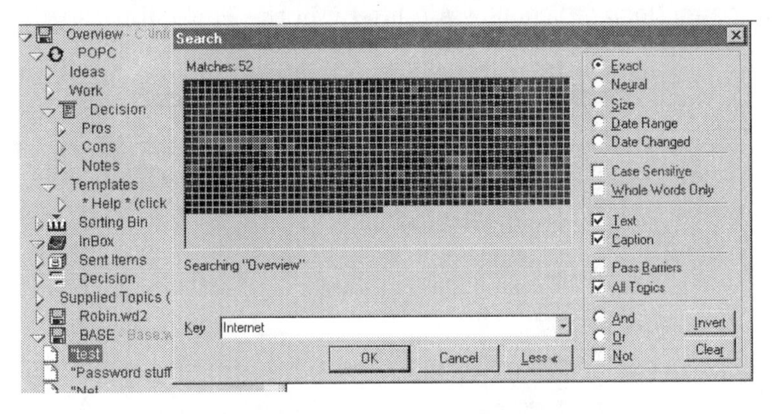

Figure 19-1. The search box in Info Select.

Scholar's Aid

Scholar's Aid is a shareware program originally designed, as the name suggests, so that scholars and students could create correctly formatted bibliographies. Later versions, including the current release, Scholar's Aid

2000, come with an accompanying program called **Notes**, which as the name implies, is used for taking notes.

The creator of Scholar's Aid calls the software Reference Processor and thus it has a slightly different approach than the traditional free-form database. If you write all your original notes in the Notes module of Scholar's Aid, you can then select text and click the transfer button. Notes then transfers the selected text into your word processor and, at exactly the same time, inserts a citation into the document as a footnote, endnote, or parenthetical reference.

Scholar's Aid, both for the citation/bibliographic module and the Notes module, uses a split-screen technique similar to Info Select. For the notes module, it is called Note Tree (the equivalent of Info Select's Selector) and the Note List (the equivalent of Info Select's Workspace).

Notes offers several predefined note types including General, Quotation, Summary, My Idea, and Table, which is, in fact, a small, Excel-compatible spreadsheet, a feature not available in the free-form databases. You can create topic folders in the Note Tree, and then type a series of notes of various kinds in each the topic folders. I'll discuss the citation and bibliographic functions of Scholar's Aid briefly in the Appendix.

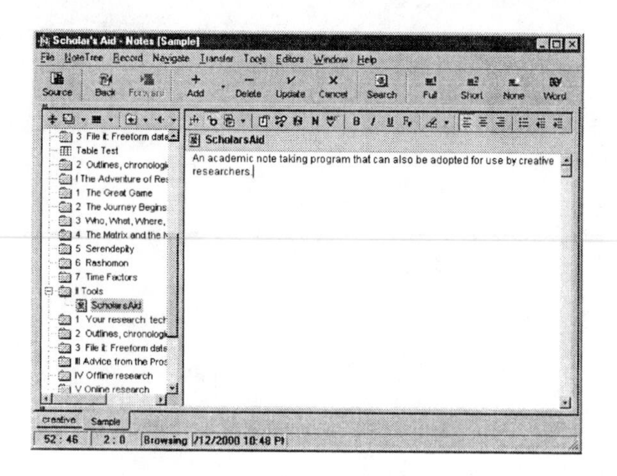

Figure 19-2. Notes in Scholar's Aid.

Scholar's Aid has a search engine almost as powerful as its free-form rivals do. You can search the current Notes folder you are using, any open Notes file or every note file.

Scholar's Aid lets you search by typing Boolean operators *and*, *or*, and brackets in the search box. Then you click the Search button. If it finds the text, it shows a set of navigation buttons that allows you to narrow down what you are looking for.

The importing and exporting functions in the current version of Scholar's Aid are a relatively weak point in an otherwise highly practical program. Because it is based on citations, Scholar's Aid uses the *paragraph* as the import unit and then designates certain paragraphs as folders and the rest as notes. This means it is difficult to import longer files.

Scholar's Aid export function is limited to Rich Text Files, which is fine if you are going to bring the notes up in a word processor. However, if you want to use plain text (for example, importing into an e-mail program), you would still have to use the word processor to strip the RTF formatting first.

As with Info Select, Scholar's Aid uses a split screen tree structure to organize its material and so reporting is not really necessary.

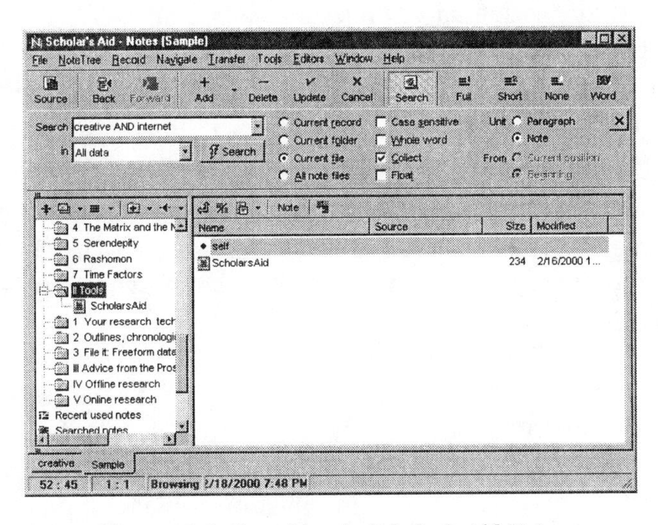

Figure 19-3. Searching in Scholar's Aid Notes.

So what do you use?

For your research project, use askSam if you are:

- ❑ A scholar working on a major project with diverse or original information.

- A journalist working on long-term enterprise projects.
- An investigator.

AskSam is best for those who have to deal with huge amounts of information stored in one file or several. On the askSam listserv, one scholar recently mentioned, "I have summarized circa 8,000 historical documents in a 4.5MB askSam database."

You can use the various templates supplied by askSam or create your own. (For example, you can create combination structured and unstructured information in one document, such as a contact name and address, and then add lengthy interview notes or a bibliographic entry form and then notes based on that source.)

Use Info Select if you are:

- A journalist in daily news or who works on many short-turnaround projects.
- A student with a lot of projects and assignments.
- A fiction writer or dramatist.
- A musician, artist, or professional in other creative fields.
- Interested in combining structured and unstructured information for the price of one software application.

Info Select is better for smaller chunks of information and in situations where you are working on several projects at the same time. Then you can quickly find whatever project you are working on in the Selector and bring up the appropriate notes.

I use Info Select for storing ideas and notes on more creative projects. If I get an idea, I pop it into my home desktop or into the stripped down Info Select for the Palm.

If you don't have Outlook or a similar program, you can also use Info Select as your structured personal information manager, using the calendar, its tickler for to-do's, and creating a database of names, addresses, and phone numbers. (You should note that you cannot, at this time, integrate Info Select's structured information with your Palm.)

Use Scholar's Aid Notes if you are:

- A scholar working extensively with "the literature."
- A student writing academic papers.

- A creative or narrative nonfiction writer who wants to include bibliographic and source notes in a long magazine article or book.
- Interested in using a simple spreadsheet or table while taking notes.

Scholar's Aid was originally designed as a bibliographic program for academic writing and there it shines. The Notes module, a relatively recent addition to the program, is strong where it follows its academic legacy but weak as an overall note storing program, although an experienced computer user can find workarounds for most of its current limitations.

Links

askSam
www.asksam.com

Micrologic
www.miclog.com

Eudora
www.eudora.com

Palm
www.palm.com

Scholar's Aid
www.scholarsaid.com

Chapter 20

People Who Need People

Tracking and finding people are key parts of creative research. Reporters, investigators, documentary producers, and other researchers work to find good people for their stories or research. There is also a special group of men and women who track down people day after day in television and sometimes in radio. They're called chase producers, booking producers, or just plain bookers.

They're called chase producers because that's what they do: chase people to get them to appear on television. They're called booking producers or bookers because that's their goal: booking a guest.

Any executive producer will tell you that a good chase producer or booker is worth his or her weight in gold. The best bookers are as smooth and persuasive as an accomplished diplomat, as tough and determined as a police staff sergeant after 20 years on the street, and as pushy as a stage mother.

If you want to find someone, learn from a chase producer.

Cut to the chase

The Internet is the equalizer when it comes to the chase. It's now easier to find people, through personal Web sites, online phone books, and e-mail, and, in the United States, the pay-for-view personal information sites.

The telephone is still the most important tool that you have. After all, once you've found a number on the Internet, you still have to pick up the phone and make the call.

Once, it was a lot harder. A reporter had to hope that the newsroom library had up-to-date phone books; the independent researcher hoped that the local public library was well-stocked.

If the books from the phone company don't help, all kinds of directories come in handy.

During the upheavals in Rwanda, I was working the phones, trying to find a civilian trapped by the violence. I grabbed a huge international directory of hotels, the kind a newsroom normally uses for booking rooms for reporters and started dialing. When I got through to one hotel in Kigali, I asked the hotel desk, "Do you have any Canadians staying there?" and they rang a phone. A moment later I was chatting with a Montreal man trapped in his room.

Investigative reporter Ira Silverman was working for NBC News in the 1970s when he received a tip that Michigan police were looking for a possible burial site for the Teamsters boss Jimmy Hoffa.

"If it was Jimmy Hoffa's body in Michigan, it would have been a very big story and I would have wanted to have cameras there if I could," Silverman says.

"I knew the names of two investigators who might be involved and no idea other than it was the state of Michigan and it was happening the next day. I was in New York and I got Michigan phone books and started calling every hotel in a radius of 25 to 50 miles asking for those two individuals. Finally after a dozen hotels, they rang the room and I hung up, and then I knew in what city it was happening."

Speed, accuracy, and tenacity

So what makes a good booker, chase producer, or combined field and chase producer?

"You have to be fast, accurate; you have to move a story forward," says Ian Kalushner of CBC's *The Magazine*. "You have got to think on your feet. You have to be aggressive, you can't be afraid of picking up the phone and talking to people. You can't be bothered by rejection.

"You have to be able to synthesize an issue relatively quickly, in terms of trying to figure out what the details of an issue are. And also, in terms of a journalistic perspective, take a new angle. The question that you always need to ask yourself and you want to be able to do is to say, 'How am I going to move the story forward?' as opposed as simply regurgitating everything that's been heard every day."

Collecting information

According to Jet Belgraver, a chase producer for CBC's *The Magazine,* "There are very few people who are not findable." She suggests using telephone directories or doing a Net search to find anything that may have been written by the person you are seeking. Building up contacts is also critical.

"You really do have to collect as much information as possible...a work number...an assistant's number...a pager...or a cell number....I keep all that information."

Persistence and ingenuity are also important for chase producers. Belgraver says, "If you want to get that person, you keep calling...go to their assistant...go to somebody else in the building...there is always a way." If all else fails, and your story idea is based on a print story, call the journalist who wrote the original article. Usually, says Belgraver, you'll get the help you need.

Silicon and paper

"A story will break. If you want a story and you want...to be the first one to get this person, you have to get there fast. You have to find your people, put in your request, convince the guest to do it. That's where having your personal files and having things like the Internet at your fingertips helps," Belgraver says.

"Do a quick [Web] search and get some really good basic information, really fast, so that within five minutes, even while you're chasing somebody, you get up to speed on what you want to ask them and what you want to talk about.

"I have extensive files," she adds. "What goes into those files are clippings, newspaper clippings, whatever papers I read during the day, if I see an article either that intrigues me or interests me. For example, I have a huge folder when it comes to the Balkans, and especially Kosovo. So whatever I spotted that was of interest to me, that mentioned names of people.

I would cut that out. I would highlight the names, so that even when I am flipping through the clipping file, the names jump out at you in bold."

Belgraver writes all phone numbers on the front of the file folder so that they are immediately accessible. And she bookmarks similar sites (for example, newspapers, government agencies) in order to have basic information at her fingertips.

The approach

So how does one approach a person you want to interview?

"Pleasant but firm is what it really comes down to," Kalushner says. He notes that how you phrase your request is critical, particularly if your interviewee is reluctant. "Especially with people who are hard to get, it is not necessarily, 'we would like to request [an interview]' because one of the things you have to consider is what is in it for them, especially if it's an accountability interview or anything like that, then there is nothing really in it for them.

"So, it's about trying to not say 'We request an interview.' But it's more... 'We want to know what time we can set up an interview.' I take it as a given that, in fact, the person is actually going to do the interview as opposed to giving him the opportunity."

If your interviewee still declines your request? Just keep trying, says Kalushner, and work around any obstacles they may put in your way. "Trying makes it very difficult for them."

When your interview subject is not a public figure, convincing the person to tell his story requires tact. "Let them reach their own decision why it's important for them to tell their own story. Clearly you want the interview. But you're not going to promise them something....They have to reach that decision themselves....There has to be a mutual trust and a mutual respect.

"We all have different approaches....What works for me doesn't work for someone else," Kalushner adds. "I have already said, you can be aggressive with a smile on your face. It's also knowing and being focused on what you're trying to accomplish, how you're actually going to do it and do it with integrity and ethics and not in an underhanded way. I will never promise something to someone. I never have lied to someone. My integrity is important."

Finding people

The Internet has made it much easier to find people. The first step to finding a person is to use your favorite search engine and check the name. Hotbot is a good place to start, with its drop-down menu option on its main search page that lets you look for a person.

Don't just stick with one search engine; try your meta-search engine and other favorite search engines as well. That will give you some indication of the person you are searching for, and that is why I recommend you do the search before you go to an online phone book. Because if you don't know that much about the person you are looking for, finding sites that eliminate certain people is just as helpful as finding sites that include information on the person you are looking for.

You can also gauge how active the person is in life or on the Net by counting the number of links to various pages. More and more people are creating personal Web pages and while you should, of course, verify and evaluate those pages just like any others, a personal Web page will certainly become part of your research material.

There are now a number of personal Web page directories, and I've listed them in the Links section of this chapter.

Online phone books and people finders

The Web-based phone book has made life a lot easier for researchers, reporters, and people finders. If it doesn't give you a phone number, it may give you an e-mail address.

The first question to ask is if you are looking for a home or business number. If it is a business number, of course, you have to know the name of the company, and then it's a case of calling the switchboard (or the automatic voice mail and spelling the name on your telephone keypad). Individual names in online directories are usually home numbers.

Most businesses do not include internal phone numbers on their sites; universities often do. You can also find some government phone books on the Net.

You should use all the resources of the Net and use a couple of online sources before picking up the phone. I did a number of test searches in the United States, Canada, and the United Kingdom for this chapter and often found some numbers (which I knew) were a year or so out of date.

The first place I usually try when I am looking for a U.S. number is Yahoo!'s People Search. In the United States, Yahoo! took over the old **www.411.com** and a return will often give you a phone number and an e-mail address.

For people living outside the United States, Yahoo! is better for e-mail addresses than phone numbers (except in Canada, where Yahoo! is affiliated with the online directory **www.yellow.ca**). Click on the regional Yahoo at the bottom of the main page, and then when it comes up see if a people search is available. You then get a search dialog box and can enter the name. Note: You should know the local language.

Yahoo! also has a directories section under "Reference" in both its main and regional sites, which can provide links where you might find the person you are looking for, as well as an index of personal web pages.

As well as Yahoo!, you can check InfoSpace at **www.infospace.com**, which also searches Canadian, British, and European phone numbers.

In the United States, Switchboard, which is now owned by CBS, at **www.switchboard.com**, has always been a favorite among American journalists for finding numbers. In Canada, **www.canada411.com** is owned by a consortium of Canada's phone companies; it is considered reliable and contains both business and residential numbers.

In the United States, there are also a number of commercial online records sites, which buy public records from various states and offer background information on people for a fee. You will not find similar sites outside of the United States, where privacy laws are much more stringent.

One additional place to check a name is in Deja, **www.deja.com,** just to see if the person you are searching for has posted a message in a newsgroup. That may provide an e-mail address for the person you are searching for.

The old-fashioned way

While searching the Net, don't forget that finding people the old-fashioned way often works just as well, or better.

If you are talking to other sources, ask them for a phone number of the person you are looking for.

Find out if the person is a member of an association or professional group and then try to reach him or her through that organization. The association or organization may have a Web site, with a list of members or at least a contact number, which may prove helpful.

If someone is not in the office, most businesses will not give out home phone numbers, especially for well-known people. But if the matter is urgent (such as a missed appointment), someone at the business will usually call that person at home and pass on your message, if you ask politely.

Use the phone book and the city directories, which are often organized three ways: by street address, by phone number (also called a reverse directory), and by name.

Use the library to find hard copy phone books, directories of associations and organizations, and other information.

Indexes of periodicals and academic journals may indicate if your subject has ever written anything. You can then contact that magazine or journal and ask, if possible, to be put in touch with the person you are trying to reach.

Working backward

In doing research, you sometimes have to work backward and then go forward. While people often search for their ancestors through genealogy, often the researcher, especially one dealing with history, uses what is sometimes called *reverse genealogy* to find sources of information.

When I was researching the life of the RCMP's Frank Zaneth, who as I have said, kept his private life very private, I did know one thing: His father, Ambrose Zanetti, had died in Springfield, Massachusetts, in the winter of 1940. So I visited Springfield and one of the first things I did was go to the local library and spend some time going through newspaper microfilm. There I found his death notice, which, as is usual, gave the names of the surviving relatives. I then went to the phone book and started calling until I found one of Ambrose's grandsons, Zaneth's nephew, who was still living in Springfield. I arranged an interview and found out more about Zaneth's last years and in addition, I was able to arrange to copy some priceless family photographs for my book.

Public libraries often have old phone books, which investigators sometimes use to try and track down people who have moved away by finding an old address and then going out and checking with neighbors.

For older history, old city directories are helpful as well, because they often mention all people living in a household and thus give the researchers the names of children or other relatives living at the same address at a certain period of time.

Links

Government

CIA Leadership Views

www.odci.gov/cia/publications/chiefs/

CIA lists of chiefs of state and government.

U.S. Federal Telephone Directories

www.info.gov/fed_directory/phone.shtml

U.S. government online phone book.

Canadian Government Electronic Directory Services

canada.gc.ca./search/direct500/geds_e.html

Canadian government online phone book and e-mail directory.

European Governments online

europa.eu.int/abc/governments/index_en.html

European Union gateway to listings for members and other governments.

Experts

Profnet for Reporters

www.profnet.com/reporters.html

Gives access to experts for members of the working news media.

Universities

General Education Online

wsdo.sao.uwf.edu/~geo/

A directory site listing universities around the world.

Canadian Universities/Universites Canadiennes

www.uwaterloo.ca/canu/

Directory and guide site to Canadian universities.

American Universities

www.clas.ufl.edu/CLAS/american-universities.html

Directory and links to U.S. Universities.

Online People Finders and Phone books

Yahoo! People Search (U.S.)

people.yahoo.com

Yahoo! People Search (Canada)

ca.people.yahoo.com

Yahoo! People Search (U.K and Ireland)

ukie.people.yahoo.com

Yahoo! People Search (Hong Kong)

hke.people.yahoo.com

Switchboard: The Internet Directory
www.switchboard.com

Canada411
canada411.sympatico.ca

Yellow.ca—People Locator Canada
www.yellow.ca
Includes a reverse directory.

InfoSpace.com
www.infospace.com/
U.S.people search site.

InfoSpace Canada
www.infospace.com/canada/

InfoSpace U.K/
www.infospace.com/uk/

BigBook
www.bigbook.com
U.S. and Canada phone book site.

People Meta Search Engines

All-in-one PeopleSearch.net
216.157.48.112/peoplesearch
People finder, multiple search engines includes U.S. and international listings and reverse lookup for U.S.

The Ultimate White Pages
www.theultimates.com/white
A people Meta-search engine, mostly U.S. with reverse lookup.

Personal Web pages and Web rings

WhoWhere? Personal Home Pages Directory
homepages.whowhere.lycos.com
Lycos directory of personal home pages.

Yahoo! Society and Culture: People: Personal Home Pages
dir.yahoo.com/Society_and_Culture/People/Personal_Home_Pages/
Yahoo Directory of personal Web pages.

WebRing
www.webring.org
Home page for Web Rings, where pages with similar topics link to each other.

Chapter 21

The Interview

Good creative research, of any kind, is based on structured or unstructured interviews aimed at getting information, whether it is a 10-second sound bite or 10 hours of oral history.

Books have been written on how to interview. At conventions, journalists flock to seminars on how to do it. Professional oral historians are trained in interviewing. So are professional investigators, such as police officers.

In this chapter, I am again using cross-fertilization to show how there are basic rules for a good in-depth interview, whether or not it is an on-air accountability interview with a politician or corporate executive, or a more relaxed, longer, oral history with a war veteran.

Often the person who is interviewed is dissatisfied with the interview. The interviewer missed something the interviewee thought was important, the interviewer didn't listen, the interviewer had a different point of view or agenda, the interviewer didn't listen, the interviewer wanted to debate rather than ask questions, the interviewer didn't listen....

So before we talk about how to interview, I am going to take you to a place where absolutely everyone has been interviewed, to a place where seven times out of 10 it's a bad interview, an interview usually with someone else's agenda, an interview that's hurried, over too soon, and in many cases leaves you dissatisfied—sometimes despite the best efforts of the person conducting the interview.

That place is the doctor's office.

What the doctor ordered

Dr. Maurice Pappworth was a brilliant and radical British physician who began his career in 1936 but was excluded from a hospital consultant's job. He was Jewish. Pappworth set up in private practice in London's Harley Street and soon began coaching young doctors for the exam set by the Royal College of Physicians. It is said that his pupils had a higher pass rate than some of London's great teaching hospitals. He also taught the young doctors a lot more than how to pass an exam. One of his most radical ideas was that doctors (then, in the 1940s and 1950s, at the peak of their authority) should actually listen to patients. When Pappworth died in 1994, the *British Medical Journal* noted that he was "regarded as a pestilential nuisance" by the establishment. Just a year earlier, he had been elected to a Fellowship in the Royal College of Physicians, after almost 60 years of exclusion, and was given a standing ovation at the induction.

In 1960, Pappworth collected his 20 years of experience as a coach into a book called *A Primer of Medicine*. He considered taking a patient's history crucial and he wrote this sentence:

> Another essential quality to possess is that of being a good listener, allowing the patient to talk freely and in simple language and yet skillfully guiding him away from irrelevancies and towards a logical continuity of his story.

Remember what Dr. Pappworth ordered and 99 percent of your interviews will be successful.

Pappworth also said a doctor must not be "arrogant and blown out with the air of feigned superiority or ultra-sophistication." How many interviewers does that describe?

To be fair to doctors, there are factors for this poor performance that go beyond the mechanistic, here-pop-a-pill training many receive. They are often dealing with the ultimate questions of life and death; they are often dealing with people in pain; some are overworked and overtired; some have seen too much; and some build barriers to protect themselves.

If you are going to be interviewing people, the best stories come out of life and death, pain and misfortune, and sickness and adversity. Three of the writers I interviewed for this book wrote about life and death in hospitals. Others write about death in war.

In all but the most routine for-information interviews, people are telling you the story of some crucial event in their lives—that's why you are interviewing them. So, as you are fiddling with your tape recorder and scribbling in your notebook, while probably struggling with your own emotional involvement in the story, think back to sitting on the side of an examination bed, when the doctor was interviewing you. Then remember Dr. Pappworth's prescription.

Do your homework

A reporter faced with deadline pressure and a limited budget is often tempted to pick up the phone and start asking questions. That's a mistake. No matter what your final aim, you should do as much homework as you can before you ask that first question.

Interviewing coach John Sawatsky advises, "First figure out the story before you jump, before you chase an individual." Sawatsky and other veterans all note that outer circle—pure research—means that an interviewer "comes up with better questions."

Science fiction writer Robert J. Sawyer writes what is called "hard" science fiction, based on science and background research essential to his stories.

"The hardest thing for any person, young or old, is to admit how ignorant they are," Sawyer says. "If you are going to do any research you are going to have to open your eyes. I am often doing research from a cold start, so I always start out by getting the 'cartoon guide' to whatever it is. You can find them at university bookstores—the beginners guides are often remarkable." Sawyer then goes to his local library and does a full text search of general interest publications and general science publications, such as *Discover* and *Astronomy*.

"At that point I am ready to start technical literature. It means a trip to the library, or getting them online if the journal has a site and makes them available, or the abstract," Sawyer says. "After I've read enough of the technical literature that I am not daunted by the vocabulary any more, then I question the experts.

"As a science fiction writer, I've approached dozens of scientists, engineers, doctors, lawyers, and philosophy professors over the years and never once did they decline to be interviewed.

"The reason is that I already know the material. Nobody has the time to spoon-feed you what you could have gotten at the library. I tell them I already know the basics...what I need to know is the more advanced stuff...and they always say 'Come on over.'"

Oral historians recommend doing as much background research as possible before an interview. For someone famous who has had a major role in history, it may take months of careful research before the first question is asked. Even for the "ordinary person," it is best to know about that person's town, unit, company, whatever it is you are asking about.

Research will give you names, dates, events, places, and data that can add to your interview. It will give you a better sense of your subject. You'll ask better, more focused questions once you get to the interview. Countless unprepared talk show hosts have found that out over the years. Preresearch is also a sign of respect for the person you're interviewing. If you ask appropriate questions, the subject will usually respect you—and then you can get to the heart of the interview faster.

Tip: Get to know the language, if possible, before you make your first calls, and certainly before any major interviews. By language I mean anything from the technical talk of a profession to slang, whether you're talking to scientists, cops, or members of a street gang. As Kevin Donavan of the *Toronto Star* recommends, get to know the acronyms as well, because the people you are talking to on a regular basis will start soon start talking in acronyms.

To tape or not to tape?

The question to tape or not to tape an interview is usually debated long and hard among print journalists. For oral historians there is no question; oral history is based on a good quality tape. For broadcast journalists almost every interview is taped, either for audio or video.

If you are writing for publication—especially if there is a chance of litigation—your lawyers may recommend that you tape. You should tape even if the lawyers don't demand it. If you have a tape, you can defend yourself if you are accused of misquoting someone.

Taping also may depend on the stage of the interview. Veteran broadcast investigative producer Ira Silverman says of meeting sensitive sources, "I don't like to tape; I think it hurts spontaneity." Silverman also says he seldom takes notes in those kinds of meetings. Instead, he says, he goes to his car or some place after a meeting with a source and makes extensive notes. As for telephone interviews, he says, "Working at the keyboard is very inviting and I particularly like it because it's quiet. With phone conversations I can type and not be heard, so I feel it's okay to take notes [during] phone conversations."

There are times when taping won't work. Meeting in a restaurant or coffee shop adds too much noise unless the subject is directly miked. There are subjects who are intimidated by a tape recorder, and you will run into people who are eloquent in casual speech and then become stilted and formal when the tape recorder is turned on.

Oral historians frequently deal with that problem—and they have to tape. A solution, according to one guide, is to turn on the recorder, engage in some small talk, stop and rewind, and then play it back to "put the narrator at ease."

Tip: Never turn the tape recorder off until you have seen the interview subject walk away after saying goodbye. It's happened to me and to almost everyone else: The person usually gives you a last minute gem after the formal interview has wound down. Pat Stith of the *Raleigh News and Observer* calls it "now or never time" when people open up.

If you do tape, then there is the problem of transcribing. There are two possibilities: transcribe it yourself or hire a transcription service.

"I do serious transcripts and I do them myself," author Martin O'Malley says. "I tried sending them away to a transcription service, and I just wasn't happy. It's very labor intensive, listening to every single interview. I'll paraphrase. I can type fast enough almost to keep up. When I come to something that is really germane, that I know I am going to actually put into quotes, then I will stop and do it verbatim.

"Often I will shut the tape recorder off...and I will write thoughts. Relistening provides them to me. I put all those thoughts in capital letters just so they'll stand out and then I'll lapse back into strictly transcribing.

"It could take me a whole day to transcribe a 90-minute interview—a six- or eight-hour day. I deliberately set up an oven timer for an hour or so, then just stop. Otherwise you get fatigue when you start to go too fast. This way it forces you to do it very methodically.

"It's very laborious, but at the end it's really useful. You already have begun to write....When you listen to that person's voice you can pick nuances or phrases and you can see that person as a character...so it's worth the effort."

I began taping interviews years ago because my handwriting is so bad. I soon realized that taping has advantages. You can really listen if you are not fiddling with a notepad or scrunched over a laptop. You can watch the person you are interviewing as she speaks.

Like Martin O'Malley, I know when to paraphrase and when to go for the exact quote. For me transcribing is not a chore, but a gateway to the subconscious, as I hear the interview again, and I begin to make connections that help the writing.

If you are going to tape and transcribe and you're going to do it all verbatim—rather than just transcripts as notes—your best sources of advice are oral historians, who are very careful about transcribing accurately (often more so than many commercial transcription services). Oral historians also have established ways for conveying speech, by reflecting as much as possible what the interview subject said (not just cleaning up words, as is common practice among journalists). They also know how to accurately reflect the emotion of the speaker and punctuate for clarity of meaning, while preserving readability.

The game plan

Once you've done your research, prepare a list of questions to ask. Have a plan of action (you may not stick to it in the actual interview, but it's part of your preparation). Your research should have given you an idea of what questions to ask, at least initially, and helped you plan how you are going to do it.

The idea of the outer circle for research began with the investigative interview, with the idea that the interviewer should begin with an outer circle of more general questions and then, as it progresses, get closer and closer to the crucial questions, whether it is in one lengthy sit-down interview or several.

McGraw's rule of three

Mike McGraw, a veteran investigative reporter for the *Kansas City Star,* approaches interviews in three stages, not only getting key general information, but also gaining the trust of the people he is talking to.

"On a long-term project I usually do three rounds," McGraw says. The first phase is usually questions that are general. That helps McGraw find out how things work and who runs the show, which helps stimulate further research.

"The first time usually is a chance to lie," he says. "I basically get people to say there are no problems. If I am looking at the B-2 Bomber, I will go to Air Force officials who are in charge of the bomber and say 'How did it go? Were there any problems?' And, of course, I get 'There were no problems at all.'

"Then I will find out that maybe there were a few problems. So in a second round of interviews, I ask about them." By the second phase, which McGraw calls an interim interview, he has learned more about the subject and tries to see things from the point of view of the person he is meeting.

"If someone's even peripherally involved in some sort of wrong doing, and they want to explain how things work and why things like this can happen, you're a lot better off giving them the time to explain it than cutting them off and saying 'I don't want to know how it happened I just want to know that it happened,'" McGraw says. "To me that is the wrong approach, because what you're telling them is 'I don't care about any of the information that surrounded this incident,' all you care about is this incident.

"I think as journalists we have to understand about how and why things happened, not just that they did happen. If we don't get across to those who we are interviewing that we are interested, I think they are less inclined to be truthful."

He has called the third stage the "come to Jesus encounter."

"Usually by the time I'm all done they're ready to tell me what the problems are in the third interview," McGraw says. "If you have enough time to do long-term research, you're going to bring these people around to being quite honest with you."

The pre-interview

Pre-interview is a broadcasting term. A researcher, producer or reporter is looking for a good on-air subject for an interview. The pre-interview is used to check the person out. Is the person a "good talker"? Does he or she know the subject at hand? If the source is a bureaucrat or company official, is he or she high enough in the hierarchy to answer the questions on the record, on the air?

There are rules for the pre-interview. A key one is that the researcher tells the source that she or he is looking for information. There's usually no commitment to booking a guest on a show, so the interviewer can draw out information over the telephone. Print reporters will often do the same thing, asking a few questions before deciding whether to go ahead or to give the source a polite "thank you" and hang up.

The pre-interview is a valuable tool for anyone conducting research:

- It helps establish whether the source knows about the subject that you're interested in.

- It helps you avoid costly duplication. Does the source have new insight or is the source just repeating what someone else has said better?
- It eliminates "housekeeping" questions such as general biographical information. (Many people keep a copy of their resume on their hard drives or post it on a personal Web site. Ask for an e-mail copy.) Asking basic questions helps you prepare. It will give you ideas for questions you ask when you're honing in or meeting the subject. It may give you ideas where you can do more research on the subject before you conduct the in-person interview.

What time and place?

If you are ready, again wait a moment and ask what time you should set for the interview and where you should do it.

You may not always have a choice. The person you wish to interview may be only available at a certain time and place.

But if you have a choice, you should always consider a place and time that will make for the best interview:

- **What is the best time for you, the interviewer?** Are you a morning person or an evening person? When are you sharpest? Can you make the time before the interview so that you are warmed up mentally and not rushed either to get started (or finished)?
- **What is the best time for the interview?** The person who controls the time controls the interview and can cut it off or extend it. One police investigator believes that for office interviews, bad times are often just before lunch and just before quitting time, or any other time where the interviewee has the ability to abruptly cut it off and go to lunch, home, or to a meeting. On the other hand, Eric Nadler of the *Seattle Times* notes, "If you arrange a lunch appointment you can force a person to spend at least an hour with you."
- **What is the best time to get the facts?** Are you going to interview the subject during office hours, at lunch, after work, or in the evening? What time is best for the facts that you are

seeking? Some people may talk more freely outside of their office environment, while others won't want to be bothered about work once they leave for the day.

A private office or a living room is usually quiet, and you can concentrate on the questions and, if you are taping, have a good clean recording.

A coffee shop or restaurant is less formal, and you may end up with a different interview. But it is harder to have a confrontation interview in public than it is in private and, as I noted, if you are taping, your interview could be drowned out with background noise.

Preparation

The best interviewers prepare themselves mentally before going in. Eric Nadler calls this the "inner interview," and he recommends imagining the successful interview, noting, "Reporters who don't believe they will get the interview or the information usually fail. As far as I'm concerned, no one should ever refuse to talk to me. It works."

Claude Shaver of the RCMP, in a lecture at the Canadian Police College, recommended that an investigator ask two questions when planning an interview:

1. What is the best thing that can happen. How *should* I *react?*
2. What is the worst thing that can happen. How *must* I *respond?*

The good listener is the best approach.

McGraw says, "What I often find with young reporters [is] that they are kind of bossy. They wear their egos on their sleeve and they [think they] deserve things because they are the press. I think...a better approach is [to act like] I am just like the general public. My job is to go and try to tell the public what happened here. I am no better than you are. I am no better than the public. I do this for a living and I need some help here. You will be amazed how willing people are to help you, if you take that attitude."

Getting there

It's best to arrive early; it gives you an advantage.

You should start observing and making notes long before you enter the building. Be polite to everyone: the security guard, people in the elevator, the receptionist, people you meet in the hall, the public relations officer taking you to meet the executive, the desk sergeant, the subject's spouse and children. You may soon be asking these people for help, and they may turn into sources of information. Make notes about the people you meet. This is especially important if you are doing any kind of immersion project.

You will get a clue of how things are going to go by how you enter the office. Being told to go right in, or having the person come to greet you is a sign of openness and neutrality. Being ushered into the office by a subordinate may be an indication of the power of the person you are meeting.

If you have prepared properly, if you know something about the person's background or hobbies, look around the office for something that reflects character—books, paintings, awards, kid's drawings. Always look at the desk and see what's on it.

"The first thing I do is survey their office when I go in," McGraw says. "I was interviewing a regulatory official at the Department of Agriculture some years ago. I surveyed the office and one of the things I saw was a beautiful bronze statue of a cowboy on a horse lassoing a cow. It was a beautiful piece—it was kind of off to the side and still dominated the office. I made note of it and later I asked the official about it. It was a very expensive gift given to this regulatory official by the industry that he was charged with regulating. We added that to the story and noted it was obviously a violation of USDA policy."

It's also important to note where the interview takes place. If you are seated in an interview area, either a couch or a couple of chairs, the situation will be less formal, and the interviewee is exhibiting less power than if you are sitting across a desk. In that situation, Shaver also recommends noting objects that tend to obstruct the view, especially a desk light.

The best situation is to sit as close as possible to the person you are interviewing, either face to face or at right angles, usually around three feet and no further away than 10 feet.

On the record

It's always best if the entire interview is on the record, meaning you can use everything you hear—although you may decide not use it.

Anyone doing interviews for publication should be aware of four levels of giving and yet withholding information:

- **Off the record** means that you can't use the information. Always ask yourself why the person is telling you this bit of information if you can't use it.
- **Condition of anonymity** is routine information officially or semi-officially released by someone in government or authority. This is usually seen in news stories with such phrases as "a police officer at the scene, speaking under the customary condition of anonymity, said...."
- **Background** is a term that originated in the coverage of diplomacy to allow officials to brief the media without saying something they would have to defend later. You see this in statements such as "a high-ranking official traveling with the president..." which could likely be the president himself or someone close to him. Background now also refers to information that has to be attributed to "sources."
- **Deep background** is another diplomatic term. Researchers and writers should avoid deep background, which means that the information cannot even be attributed to sources, and that the researcher has to go out on a limb and float a trial balloon.

Opinions differ on how to deal with a request to go off the record. Eric Nadler says off the record information is useless and so a reporter should avoid it.

Mike McGraw has a different approach. "I think I am unusual among reporters," he says. "There are times I will approach a source, whether on the phone or in person, and say I'd like to have this first conversation off the record. A lot of reporters may scream heresy, but I find that if you start off that way, people relax and you get a lot more information about how things really work, whether it's the Air Force, the FDA, college sports, or whatever. Often then when you come back to them, you can get a whole lot of things on the record, that [they] initially said off the record, sometimes all of it."

The task then, whether the person is trying to talk off the record, or on background, is what Nadler calls *ratcheting*, by then going over the statements and asking why they should be on background or off the record. I would note that there are sometimes good reasons for off the record (such as sensitive personal or family information that is only marginally connected with the subject of the interview). If the source insists on staying on background, respect that request.

Who are you dealing with?

"I sort of size people up when I go in and decide which approach is going to work," Mike McGraw says. "I am going to have to warm this person up. They're going to have to get used to me, they're going to have to decide whether I'm honest or not, whether I'm lying. Then I will take the slow approach. I'll always try to go into an interview with a list of questions. I will try really hard not to control the interview because that can be mistake also, if you don't let it breathe on its own.

"I see interviews as living things. If you let them breathe on their own, and let them go on their own, without completely letting go and giving control to who you're interviewing, you're going to have a lot better luck in the long run."

The researcher/interviewer must also be aware of the person they are dealing with. Is the person experienced dealing with an interviewer? Someone who is inexperienced in dealing with any kind of interview needs a little help, perhaps some prompting, help in relaxing, and encouragement.

Boston University's Mark Kramer notes that an interviewer must always play fair and be ethical. For Kramer agreeing to be interviewed is "a form of informed consent" where the person's "well-being is naively in your hands."

Someone who is unfamiliar with the media or other forms of interviews may also be unfamiliar with the idea of "off the record." An ethical interviewer should always say something like "Are you sure you want to tell me that?" at the appropriate time.

If the person understands the basic ground rules, if he or she is familiar with the interview process, then follow your game plan. If both sides of the interview respect each other, then it should go smoothly. If the person being interviewed has something to hide, in many cases, you will get a sense of that and can hone your questions appropriately.

The biggest barrier to a good interview these days is "the message." Spin doctors craft a message for the clients and tell them to stay "on message." Spin doctors try a couple of ways to get their clients to stick with it, both named with appropriate metaphors:

- **Bridging** is answering, no matter what the interviewer asked, by using a bridging phrase to make it seem as if you are answering the interviewer's questions. The answer, however, is really "the message." Faced with that, an experienced interviewer will gently, politely, and firmly say "And to get back to the question at hand...."

- **Punting** is answering, no matter what the question, by making some sort of statement you want to get across, sometimes without a bridging statement. For the interviewer the appropriate response is :"And now to go back to the question I asked...."

Spin is most effective on live television, either in a one-on-one interview or in a news conference, where the idea is to get the message over the heads of the media and on to the public. In some interviews, the subject never actually answers the host's question.

Questions

The interview actually begins the moment you enter the room, as you shake hands and begin with a little small talk. If you are meeting in an office or home, you can usually quickly find something to talk about, even if it is just the view, whether it's a cityscape, a back garden, or a parking lot.

Try to find something in common with the person you are meeting in those moments of small talk. It creates a human bond between the two of you, even if the rest of the interview is strictly business.

Plan your questions carefully:

- **Remember the focus of your story or research project.** Know *what* you want and *why* you want it. But remember the military adage that no plan survives contact with the enemy. Throw out your plan if you aren't getting anywhere or if the unexpected happens.
- **Keep your questions simple—but open-ended.** A simple question doesn't intimidate the source. An open-ended question allows the source to think about the answer and could lead to an answer you, the questioner, did not think of. Answers to simple questions also often show that you don't know as much as you thought.
- **Ask just one question at a time.** It's not only easier for the source, but it's easier for you to find that answer in your notes or on tape.
- **Ask questions; don't make statements or answer your own question.** Check your preconceptions or biases before you walk in the front door. You're a researcher, not a prosecutor. Also, it doesn't work. John Sawatsky notes that in these cases the person answers the comment and not the question.

- ❑ **Keep it businesslike.** Don't take sides, either for a character who appears to be sympathetic, or against one who appears to be unsympathetic. (Take a hint from the actors who have to find something human, something sympathetic, to play the most repulsive characters. Reporters and nonfiction writers should remember what good fiction writers and dramatists know: In most cases, no one sees him or herself as a villain).
- ❑ **Don't be afraid to ask difficult questions.** Most often, your source will answer.
- ❑ **Personalize the question, even if you're using a basic boiler plate template.** Use your research to find and ask that question that no one else has asked.
- ❑ **Ask for anecdotes.** It doesn't matter whether you're a journalist, student, or academic, anecdotes and stories illustrate your research. If you're an academic with a fear of "anecdotal evidence," do your research first and the find the anecdotes that illustrate and dramatize your data and your thesis.
- ❑ **Although the experts recommend going slow, have your key questions ready in case something interrupts the person or if the person tries to cut off the interview.**
- ❑ **Never underestimate your source.** She or he probably does know more than you do—at least in some fields.

The outer circle

Begin with the outer circle, the easy questions, the general questions. Ask housekeeping and biographical questions first. That not only gets them out of the way, it starts your subject talking and makes it easier for them to answer the next questions.

Eric Nadler recommends asking for someone's life story, even if you don't plan to use it. It almost always brings out useful information.

If you have a good chronology, then you will have some idea of major events that happened along the way. Oral historians use this technique, asking for date cues such as "Where were you when...Pearl Harbor was bombed...John Kennedy was shot...man landed on the moon in 1969...the day of the Oklahoma City bombing?" Reporters will look at their chronology and begin to ask, "Where were you when the decision to do this was made?"

Good interviewers use props: investigators and investigative reporters with documents; oral historians with photographs, clippings, artifacts, or maps.

Oral historians often ask a person for a physical description, not just for information (which you would have to confirm given that memory is sometimes unreliable), to trigger associated memories and new information.

Similarly, you can use dialog as a memory trigger, asking, "What did you say then?" It may be hearsay to a court, but it tells the story from your subject's point of view and also can trigger vivid memories.

Remember 5W+

Using the five W+ how is especially useful to bypass asking someone point blank if they did something. Ask how something happened, using, if possible, details from your research. Then ask why it happened. An outright question could bring an outright denial. Edging around it can bring an explanation.

Use any of the five Ws to get around a strict confirm or deny situation, especially with officials. Instead of "Are you investigating?", ask "At what stage is your investigation?" or instead of "Are you working on such and such?", ask "Who is in charge of the project?" or "What is the budget for the project for this year?"

Eric Nadler recommends confirming credibility and fact by asking, "How do you know that?"

Oral historians use "how" to bring out emotion by asking, "How did you feel at that point?" John Sawatsky recommends "What went through your mind at the time?" as an alternative to "How did you feel?"

Sawatsky also says, "What was the turning point?" and "What were the options?" are questions that often get results.

Liar, liar

People may lie, or they may spin. So what do you do? If your interview is backed up by extensive research, you are in a good position, even with the most unreliable characters.

Investigative producer Ira Silverman says, "Often when the source has a terrible reputation, perhaps a criminal record, I will say, 'Give me one piece of information that you're telling me that you think would be the easiest for me to validate. And tell me who to go to that will validate this.' That is the important first step, to take that piece of the material and check it thoroughly before going further."

Intelligence analyst Sam Porteous recommends that interviewers "start off by testing his knowledge and response to information and knowledge you are very familiar with" before going on to more detailed information.

Beware of phrases such as, "Now let me be frank with you," "to be honest," "I swear to God," "on my honor," "on my mother's grave," "honest to God." It probably means that you're being set up for a lie. Beware of "I'm glad you asked that question." It probably means you're being set up for spin.

If a story seems mendacious or outrageous, ask the person to imagine how it will appear to the public. It's one thing to try to lie one-on-one, another to lie to the entire world (although it's been tried many times).

Never call a person a liar, but do look him or her in the eye and say something along the lines of "oh really," or something a little stronger. Just don't call them a liar.

In turn, never lie about yourself or your aims.

Body language

Many people think they can become quick experts on body language. The experts prefer the wider term of "nonverbal communication."

"A lot of people probably think they can look at people's eyes and tell if they are lying or not. I think it depends on the person and whether they've got the experience," Mike McGraw says.

"Really there a lot of people who can lie and not give anything away, not have body language that will betray them."

Anyone who has met a functional psychopath, a sociopath, or pathological liar will know that they can lie so convincingly as to fool their victims and even experienced investigators.

Beware of clues such as demanding people look you in the eye. It could mean a cultural difference where people are taught to look away or perhaps a history of traumatic abuse. Don't automatically assume that fidgeting, constant crossing and uncrossing of legs, or rapidly changing the subject means the person is lying. The person could be an adult with Attention Deficit Hyperactivity Disorder.

Instead, you should look for the overall pattern of behavior. First you will see what the experts call *core patterns*, the habitual patterns that people exhibit all the time. Core patterns are comfort patterns, do not vary, and can be seen lasting for a long time. *Ad hoc patterns* are breaks from the core patterns, last for short periods of time, and "are generally associated with discomfort or tension." In his lecture on nonverbal communication,

Claude Shaver of the RCMP gives examples of a raised eyebrow, a nervous laugh, a quick shift in a chair, or a pattern crossing or uncrossing of legs.

The inner circle

The inner circle is the key moment in the interview. In a series of interviews, it is the last one, Mike McGraw's third "come to Jesus" moment.

When a series of people are interviewed, the most important one—the target of an investigation or a subject of a biography—should be interviewed last, after all the background material possible has been gathered.

It's in the inner circle interview that you ask for the embarrassing details, the key decisions, the pivotal and historic moments.

It's in the ultimate interview when you ask the person to correct the mistakes, whether they are mistakes in the public record or your own research.

It's in the inner circle interview where you ask people to bare their souls, to explain what happened.

Don't let the person cut off the story. Tell them that you need clarification on the points they are avoiding, but don't get into a debate. Try pointing out that there will be a hole in the story, or that that part of the story will be told only by others.

If the interviewes says, "no comment," politely point out how bad "no comment" looks when it appears in print or television.

Don't show off. Remember you're not there to prove what a good researcher you are. You're there to ask questions.

Silence is golden

There will be moments of silence in an interview. Use them. Oral historians, who most often deal with elderly people, give them time to collect their thoughts, to bring up long-stored memories. If the interviewer jumps in too quickly, the thought could be lost.

A badly trained television interviewer jumps in too quickly, more afraid of dead air than a bad answer. A good television interviewer is aware of the time and waits a few seconds before coming in. Only if there is silence after the question is repeated do you try something new. Often the person will answer the question anyway a little later on. If not, return to that question before the interview is over.

Be patient

Be patient in the interview. Get the most detail you can. Eric Nadler advises going in "slow motion" and "getting it in Technicolor." Slowing down and finding the details is how you get a story, not just facts, he says.

Don't interrupt. Interviewers always seem to want to jump in at the wrong moment. Always let the person finish what he is saying. Then ask your follow-up question. Again, oral historians note that an interviewer should allow the person to go where her "memory leads." The interviewer can always return or follow up the question later.

Patience can be rewarded long after the formal interview is over. On a number of occasions, a person has phoned me to give me more details on something we discussed, or called to say, "I just remembered...."

Listen

Listen. It must be repeated that you have to *really* listen to the person you are interviewing.

"You have to hang on every word, you have to look at them in the eye, be completely absorbed, listening to them," Mike McGraw says. "You have to let them know you've heard their answer by reacting to their answer and by asking follow up questions where the answer isn't specific and clear.

"I often work with a lot of young reporters....they're so busy thinking about the next question, that they don't hear the answer to the last one.

"I think the most important part of an interview [is] following up on answer that's been given. 'I don't understand that, can you expand on that?' If they're reading from a piece of paper, 'Can I have a copy of that document, why or why not?"

The last 2 questions

Every interview should end with two sets of questions (usually, but not always, in this order):

1. **Who else should I talk to?** For in-depth interviews, ask for people who support them, who know them well, who will provide additional positive information. Then ask about those people and that information. It will bring new and different details to the questions you've already asked. Then ask for the names of critics or even enemies. Ask what these people will say. The reaction may be enlightening.

2. **What have I missed? What else is there that should be in the story? What should I have asked?** This almost always leads to new information, perhaps to new stories.

You will usually end the interview with some more small talk. As I said earlier, if you are taping, keep the tape machine running if you can. Nine times out of 10, you will get valuable information or insights once the formal interview is over. Always give the person your business card, a phone number, and an e-mail address and invite them to contact you if they think of something new or more details that will be useful.

Fact checking

Never be afraid to call back, or these days e-mail, to check facts or ask for clarification. Go over your notes with the person if necessary to make sure everything is accurate. As long as you stress you want to ensure accuracy, the person will usually be cooperative. If you are writing an article for a major magazine, a fact checker will probably call the person to verify everything in the interview.

Links

Oral History Association

www.dickinson.edu/organizations/oha/Othersites.html

Oral History Association links page.

The One Minute Guide to Oral History

library.berkeley.edu/BANC/ROHO/1minute.html

A brief guide to oral history techniques from the University of California, Berkeley, library.

Oral History Techniques Pamphlet

www.indiana.edu/~ohrc/pamph1.htm

A web page from the University of Indiana with a basic how to interview, form the point of view oral history, with a bibliography.

Oral History Research Center

www.indiana.edu/~ohrc/

Oral History

www.gcah.org/oral.html

A basic guide to oral history interviews, from the United Methodist Church.

Acronym Finder

www.acronymfinder.com

Look up 132,000+ acronyms/abbreviations and their meanings.

Kansas City Star

www.kcstar.com

Toronto Star

www.thestar.com

Raleigh News and Observer

www.nando.net

Seattle Times

www.seattletimes.com

Chapter 22

The E-mail Interview

The e-mail interview is seldom a complete substitute for an in-person or telephone contact. It is, however, a means of smoothing the way and finding insights you might not otherwise find. The e-mail interview is also becoming more important, in these days of shrinking budgets, as a way of getting information or interviews that would otherwise be impossible to obtain.

Why an e-mail interview?

What are the circumstances when you should use an e-mail interview?

- To answer short puzzlers, those questions where reference material isn't easily available.
- To track down new sources for your research.
- To overcome the "cold call barrier" that even experienced researchers face. Once you've exchanged a couple of e-mail messages with your source, picking up the phone is easy.
- To pre-interview a source you will later telephone or meet in person.
- To assure yourself that the technical information is as accurate as your source can make it.
- To follow up and fact check an earlier telephone or personal interview.

- To create an ongoing relationship with sources and potential sources, especially if a reporter or researcher is established in a newsgroup or mailing list.

You should always remember that the suggestions for good e-mail Netiquette also apply to the e-mail interview. Keep everything as tightly focused as possible.

E-mail pre-interview

E-mail is an ideal way of doing a pre-interview (or in the case of broadcasters a pre-pre-interview):

- It keeps down the cost of long-distance calls. If you get the preliminaries out of the way, then you and the subject know what you're going to talk about ahead of time. The farther away the subject, the more valuable this information.
- If you're traveling out of town, e-mail is a cost-effective way to set up appointments. The questions you ask online provide an opening focus for the interview. This is especially helpful if you have limited time with each subject.

The computer cocoon

One experienced interviewer I talked to doesn't believe in the e-mail interview: "An interview by e-mail is not an interview, it's basically an invitation to give you a series of press releases....An interview requires some element of cross-examination, and you can't do that by e-mail." Another says, "You have to understand that what you're being fed is flack, it's PR."

I have done many successful pre-interviews and interviews by e-mail, so I am going to respectfully disagree. Success depends on the source and the research project, but I often get more valuable information by e-mail than I would by phone or in person.

To consider why, let's look at what happens when a television crew shows up at someone's office or home. There's a reporter and cameraperson, perhaps a sound person, and sometimes a producer as well. There's all that equipment, and it's the job of the reporter to make the subject forget about the camera, the lights, the lavaliere microphone on his shirt, and believe that there's just a one-on-one conversation between the interviewer and the interviewee.

So it's the job of the interviewer to make the subject relax and concentrate on the questions. It's called *cocooning*.

When you conduct an e-mail interview, your subject is, most often, already in a cocoon.

For years there have been anecdotal reports that someone reacts differently if they're in their basement or den, or even their office, typing e-mail or newsgroup articles alone, with no one to bother them. We know that human emotions don't come across in cold electronic type. That's why emoticons such as the smiley **:-)** were invented. It seems that people will often feel that if they're typing away in the privacy of their own home, laws in the outside world may not apply to them and hence we see rash statements, flame wars, and sometimes even libel suits.

So if your source agrees to answer a few questions by e-mail, he or she will be often answering those questions in his own cocoon. His fingers fly over the keyboard and type answers in a different way than the person would if he were talking on the telephone or facing a microphone. Thus, if your aim is to go to the heart of your subjects, you may find some interesting insights into their character and their life and work from an e-mail interview, something you might not get in person.

Then again, you might not. A number of people who had worked with computers and the Net, the same people who send out scores of e-mail messages, were reluctant to do e-mail interviews for this and other books, and they were interviewed the old-fashioned way. Others were the opposite; they were too busy to come to the phone but supplied long e-mail messages.

Is there evidence to back up the idea that people are often more candid on the computer? The answer appears to be yes.

A series of studies over the past 17 years, of both the survey data so beloved by social scientists and e-mail itself, seem to indicate that people sometimes are more forthcoming in e-mail and even use significantly less distortion in e-mail than they do face to face.

One of the first studies was carried out by Sara Keisler and Lee Sproull at Carnegie Mellon University in the fall of 1983 and published in 1986. The authors reported that in traditional paper surveys, people refused to answer certain questions, gave incomplete answers, underreported socially undesirable information, and overreported socially acceptable or conventional behavior. They noted that "face-to-face and telephone interviews increase respondent's desire to please over self-administered paper questionnaires."

So the two professors conducted an electronic survey among students, faculty, and employees at Carnegie Mellon, then one of the more wired universities. The results showed that compared to a paper survey, those who participated in the electronic survey admitted to "more socially undesirable responses in the electronic survey than in the paper survey"— including use of illicit drugs.

The authors say that his study and others indicate that "people tend to be both more self-absorbed and uninhibited when they communicate using a computer." The respondents to the electronic survey also left fewer items blank, refused to answer fewer questions, and made fewer mistakes than the people in the paper survey.

In a later summary of their work, Kiesler, Sproull, and John Walsh noted that "computer surveys and interviews can be highly motivating while minimizing anxiety. They therefore elicit a high number of responses, good accuracy, and much disclosure."

A new study by Stephanie Watts Sussman of Case Western University and Sproull, now at New York University, was published in June 1999. It indicated that people are "more likely to communicate bad news honestly" through a computer than face-to-face.

Summing up the research over the past decade, Sussman and Sproull say, "People find social context and recipient less salient in electronic communication, are less concerned about presenting themselves in a positive light or 'looking good' to the recipient and so are more honest." They also say the people who use computers "reported higher levels of comfort and satisfaction than those in either face-to-face or telephone conditions."

E-mail, the authors say, usually means less "negative politeness," what social scientists call the mum effect or the "desire to distort negative information in a positive direction."

In the conclusion to their paper, Sussman and Sproull offer a way of understanding flaming. They say "People seem to do less 'cushioning the blow' of negative information" when they use the computer. In face-to-face situations, it is a human tendency to suppress straight talk, especially if people find it discomfiting or offensive. So while, earlier social scientists had proposed that the computer "caused" flaming, Sussman and Sproull argue the computer causes more "straight talk."

That may be changing. In an e-mail to the author, Sussman warned: "I would say that e-mail is potentially an important research tool. But there is evidence that people don't appreciate the unsolicited, so the challenge is contacting the person first and getting their permission to send an e-mail. People are increasingly installing filters on their e-mails systems so that unsolicited requests get filtered out. This is simply an indication that people should be getting permission first and not sending unsolicited e-mails. People are having to spend so much time on e-mail that the noncritical activities don't get done....people have very limited time, so it may be faster to use the phone if you are looking for in-depth, qualitative materials.

"I would say that e-mail is ideal for research that utilizes quantitative analysis of short-answer questions, [because] it doesn't require much typing on the part of the respondent, and you can use software to do the data analysis without having to do transcriptions."

There's much more to the e-mail interview than simply public relations and flack. It is a new field—one that must be explored by the serious researcher.

The e-mail interview is a good tool, but the information you receive must be evaluated and verified no differently than an in-person or telephone interview

How to do it

Although the techniques for conducting an e-mail interview are still evolving, some helpful trends have emerged:

- You're ahead of the game if you have participated in a mailing list or newsgroup. That makes you a known quality for the people involved. If you have lurked first, learned about the culture of the group, and then participated, it is more likely that people in the group will respond.
- Keep your initial queries *short and to the point.* During the research for this book I conducted an unscientific survey among the people from whom I requested information. In most cases, I got a faster and better response to a short message than to a long one.
- Send individual e-mail, addressed to the recipient, rather than a bulk mailing with a long list of e-mail addresses, nor using the blind carbon copy (bcc) function that spammers like to use.
- If you follow up with a questionnaire, ask about five questions, certainly no more than 10. If you have created a template questionnaire, personalize it for each recipient.

- Expect a low response rate and late answers.
- The e-mail interview is best when the person is willing to give you personal information, either about certain events, or experience in a certain area. For this book, people did send me long e-mail messages about their research experience.
- Use an e-mail interview as an *absolute last resort* in cases where you are trying to get a response on the record for investigative research. In the past, you could be stonewalled or given a simple "no comment." These days it appears that more people and companies are willing to respond by e-mail to that sort of query. The answer will be spin and perhaps even cleared by the subject's lawyers, but it will be, as much as possible, an on-the-record response, and better for both sides than a "not available" or "no comment" response in the final story.
- Go from the general to the specific. Ask the biographical and housekeeping questions first, before going on to the meat of the interview. That gets the person typing and creates that level of "comfort and satisfaction" that Sussman and Sproull talk about.
- Follow the rules of the in-person interview with simple, open-ended questions.
- Always make it clear in your initial contact that the questions the source is answering are for publication either in the media or in an academic paper and they will be quoted. With asynchronous communications, there are many possibilities for misunderstanding. No one can ask online to go off the record, as they might in a personal interview. It's also the interviewee's responsibility *not* to include confidential or off-the-record information in an e-mail interview without reaching an agreement first with the researcher.

The follow-up

Once you've completed the e-mail interview, you should do a follow-up in person or by telephone.

First, many researchers are aware—and wary—of the problem of identity hacking or mistaken identity on the Net.

A telephone call or a visit will also give you the chance to get an all-important "feel" of the person that you need to judge both the e-mail and in-person answers. Just hearing the person's voice will change the way you view that person, adding another dimension to your research. An in-person visit, of course, will give you the color that you won't ever be able to get by reading an e-mail message. You will be able to see if that e-mail message came from a glass and steel corporate office tower, a one-bedroom apartment home business, or an ivy-covered stone quadrangle at a university.

There are, of course, times when you can't do that follow-up, for example, if your subject is on another continent and you don't have the budget for an airline flight or long-distance call. You should learn to judge and evaluate the answers from an e-mail interview just as you learn to evaluate material on a Web site or in a paper file. That comes with experience.

Links

Informs PubsOnline

pubsonline.informs.org

Sussman and Sproul article: Straight Talk: Delivering bad news through electronic communication. Select Guest Login, and then the Journal: ISR (Information Systems Research). The article is the last one in Vol. 10, #2. Requires Adobe Acrobat.

Chapter 23

Books and Libraries

At one time most researchers worked in great halls—and they still do today. Five thousand years ago, the archivists of ancient Mesopotamia gathered clay tablets written in cuneiform. Two thousand years later, philosophers and scholars from around the Mediterranean came to Alexandria to study at that city's magnificent library with its half-million scrolls. Students at Alexandria's schools of astronomy, medicine, and mathematics used the great library for research.

In Europe, monks used parchment to copy ancient manuscripts and preserve them in libraries safe from the Dark Ages. The great universities grew out of the bosom of the church and flourished in the Renaissance. The founding of the universities created a new form of scholarship and new libraries. Gutenberg invented movable type and printing spread new knowledge across Europe.

New national governments founded great national libraries. One was the British Library, with its circular Reading Room, part of the famed British Museum, with walls of old leather-bound books reaching up to the building's dome. Until recently, researchers, with the privilege of a Reader's Ticket, worked at the same tables as people generations before them, such as Karl Marx and Charles Dickens. Now the researchers toil in a modern brick box a few miles away.

There are the Library of Congress in Washington, D.C., with its own magnificent reading room, and *La Bibleothèque Nationale* in Paris. In the

19th century, public free-lending libraries were born, some bankrolled by the steel baron Andrew Carnegie.

For those who research, it has always been a joy to walk through those great libraries where one still has access to the stacks. The late historian author Barbara Tuchman loved research so much that she wrote a book about it, *Practicing History*. She says wandering through the stacks at Harvard's Widener Library was "my Archimedes bathtub, my burning bush, my dish of mold where I found my personal penicillin."

For all those centuries, people had to go to the library. It may have been a perilous journey through dangerous times to a far off monastery or a gentle spring walk around the corner from home.

You still have to go to the library, but the Internet and the Web have made it a lot easier to enter the library prepared to do a more thorough and focused search for material.

Librarians were among the first to embrace the Internet, to migrate to the Web, and to act as guides to material offline and online.

The Web has made it a lot easier to find books and other material in your library. In fact, it is best to start your library search at home, in front of your computer. Do a check from your home or office computer. It saves time in several ways.

In the precomputer days, when libraries had banks of file cards for their catalog, there was room for many people, each checking an individual file drawer. Now every library is wired, and usually there are limited numbers of computers. So, if you don't check the online catalog from home, you may have to stand in line once you get to the library. Most library catalogs are available through an online gateway and so the Web-based catalog is becoming standard.

What kind of library?

First you have to decide what kind of library you are dealing with (for a major project you may end up dealing with all kinds):

- **Public libraries** are local or regional, and they are supported by local, state, provincial, or federal taxpayers. They are there to serve a wide cross section of the public from toddlers to seniors, from students writing two-page reports to scholars. Many regional library systems have integrated computer catalog systems that give you a wider field to search. Major local or regional public libraries may have special collections that can draw researchers from outside their region.

- **University libraries** are aimed at the university's students and the scholarly community. While you certainly can search the catalog online, that doesn't mean you will have access to the library itself. It all depends on the rules set down by the library and the university. You may have to apply, have your project screened, and pay for access. Many university libraries, however, have special deals for alumni, so if you still live in the university community where you got your degree, it is something worth checking out.
- **Private and corporate libraries**, usually called **special libraries**, serve a company and industry and often have highly specialized collections that may be of interest to a researcher. Access to such libraries varies, for the main purpose is to serve their employer or sponsor. Special libraries often have limited staff and resources. Usually, if the material the library has is unique and not accessible in a public system, you may be able to get the information through interlibrary loan or by requesting access and making a good case for yourself. It all depends on the policy of the library.
- **Government libraries** exist to serve government employees and, as with special libraries, access may be limited. If the government library does have unique information, you may be able to get access if there is a reading room.
- **National libraries** are the information central for any country's libraries, where cataloging information for all libraries is decided. Library of Congress, the British Library, and the National Libraries of Canada and Australia usually get one or two copies of every book published in that country and many more published in other countries. National libraries are also a good source for rare books, but unlike popular belief, national libraries don't necessarily have everything.

Numbers and letters

In North America, most school and public libraries use Dewey Decimal classification, and that is what most people are familiar with since the first day they toddled into their neighborhood library.

Most research libraries and academic libraries use the more comprehensive and flexible Library of Congress classification. Medical information is usually based on a system devised by the U.S. National Library of Medicine.

The Dewey system, created by Melvil Dewey back in 1876, divides human knowledge into 10 categories, each represented by a three digit main number, and then a decimal that creates subdivisions:

000	Generalities
100	Philosophy & psychology
200	Religion
300	Social sciences
400	Language
500	Natural sciences & mathematics
600	Technology (Applied sciences)
700	The arts
800	Literature & rhetoric
900	Geography & history

The Library of Congress system uses letters and then numbers and letters to create subdivisions:

A	General Works
B	Philosophy. Psychology. Religion
C	Auxiliary Sciences Of History (including genealogy and biography)
D	History: General And Old World
E	History: America
F	History: America
G	Geography. Anthropology. Recreation
H	Social Sciences
J	Political Science
K	Law
L	Education
M	Music And Books On Music
N	Fine Arts
P	Language and Literature
Q	Science
R	Medicine
S	Agriculture

T	Technology
U	Military Science
V	Naval Science
Z	Library Science

The catalog entry

Before you go searching for a book, you have to understand how the catalog system retrieves information, so let's take a look at a couple of catalog entries. One, for this book, you will find near the title page. Here is the Library of Congress entry for my earlier book, *Undercover:*

Author:	Dubro, James.
Title:	Undercover: cases of the RCMP's most secret operative / James Dubro and Robin Rowland.
Published:	Markham, Ont.: Octopus, c1991.
Description:	314 p., [12] p. of plates: ill. ; 24 cm.
LC Call No.:	HV7911.Z36D93 1991
Dewey No.:	363.2/32 B 20
ISBN:	0409905399
Notes:	Includes bibliographical references (p. 298-300) and index.
Subjects:	Zaneth, Frank, 1890-1971. Royal Canadian Mounted Police Biography. Undercover operations Canada History.
Other authors:	Rowland, Robin F.
Control No.:	1573322

So let's look at the card more closely and the important parts for the researcher:

- **Author:** I wrote the book with my colleague Jim Dubro and his name came first on the title page, so he is listed first. The **Other Author** entry makes sure those searching under my name for the book get a hit.
- **Title:** The card gives the complete title
- **LC Call No:** This is HV7911.Z36D93 1991. In the general category of Social Science, HV is described as "Social pathology.

Social and public welfare. Criminology." The numbers 7551-8280.7 include Police. Detectives. Constabulary, appropriate for a book about an undercover cop.

- **Dewey No:** This is 363.2/32 B 20, which is roughly under the general category 363: Other social problems and services.
- **Subjects:** The CIP data includes three subject categories, which are part of the *controlled vocabulary* system I mentioned earlier in the chapter on searching. I'll discuss the subject system in a little more detail shortly.

Who decides how this information gets on the card?

Because so many books are published today, the national libraries have created Cataloging in Publication. That means the book's catalog entry form is being created often as the author is still writing the book. By international agreement the process is similar in the United States, Canada, Australia, and Britain.

In the United States, for each title, publishers send a completed CIP Data Application form and the full text of the title, the table of contents, and other information to the Library of Congress. At the Library, the application is reviewed, assigned a Library of Congress Card Number, and then sent to the cataloging division.

Catalogers complete the subject cataloging; assign subject headings, including creating new headings as appropriate; and assign Library of Congress and Dewey decimal classification numbers. The completed CIP data is then sent back to the publisher, who prints it beside the title page. At the same time, a computerized record is distributed to large libraries, bibliographic utilities, and book vendors around the world.

When the book is finally published, the librarians update the record and make sure it is accurate. Changes in title, subtitle, series, author, or subject may be made. Then a new and updated record is distributed by computer.

It's not always an exact process. One CIP librarian told me that he sometimes gets irate calls from authors who say their books have been put in the wrong category.

Sometimes, librarians make a decision that is different from the CIP data. A search for *Undercover* in library databases shows that while most libraries followed the CIP and shelve the book under 363, crime section, many chose to use 921 Z, for a biography of Frank Zaneth.

Unfortunately, the British Library does not require U.K. publishers to publish the CIP opposite the title page, which means that information is not immediately available to researchers looking for similar books.

Subject entry

When you are looking for a book by subject in a library, you are looking for terms that professional librarians with many years of experience have chosen.

Main subject headings are chosen by the Library of Congress and published in a multivolume set every year, the LCSH (Library of Congress Subject Headings). The LCSH is supplemented in each country by a supplemental volume of subject headings; in Canada it is, CSH, Canadian Subject Headings.

If we look at the two of the headings for *Undercover,* you will see subheadings, called Narrower Term (NT) headings by librarians:

Royal Canadian Mounted Police Biography.
Undercover operations Canada History.

For *RCMP*, you have the narrower term, biography, to differentiate from other books about the RCMP. For *Undercover operations*, you first have the geographical qualifier, Canada, and then the NT, history.

With the computer and retrieval systems, the number of categories has actually increased. It costs little more to add a category to a computer system, whereas in the old days, it would have meant physically typing and filing a card.

The subject headings also change over time. The most common example used is the changing subject headings for people of color in the United States. It began as *Negroes*, and then became *Afro-Americans*, (*Afro* because the Library did not want to file the subject in the same category as topics from the continent of Africa) and now *Blacks*.

Geographic changes also bring updates to the subject headings. The Soviet Union no longer exists; it is now Russia and other states like Ukraine or Belarus. But the USSR did exist for many years, and histories are still being written, so you have a number of subject choices there.

One geographical change can mean changing a whole series of categories. On April 1, 1999, Canada divided the Northwest Territories, and created the new territory of Nunavut. That created a whole new series of main terms under Nunavut and brought in the use of Nunavut as a geographic qualifier and subdivision. So on that date, the National Library of Canada issued a whole series of new subject headings.

Not all changes come that fast, especially in scholarly fields where terms take years to be accepted, and older books in a field may be subject cataloged under earlier subjects or more general categories.

The British Library has used various subject indexing systems over the years, and so a Web search may bring up older systems called Precis or Compass as well as the LCSH. A British Library web search for *Undercover* returned:

Subject: Royal Canadian Mounted Police
Subject: (Compass) Mounted police
Subject: (Compass) Canada

The British Library Web catalog, OPAC, notes that a subject search will also pick up words in the title of a book. The Help page recommends entering as many search terms as possible to overcome the limitations of the older systems.

Searching by subject

Searching by subject is why even library research can be an adventure. You have many choices, many paths to go down as you look for the material you want. So where do you start?

If you already have a book published in the past 20 years in the United States, Canada, or Australia, you should find the CIP data across from the title page. That will give you some data to start with: the CIP subject headings, and the Library of Congress or other library's subject headings.

Then you have to do your search on all three (or more)subject headings, plus the call number.

Each search will give you new titles and often new subject cross-references. Some systems allow you to save your search to disk. As you go along, you will get a sense of where the best places are to search; often there is more than area to look.

Figure 23-1 shows the advanced search page for the Library of Congress Web site, which allows you to do a Boolean search within three sets of dialog boxes. It lets you search for any term or use a drop-down menu that searches through specific catalog categories. The advanced search pages at the Canadian, British, and Australian libraries are similar.

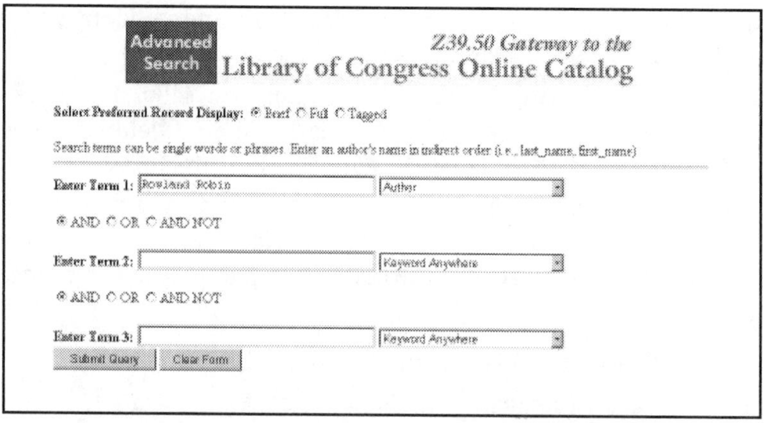

Advanced Search
Z39.50 Gateway to the Library of Congress Online Catalog

Select Preferred Record Display: Brief Full Tagged

Search terms can be single words or phrases. Enter an author's name in indirect order (i.e., last_name, first_name)

Enter Term 1: Rowland Robin Author

AND OR AND NOT

Enter Term 2: Keyword Anywhere

AND OR AND NOT

Enter Term 3: Keyword Anywhere

Submit Query Clear Form

Figure 23-1. Advanced search page at the Library of Congress.

Before you go to the library

You're now ready to go to the library. It's time to get on the Web and do your initial search before you step out of the house or your office.

One thing you should note before you do your search, no matter which library, is the date the catalog went from file card to computer. For the Library of Congress, that year was 1968.

Depending on the size of the library and its budget, the entire catalog may be available for a search, or the Web page may tell you the year the electronic catalog started.

To start your search for books, I recommend three initial searches: the online library catalog, *The New York Times Book Review* index, and online bookstores. That will give you a good overview of what is available in your subject area.

Library catalog

Start with your local neighborhood, main downtown metropolitan, or regional reference library, or if you are a student or scholar, your university library. Search first using the authors, titles, or subjects you already know. Save that initial list and do some cross-reference checks using first the specific call number for the book, and then the more general call number.

That will quickly give you an idea of what books are available in the system. If the library catalog is tied in with the circulation system, as it is with the Toronto Public Library system, you will be told not only the branch that has the book, but also whether or not it is in the library. If it is not, you should be able to put a reserve on the book.

Print everything out. Most public and university libraries have books on open stacks, so when you get to the library you can locate the books you want and see what else there may be nearby.

The New York Times Book Review

The New York Times has put online all 50,000 book reviews, from the daily and Sunday editions, from 1980 to present on the Web. The *New York Times* online requires registration, but the service is free. The *Times* reviews only a fraction of the books published each year, but as one of the more definitive book reviews in the United States, it may be that a search will turn up something missed in a more narrow controlled vocabulary search. The return also has the advantage of being a complete descriptive review of the book, rather than just a few words in a subject heading.

Tip: Check out who wrote the review. The author of the review is often an expert in the same field and has written on the subject so do a search on that author both in *The New York Times* and back at the library.

Other book reviews may be available from local newspaper sites, but none would go as far back as the *New York Times* nor would they be as easily available.

Online bookstores

The online bookstores **Amazon.com**, **Amazon.co.uk**, **bn.com** (Barnes and Noble), **Chapters.ca,** and **Indigo.ca** are good places for current and forthcoming books.

Library bureaucracy often moves slowly, so it may be a while before a new book becomes available in a library online catalog. It will show up in an online bookstore often before it is published. Then you will have to make a decision whether or not to buy the book, or wait until it becomes available in the library.

Subject searching is often poor in the online bookstores. Usually you cannot do a subject search from the initial search box you find on the home page. The advanced search feature is usually found as a link on the books page and you should use that to do your search.

When the book page comes up, look for cross references, such as Amazon.com's "People who bought this book also bought..." It's a good marketing feature, and it is helpful to researchers as well.

Another advantage to online bookstores is the availability of small press and limited run books. You may not find such books in bookstores. Nor will you find them in most smaller libraries. This type of book takes up space that can be more profitably used for buyers or borrowers. If the small press is registered with the wholesaler that deals with the online bookstore itself, a catalog entry takes up a minuscule amount of disk space and still makes a small profit for the online bookstore when you order it.

Tip: Search in all three countries, perhaps using Amazon.com, Amazon.co.uk, and Chapters.ca. That way you can pick up books available in one country but not yet available in another.

In the library

In the library you will find a vast amount of material available to you. If you did your initial search at home and have a good printout, go straight to the area of the call numbers, locate the book you want, and then look around. Look at the books beside the ones you want, and then check nearby stacks, especially in more general categories. Grab a few books, sit down and leaf through the bibliography and citations at the end, and see if anything interesting shows up.

It's called *stack serendipity,* that chance discovery in the library stacks of the book not on the shelf in front of you, but on the shelf behind you that you never thought of. And then you're in a whole new area of research.

Card or computer catalogs, while helpful guides, are not always as favorable for serendipity. You have to be there and see what's in the books themselves.

That is the problem with closed stacks, where the library retrieves the book for you, and you don't know what you're getting until it arrives (sometimes after an hour's wait on a busy day). Quite often, in that situation, the books are duds, with little or no relevance to your project. Sometimes there are unexpected gems. In libraries with closed stacks, subject and call number searches help narrow the search and help you find some relevant material, but, unfortunately, limit the possibility of serendipity.

Encyclopedias and indexes, directories and guides

A library is much more than books you can take out. Libraries are the source of reference books, specialized encyclopedias, directories, guides, and indexes to all kinds of information.

So once you are in the library, you should also look for such sources of information as:

- **Specialized encyclopedias and dictionaries.** There are many kinds of highly specialized encyclopedias that cover specific geographic or subject areas. They can be called dictionaries or encyclopedias, or have a more general title. All have alphabetical listings of highly specialized information, from biographies of famous and not-so-famous writers, musicians, painters, or politicians to highly technical medical and scientific information. There are a number of guide books to specialized and general encyclopedias, including encyclopedias and dictionaries published centuries ago (which give a interesting insight to what people thought in the past).
- **Scholarly indexes.** These are guides to the "literature" and often the first place that scholars go to when researching a subject. The indexes are available in print until the dawn of the computer age, and after that usually available both in print and online or on CD-ROM. Key areas are the social sciences, humanities, business (including popular, specialized, and academic), general science, applied science and technology, biology and agriculture, law, education, and art. Anyone doing any kind of in-depth research should consult these indexes. Not all scholarly articles are dry as dust and many provide insight, information, and possible contacts for interviews. **Note:** The scholarly indexes often have their own subject conventions and may not match the commonly used Library of Congress subject headings.
- **Periodical indexes.** The best known is the *Readers Guide to Periodical Literature,* which indexes popular magazines. The Canadian equivalent is the *Canadian Periodicals Index*. The periodical indexes are good for subject searches and for looking for articles either by or about authors whose books you are reading.

- **Citation indexes.** Part of the scholarly world, they are a good way of cross-referencing an author. If you look up an author in the citation index, you will see which other scholars have cited that author in footnotes or a bibliography, and then see what their article is about. That is one way, at least in the scholarly world, of getting around the possible limitation of subject indexes. You can follow the trail as long as you want, seeing who cited the authors who cited your original author.
- **Directories.** These books are a good source for finding people, ranging from the *Who's Who* series to law lists and members of associations.
- **Vertical files.** This is the librarian's name for clipping files held in file cabinets. They are often a good source of information, especially from the days before computerization of newspapers and magazines. Vertical files can be still be valuable sources of information especially on local history and personalities. Older vertical files have quite likely been converted to microfiche or microfilm.

Reference books are often shelved separately from more specialized stacks. You will usually find these books in the "General" information section of the library, the 000 in the Dewey system and the A's in the Library of Congress system, or for specialized subject areas, at the beginning of each section. In most cases, it is best to ask a librarian for help.

Working with librarians

It's the librarian's job to help you find what you want. A librarian is your guide, not only to the stacks in that library, but to others as well. A librarian is the one to help you find ways of getting books and other information you need, whether it is in a stack a few feet away, by interlibrary loan, or by actually recommending you hop on a plane and fly to Washington or London.

To go back to the idea that your research quest is a form of Joseph Campbell's heroic journey, librarians are your most important threshold guardians, heralds, and mentors. It is their job, and what they have been training for years to do, to help you to do your research, to zero in on exactly what you want.

Then, like a good mentor, guardian, or herald in the old tales, the librarian most often gives you many choices to many paths, knowing full well that in most cases there are many paths, in that very library itself, to what you are seeking.

When working with a librarian, the researcher should:

- ❑ **Do your homework.** The more prepared, the more preresearch you have done by reading, interviewing, or online searching, the more you have focused your topic, the more the librarian will be able to help you.
- ❑ **Don't ignore the herald's call.** Librarians often grimace at two traits of the scholarly community. The first is to do it yourself, as if you're not a scholar if you can't find it all by yourself. The second is the tendency of many scholars to remain strictly within a few areas of their field and too often ignore relevant material in other academic fields unless a librarian points them in the right direction. Less prevalent, but also a problem, is on the creative side, where many writers and journalists want to stay away from the scholarly and stick to the strictly popular. On major projects, I always ask a librarian if there are any additional promising areas I might have missed.

When you approach a librarian, especially in these times of budget cuts, be polite and patient; most librarians are overworked.

A librarian will then usually interview you, trying to narrow down what you want. If you have a simple question, a ready reference question that "requires a single, usually uncomplicated, straightforward answer," you'll soon be on your way. If, however, the question is more complicated, as it is with most in-depth research, the librarian will conduct what is called a reference interview, asking a series of questions that help the librarian focus in on what you—the user— need. You may then be pointed to a number of sources, including books, specialized encyclopedias and reference works, microforms, and scholarly and popular periodicals.

Old books

One of the best alternative sources for researchers is the used or secondhand bookstore. Secondhand bookstores, especially those that specialize in specific fields, such as the military, crime, or science, are often a gold mine for the researcher. If you are doing a major research project, never pass a used bookstore, anywhere, without going in. You never know what you might find.

Throughout my years of doing research projects, this rule has stood me in good stead. When I was working on my first project, about female war correspondent Kit Coleman, I was in a used bookstore looking for something else when I came across the equivalent of *Who's Who for Canada* for the turn of the last century. It had capsule biographies of almost every character I was writing about. Since then secondhand bookstores have provided me with additions to my reference library and bibliography for every project I have worked.

These days, you can also search online for used bookstores. The two best-known sites that allow you to search are Abebooks at **www.abebooks.com** and Bibliofind, at **www.bibliofind com**. Both sites allow you to search for holdings by member bookstores.

You should note that the keywords are created by the bookseller and often do not follow the Library of Congress subject headings, so there is a chance of hitting something the LCSH system might miss.

Both Abebooks and Bibliofind allow you to order directly by filling up a virtual shopping cart. It is better, however, especially if you support used bookstores, to click to the bookstore itself and order directly, ensuring better service by eliminating the middle merchant.

Note: Bibliofind is now owned by Amazon.com. Avoid using Amazon's own search service because the main Amazon site charges premium prices. Search on Bibliofind and Abebooks instead.

Links

Library of Congress Home Page
www.loc.gov

Library of Congress WWW/Z39.50 Gateway
lcweb.loc.gov/z3950/
Gateway links page for searching the Library of Congress. You can also link and search other library catalogs, including U.S. public and academic libraries, private libraries, Canadian, and international libraries.

Library of Congress Classification Outline
lcweb.loc.gov/catdir/cpso/lcco/lcco.html
Web index for LOC classification system.

U.S. National Library of Medicine
www.nlm.nih.gov

NLM Library Services
www.nlm.nih.gov/libserv.html
Catalog and database entry page for the U.S. National Library of Medicine.

OPAC 97

opac97.bl.uk

British Library online public catalog.

National Library of Canada Home Page

www.nlc-bnc.ca/ehome.htm

ResNet-National Library of Canada Search

amicus.nlc-bnc.ca/resanet/reslogine.htm

Search page for the National Library of Canada.

Library of Canada Canadian Subject Headings

www.nlc-bnc.ca/csh/csh-e.htm

The National Library decision on the use of Nunavut in the catalog is accessible from this page in Adobe PDF format.

The New York Times: Books

search.nytimes.com/books/search/

Search *The New York Times Book Review* Archives.

Abebooks.com

www.abebooks.com

Abebooks calls itself the world's largest source of out-of-print books.

Bibliofind

www.bibliofind.com

A secondhand book search site.

Amazon.com

www.amazon.com

Amazon UK

www.amazon.co.uk

Barnes and Noble

www.bn.com

Chapters

www.chapters.ca

Indigo

www.indigo.ca

Chapter 24
Archives

The boxes were filled with old records wrapped in brown paper and twine, records that had never been opened from the day they were shipped from Japan to the U.S. National Archives in Washington.

When Randy Herschaft, an investigative researcher for the Associated Press (AP) opened up that brown paper and twine, he found long-forgotten orders from U.S. Army commanders to shoot civilians during the first frantic weeks of the Korean War in July 1950.

The AP would report later that the commander of the U.S. 25th Infantry Division told his troops that civilians in the battle zone "are to be considered as enemy and action taken accordingly." The operations chief of the First Cavalry Division ordered: "No refugees to cross the front line. Fire everyone trying to cross lines. Use discretion in case of women and children."

Former U.S. soldiers who served in Korea told AP reporters that "hundreds" of civilians could have been killed at No Gun Ri in the central part of the country.

The AP report, "The Bridge at No Gun Ri," by reporters Sang-Hun Choe, Charles J. Hanley, and Martha Mendoza, which moved on the wires on September 29, 1999, would later win the Pulitzer Prize for investigative journalism.

AP first heard about the story from Korean civilians who had been pressing their case with the Korean government and sending petitions to the U.S. embassy. Sang-Hun Choe wrote a story on the petition. In response, the Pentagon said the First Cavalry Division wasn't in the area at the time.

In New York, Bob Port, editor of the Special Assignment unit (and now with APBOnline) decided to check further.

In an interview, Port told me, "The first thing we did was to get the official Army history of the Korean War, which is like a diary with maps and everything. And so we look up the location and time and the hell they weren't there, they were all around there. It was sitting right in a history book."

"Then I sent my researcher Randy Herschaft to the National Archives to retrieve all the records of all the units in those first weeks of the Korean War. And he discovers boxes of records in brown paper and twine that have never been opened, since they were packed up in Japan after the Korean war. No one had ever looked at these things. And they were just declassified automatically. So we looked inside; we found orders to kill civilians."

Herschaft and reporter Martha Mendoza kept working in the archives. "We had to pin down which unit was there," Port says. "We had to reconstruct the movements of all units over about a 10-day stretch of time. We copied the original maps, blew them up, spread them around the walls, and with markers and tape and so on reconstructed the movements.

"Then we got the names of the soldiers from another archive in St. Louis, Missouri [National Personnel Records Center], and reconstructed the rosters of the soldiers.

Months of work followed, with hundreds of declassified documents, Freedom of Information requests, and phone calls to veterans—first to enlisted men, then to officers. *[Author's Note: On May 25, 2000, the AP reported that one of the key U.S. veterans interviewed for the story "now recognizes he could not have been at the scene." He was elsewhere in Korea at the time. The AP is standing by the rest of the story.]* In Korea, Choe interviewed 24 survivors of the massacre. "We found every single one who is still alive. That took months of work. But I am very confident that between the archival records and then the veterans' organizations that we got into touch with, we were able to phone every single person who was still around. That was a good example of basic research."

Herschaft kept checking in more archives, the Truman Library in Independence, Missouri, and the U.S. Army Military History Institute in Carlisle, Pennsylvania. Mendoza later reported that Herschaft made 50 trips to public and university libraries.

Then on Sept. 29, the AP moved the story no one wanted to hear, how early in the Korean War "American soldiers machine-gunned hundreds of helpless civilians under a railroad bridge in the South Korean countryside."

"We just annihilated them," the report quoted one soldier as saying.

Within hours of the report, President Bill Clinton ordered an investigation and so did the government of South Korea.

People and paper

An archive may hold millions of pieces of paper, but for a creative researcher an archive is really all about people, set down in reports, letters, and transcripts.

While I was working on the Rocco Perri story, I read *Hamilton, An Illustrated History* by John C. Weaver, a professor at McMaster University. I noticed a footnote that said much of his information came from the files of the U.S. Consulate in Hamilton, Ontario. Until the modern era of communication, the United States had many more consulates around the world than they do now. All sent diplomatic, economic, social, criminal, and military intelligence of interest to the U.S. government back to Washington.

When I got to Washington I found that the consular files were an untapped goldmine of reports on Canadian bootlegging.

Included in the files were a series of reports from a young diplomat named Richard Boyce, who was the U.S. consul in Hamilton in the late 1920s. He decided to do some research of his own. In those days, anyone exporting goods to the United States filed an invoice with the nearest consulate, so Boyce went through each one and compared them to shipping manifests. He then discovered that Perri's gang was "laundering" liquor going to the United States by adding boxcars full of booze to the trains. In 1927, there was a shipment of hay from the area to Newark, New Jersey. But Boyce discovered that only six boxcars were legitimate shipments of hay. Eleven boxcars presumably full of booze went to other cities in New Jersey. Boyce got little satisfaction from the State Department for his trouble. He was told an investigation "would cause irritation among innocent shippers out of all proportion to its probable value in preventing the shipment of liquor." The department went on to tell Boyce to stick to his defined duties.

Whether it is soldiers fighting for their lives in Korea, or a young man frustrated by his own bureaucracy, archival documents are window into the past.

How to work with documents

There are all kinds of archives, public and private, that hold documents, audio and video recordings, and photographs. Original source material of any kind will often yield the most valuable information that you will find during a major research project. But to go back to our idea of outer circle, inner circle, and pure and applied research, a search for documents comes only as you near your goal, once you have done most of your research with secondary, published sources. Only then will you have an idea of what you are looking for.

When you are looking for documents, as with any other project, the better background information you have built up, the better questions you will ask as you open the boxes an archivist has brought to you. If your research is superficial or hurried, then you may not recognize a key name on file, a name that may become important later.

Researchers and reporters use the phrase "interviewing the document," which means you are always looking at a document and asking the same questions (to yourself) that you would ask a human being in a face-to-face interview.

Those documents, after all, were written by human beings and often betray the same weaknesses, biases, and mistakes made by other human beings. While official documents can and should be quoted as authoritative sources, the information in those documents should always, if possible, be verified by information obtained from other documents, from people who know about the project you are researching, and from published sources.

Getting there

For any project where you are seeking original documents, your reading comes first. Any good book on the subject will have a bibliography and in that bibliography will be a list of all the record and manuscript sources that the author used for that research project.

When contacting people in the course of your research, it is always a good idea to ask if they have any documents or where those documents might be found.

If a government department is mentioned in any account by a newspaper, perhaps, or by a human source, then it is likely that department will hold some paper record. Then you will have to find out if the material is available freely, if you have to use a Freedom of Information request, or as a last resort, try to obtain the information from "usually reliable sources."

Government documents are usually called *records* and archives usually give them a number such as *RG 59* (Record Group 59), which is the U.S. National Archives designation for records from the State Department. Documents received from individuals and corporate bodies (profit or nonprofit) are generally called *manuscripts* and are usually given a number with *M* or *MG* (Manuscript Group). You should note, however, that some archives use the M also to designate microform holdings. Always check with the guide to the archives before starting work.

Then and now

A government archive has two functions. The first is to be the record-keeper for the government itself, to store all those millions of documents generated each year by every department. Material is routinely transferred to the archives after a certain period of time.

The second role is to make that material available to the public for research purposes and to preserve historic material so that future generations can use them.

Just because material is in the archives, that doesn't mean that you can get hold of it immediately. As a general rule, most federal government information in the United States and Canada is restricted or classified until it is 30 years old.

Even if the material is more than 30 years old, it may not be completely open. The sheer volume of material means it is impossible to routinely declassify most documents. In the United States, in all but rare cases, mostly on national security issues, if you find and want to copy a document marked "Secret," it can be routinely declassified by a duty archivist.

Other information will require a Freedom of Information request before you can see it and then provisions of various Freedom of Information acts will apply. For example, the FBI still requires FOI requests for cases going back to the 1920s.

Some highly sensitive material is sometimes restricted for longer periods. For example, the United States restricts information concerning "intelligence activities or intelligence sources or methods" for 50 years. Canada restricts the release of personal information until 20 years after the subject's death, while the United States releases it under Freedom of Information once the individual has died.

With state, provincial, regional, county, and municipal governments, other rules may apply and material may be restricted for periods of 10, 15, 20, or 30 years.

Manuscripts and personal papers may also be restricted. That material is, after all, the personal property of the individual and he or she has the right to place restrictions on its use. Restrictions may include a period of time before it can be viewed, perhaps a number of years after it was donated, or a period of time relating to the death of the individuals involved. Although individual manuscripts may be in an archives for preservation, this does not always mean that the letters or material can be published. The original owner retains copyright. International copyright law usually says that copyright remains with a writer's heirs, whether it is a published book or unpublished letter, for 50 years after death.

Where to find it

If you are looking for material that may be in a public or private archive, the first place to check is any archive, library, or museum that you come across in your reading.

The rise of the World Wide Web has made finding things easier—but not as easy as it is for libraries. One reason is that the sheer volume of material in archives makes it harder to catalog for the Web. So far, the paper world of archives has not received the attention it deserves from the online world.

The Library of Congress has an online version of the National Union Catalog of Manuscripts, plus links to its own and other manuscript collections in North America. The U.S. National Archives has links only to its own regional offices and the Presidential Libraries. Britain's Historical Manuscript's Commission has a search engine that covers most of the country's manuscript holdings outside the Public Record Office. Canada's National Archives lists only its holdings. Australia has a gateway site to all the country's major archives.

If a bibliography or an online search doesn't provide an answer, it is time to go to a major library to consult, with the help of a librarian, the many published indexes of archives and manuscript holdings. Some of the material, especially older material, will be found in bound books; newer material may be found online, on microfilm, or on CD-ROM.

The indexes will list the archives and manuscript collections and their holdings, while others list names of individuals and corporate bodies (both for profit corporations as well as private groups, associations, and clubs).

Writing for help

A well-focused query letter will give you an idea of what is available. For small requests (just a few documents), the archives may just send them to you on a complimentary basis or include an order form allowing you to order them by mail.

For larger quantities of documents, it is worth a visit, because you could be ordering and paying for photocopies or microfilm of irrelevant material.

Not all archives are cooperative, especially in these days of staff shortages. From some, if you get a reply, you may get a condescending letter telling you to hire an expensive local researcher to do the basic work the archives should be helping you with.

Fortunately, with new online search engines that list archival holdings, finding out what is in an archive is becoming easier.

Finding aids

Once you have an idea of what you are looking for and where to look, the next step is to consult a *finding aid*.

Archives usually call their lists of holdings "finding aids" instead of catalogs, again because it is impossible to catalog individual documents.

The finding aid will usually give you a title, perhaps the original title given by the government department that originated the document or perhaps a title given to the collection by an archivist, and sometimes a capsule description.

The level of detail may also depend on what is in the file itself—or how well the original government department was organized. For example, the holdings of U.S. Coast Guard operations during the Prohibition era (RG 26) are probably more detailed than some other holdings because they are popular source of information about the boats that brought liquor to the United States along the Atlantic, Pacific, and Gulf coasts. On the other hand, while I was working on my Prohibition books, I also wanted to consult the records of the old U.S. Bureau of Narcotics, only to be told by the archivists that the records were so disorganized that no one had attempted the Herculean task of trying to find what was in those records.

An archivist is essential to helping you find material. A good archivist who has worked with the documents and researchers will have a good idea where the information you are seeking is held. I also note that the best archivists asked me as I was going along what I was finding and what was interesting to me—increasing their store of knowledge of their holdings.

The bad news is that during the past 15 years or so, budget and staff cuts in archives around the world have reduced the number of archivists. Staff cuts also mean everyone is overworked and less able to help the individual researcher. Martha Mendoza, writing about how she and the AP team uncovered the No Gun Ri story, noted that the U.S. National Archives has no Korean War specialist.

Online finding aids

The growth of the World Wide Web has brought with it the online finding aid, although researchers should note that so far, again because of the large volume of records, not all archives have their complete finding aids online. Britain's Public Record Office is the most advanced, and you will find its online catalog has an excellent level of detail and will give you a good idea of what is available.

The U.S. National Archive's online finding aid is called NAIL (NARA Archival Information Locator). Material is still being added to the lists. The National Archives of Canada online finding aid is called ArchivaNet. Finding aids are still being added in Canada as well. Australia's National Archives has an extensive online catalog.

The Library of Congress has an online version of the National Union Catalog of Manuscripts and Britain's Commission on Historical Documents has a search engine for manuscript holdings.

These online finding aids will give some idea of what is available so you can prepare for your trip to the archives.

Tip: It's now easy to check at least some of the holdings of major archives around the world, so it's a good idea to run the key words and names for your research project through all of them, just in case something turns up.

At the archives

When you arrive at the archives, you will have to register, get your pass or reader's ticket, and become familiar with the security rules. You will have to check your coat and bags, but you will be allowed to take a computer to the reading room, although you may have to use it in a special area. In most cases, you will not be allowed to take pens into the reading room, to prevent damage to the documents, but will be allowed to use pencils to take notes.

You should always ask to meet any of the archivists who have helped you by letter, to thank them and to ask for their help as you go along.

In most archives, you may be restricted to the reading room, but in some you are permitted to visit the archivists in their offices. Sometimes they will take you back in the stacks as they help you out, although the material you want will be transferred to the reading room when you want to examine it.

If you have requested some material and you are going to use it for a second day, usually it can be held overnight for you close to the reading room and reissued in the morning. If you have finished with your boxes for that day, always order your next day's request before you leave. That way it will be readily available when you get there in the morning.

The documents

You will be allowed to look at documents in two ways: either the originals will be delivered in a box, or you will have to look at them on microfilm or microfiche.

The original is always the best choice, for it is only on the original document can you find the intangibles that are lost in microform. You can hold the document in your hand, feel how thick the paper is (a flimsy carbon copy, cheap paper, or thick, embossed stationary?). You see if notes were written in ink or pencil, and if there is anything on the back. (*Always* look at the back of every document).

As documents become fragile, or if they are popular items for research, then to preserve the originals, they are copied to microfiche or microfilm. While the information and the data is intact with microforms, those intangibles, which help the creative researcher, are lost.

Documents in archives are usually organized the same way as they were received from the original agency. They reflect that agency's needs, rather than those of the researcher, which is why preresearch and consultation with an archivist is essential.

Documents will arrive in boxes, probably with a number of files in each box. Go through the boxes and the files carefully, one at a time, both to keep your research organized and to make sure you don't return a document to the wrong file.

As you read the documents, personalities will emerge, and you will catch a glimpse of the human beings who decided the issues, wrote the decisions, or opposed them.

Most documents will give a series of clues to other documents. Look for reference numbers that may apply to other cases, other departments, or other agencies. Then track down their files for a wider and perhaps alternative view. Look for names of officials or anyone else that keep showing up and then make notes so you can look for further information about those individuals.

Keep track of all the dates on the documents, especially older ones, and add them to your chronology. Putting the dates in chronology, as I noted earlier, helps put the story in perspective. For the 19th and 20th centuries, knowledge of the dates also allows you to go to the newspapers and magazines of the era. With those dates you can use microfilm to find what the media was saying (if anything) about the case.

Notes and copies

Making photocopies in most archives is usually more expensive than in your neighborhood copy shop. That's because most archives use what is known as a "cost recovery" approach to the copying, meaning that overhead and other costs are added to the cost of copying.

You may be offered what appears on the surface to be a cheaper alternative, which is microfilm or microfiche. But what you have to consider in the long run is how you are going to use the microform. Are you going to be able to use a reader in your local or university library? Are you then going to make copies from the microfilm?

This is where your notebook computer, chronology, and free-form database software come in. Make as many notes as you can on computer, create files on individual names so you can add information later from other sources, and add to your chronology as you go along. Then order just those photocopies you really need.

The Bullock lynching case

On January 11, 1922, three detectives from the Hamilton, Ontario, police department raided a local rooming house and arrested a black man named Matthew Bullock. Police said that Bullock was wanted in his hometown of Norlina, North Carolina, on a charge of provoking a race riot. Over the next two months, first local, then Canadian, and finally the U.S. national media turned its attention to North Carolina's demand that Bullock be returned to that state for trial.

A year earlier, Matthew's 17-year-old brother Plummer had been sold rotten apples by a white storekeeper in Norlina. The teenager demanded his money back, there was an argument, and Plummer Bullock was arrested. That night a mob attacked the jail and lynched Plummer Bullock and another black who was also being held in the jail.

The white mob then attacked the local black community and was repelled in the ensuing gunfight. Matthew Bullock, a veteran of World War I, helped organize his community's defense, and then knowing he was a marked man, fled to Canada.

A year later, the local U.S. consul demanded extradition. Bullock was arrested and taken before a local judge, Colin Snider.

One key factor in the case was the belief that if Bullock returned to North Carolina, he would also be lynched. In almost all extradition cases, all that is needed to send a suspect back to another country are affidavits showing enough evidence to go to trial. In one key case in 1911, Justice Oliver Wendell Holmes, writing for the U.S. Supreme Court, said, "We are bound by the existence of an extradition treaty to assume the trial will be fair." The trouble was in the Bullock case, all indications were that he would not get a fair trial. So Judge Snider demanded witnesses from North Carolina. The state refused and Bullock was freed.

I knew all that based on news accounts that I discovered while researching the Rocco Perri story.

On my next trip to Ottawa, I easily found the file on Bullock from Canada's Department of Justice. It contained letters from the U.S. State Department with reference numbers. Those reference numbers meant it would be easy for an archivist in Washington to find the Bullock file, and I was able to order it by mail. The State Department file also contained correspondence with the Governor of North Carolina. With that reference, it was easy to obtain the North Carolina file—again by mail—from Raleigh. Finally, news accounts said leaders of the National Association for the Advancement of Colored People, the NAACP, had come to Hamilton to help Bullock with the case. So I wrote to the NAACP and was able to obtain their file on the case.

The four files gave me a better idea of what was going on. I had the correspondence between the U.S. Consulate and the State Department, the Canadian government and the State Department, the Canadian Department of Justice and Judge Snider, the State Department and the State of North Carolina. I also had the reports on the lynching—and the fear in the community—from the NAACP. The Canadian Justice file also had transcripts of the hearings.

Judge Snider, 71 at the time, a pillar of the Ontario establishment, used a loophole, demanding that someone come from North Carolina to identify the prisoner. North Carolina refused, possibly facing embarrassment with the newspaper spotlight on the case.

The documents revealed some interesting tactics by both the Canadian and U.S. governments. The Secretary of State, Charles Evans Hughes, took one tack with North Carolina. He noted that in cities close to the Canada-U.S. border, American witnesses often did come to Canada to identify suspects and told North Carolina that Snider was justified in his ruling. In his letter to Ottawa, however, Hughes wrote that the Snider decision was a dangerous precedent that could "defeat the purpose of an extradition treaty."

Ottawa, which of course did not know what Hughes had told North Carolina, pondered what it should do about the letter from the Secretary of State and in the end decided, diplomatically, not to answer. "I feel somewhat embarrassed in answering the United States dispatch...possibly it will not be revived," an official wrote, adding, "put these papers on the file in order of date and hold for future consideration if necessary." That is the last official note in the file.

What happened to Matthew Bullock? It's not certain. After he was released and officially permitted to stay in Canada, the Ku Klux Klan in North Carolina threatened to kidnap Bullock. So the leaders of the black community in Hamilton used what was left of the defense fund to spirit him out of the country, saying only that he had "arrived safely on another continent."

Links

The Bridge at No Gun Ri

wire.ap.org/APpackages/nogunri/cover.html

AP's Bridge at No Gun Ri

wire.ap.org/APpackages/nogunri/documents.html

Archives

National Archives and Records Administration Home Page

www.nara.gov

NAIL Homepage

www.nara.gov/nara/nail.html

U.S. National Archives basic search page.

Visiting NARA: A Nationwide Network of Facilities

www.nara.gov/nara/gotonara.html
National Archives guide to its regional facilities and presidential libraries.

Special Collections in the Library of Congress: Manuscript Division

lcweb.loc.gov/spcoll/cdmanu.html
A guide to manuscripts held by the Library of Congress.

Library of Congress manuscript search page

lcweb.loc.gov/cgi-bin/zgate?ACTION=INIT&FORM_HOST_PORT=/prod/www/ data/z3950/rlinamc3.html
Simple search gateway for manuscripts from the Library of Congress.

NUCMC Home Page

lcweb.loc.gov/coll/nucmc/nucmc.html
Library of Congress National Union List of Manuscripts Web page.

Archival and Manuscript Repositories in the United States

lcweb.loc.gov/coll/nucmc/other.html
Library of Congress web guide to archive and manuscript collections in the United States.

Public Record Office

www.pro.gov.uk
Britain's Public Record Office.

Public Record Office, Finding Aids, Catalogue

www.pro.gov.uk/finding/catalogue/default.htm
Entry page for the PRO's extensive online catalog.

Historical Manuscripts Commission's Web Site

www.hmc.gov.uk
A guide to British manuscript and archives.

National Archives of Canada—Archives nationales du Canada

www.archives.ca
Home page for the National Archives of Canada.

ArchiviaNet

www.archives.ca/exec/naweb.dll?fs&0201&e&top&0
Entry to the National Archves of Canada search page.

Archives of Australia Gateway

www.archivenet.gov.au
Gateway page for the Archives of Australia, the State and Territory archives, and a number of other Australian archive organizations.

National Archives of Australia

www.naa.gov.au
Home page for the National Archives of Australia.

Chapter 

Freedom of Information

Freedom of information (FOI) requests are a key source of current information, government data, and historical information held by federal, state, provincial, and local governments where Freedom of Information statues exist.

Because there are so many jurisdictions, I am going to use this chapter to give you a general overview of how FOI works. I'll also provide links to how you can find out more in the jurisdiction where you are seeking information.

There are three types of laws that you should be aware of:

- **Open records laws** apply in some U.S. states, which means that all records, with certain exceptions, are open to the public. Connecticut, for example, requires "all records...shall be public records and every person shall have the right to inspect such records promptly."
- **Freedom of information** laws require a government agency to provide information on request. That information is always screened to make sure it complies with provisions of the relevant act and exemptions are almost always applied.
- **Privacy laws** exist to protect your privacy and to make sure that privacy is not violated by the government, the private sector, or researchers, including the media.

The strongest Freedom of Information legislation is found in North America. There are now 40 countries that have some form of freedom or access to information legislation, although application and enforcement is often weak. (Governments and bureaucrats generally hate to disclose anything.)

Congress passed the first U.S. Freedom of Information Act in 1966 to ensure access by the public to information held by the U.S. government. Since then most jurisdictions in North America have adopted some form of freedom of information and privacy legislation. Scholars who follow the development of freedom of information generally say that the later a law was enacted, the better it is, as legislatures build on previous experience.

That does not mean that there are not problems. Information obtained under FOI, usually by journalists and scholars, is often politically sensitive, and that makes politicians twitchy about passing strong FOI laws. The trend to the privatization of government agencies, supposedly to make them more efficient, effectively takes public information gathered at taxpayers' expense out of the public realm, often exempting it from FOI access.

Finally, governments are taking advantage of a justified and growing concern among the public by invoking privacy as a means of shielding government and government officials from public scrutiny. Often even routine requests are denied to protect the privacy of the people involved, even if those people are the ones complaining (as is often the case with both the IRS and Revenue Canada).

In this information age, privacy is eroding, and computers are giving both governments and corporations incredible power. At the same time, the same software and skills give both scholarly and journalistic researchers the ability to discover new trends and act as a watchdog. Computer-assisted reporting in the United States has, for example, exposed such practices as the policy of banks to "redline" or refuse mortgages in predominately minority neighborhoods. The task in the future will be to find a compromise between the right to know and the right to privacy.

Before making an FOI request

Once again, preliminary research is essential if you are going to make a Freedom of Information request. The more you know about your project and the government agencies involved, the better your chances are of getting what you want:

- ❑ Ask yourself which departments and agencies collect the type of information you are seeking. Don't limit yourself to federal agencies; look at state/provincial and local, and if appropriate, international agencies.
- ❑ Find out what is available already as public information. Most government agencies have a Web site and will post information that is routinely released.
- ❑ Check the Web site to find the department's or agency's freedom or access to information officers. They will be handling the information you request.
- ❑ Use the departmental Web site and a government phone book to figure out the structure of the agency. That will help you narrow down where the information is handled.
- ❑ Check any regulations or suggestions that a department may post about filing Freedom of Iinformation requests.
- ❑ Check for both fees and fee waivers.
  - ❍ Most Canadian jurisdictions charge a fee. For example, the Canadian Federal Access to Information Act has a filing fee of $5, which gives you five hours search time and 100 pages of photocopies.
  - ❍ The U.S. Federal Freedom of Information Act provides for waiving or reduction of fees if "disclosure of information is in the public interest [and] likely to contribute significantly to public understanding...of government." News media employees and qualified freelance journalists as well as some educational researchers (in limited circumstances) can request waiver of fees.
- ❑ Check for residency requirements. Canada's federal Access to Information Act limits requests to citizens and landed immigrants (legal residents). Some other countries have similar restrictions.
- ❑ Try to find out if the information may also be available more freely from nongovernment sources.

Informal or routine release

Before you file, always try to ascertain first if the information can be released without a formal request. A request under Freedom of Information, no matter what the jurisdiction, will automatically trigger the provisions of the act.

You can always try an agency's public relations office first and if the information you are requesting is noncontroversial, chances that are it can be released without a formal request.

If that doesn't work, your next step is to talk to an FOI officer in the department or agency. Again try to find out if the information can be released informally without having to file a request.

Under 1996 amendments to the U.S. federal FOI Act, information requested frequently by the public is routinely released with out a FOIA request. Congress requires that agencies create an index of that type of information.

Information previously released to others under FOI can also be released to you at minimal cost for copying and an index is usually available from the agency either on a Web site or in a reading room.

On the other hand, sometimes even routine requests for public information can trigger an unwanted FOI request. For example, a request to the State Department for basic biographical information on the consuls in Hamilton, Ontario, was handled as a FOI request. I was then given previously published information.

Filing the request

If you have exhausted all informal means of trying to get the information you want, then it is time to file formally. Write to the agency, noting that you are making a request under the appropriate freedom of information or privacy statute.

You must craft your request carefully; make sure that is neither too broad nor too narrow.

The best approach is to ask for *all records* but in as narrow a subject area as possible (without narrowing your request too far). Writing a good FOIA letter is an art.

You should add a note that all records should include a phrase like *including but not limited to* and describe records you believe will help your research project. Legally a government *record* means any reports or data on paper or in computer format and includes maps, diagrams, charts, and database data. If you want something specific, it is often a good idea to spell that out, again noting that you are not limiting your request to that specific area.

If you want data on computer disk or tape, mention that specifically; otherwise the agency may supply it to you on paper.

Some government departments and agencies will either have computer equipment so ancient that it may be not possible to give data to you in a contemporary format (although this is less of a problem after Year 2000 upgrades). U.S. law says agencies must provide data to you in the format you want if it is "readily reproducible," which may or may not be the case, depending on the agency and its equipment.

If you are asking for a waiver of fees, make sure that request is included in your letter.

Time

Freedom of Information laws require a department or agency to initially respond within a reasonable period of time. For the U.S. federal FOIA, it is 20 days; for Canada's federal Access to Information Act, it is 30 days.

Unless the information is simple and easy to find—and depending on the backlog—you will usually get a response saying the staff is searching for the material and requesting an extension.

The time line for your request can then stretch into months or even years. The FBI gets so many requests, and so many detailed requests, that often it can take as many as two or three years to fulfill a request.

There can be a number of reasons for the delay. Budget cuts have brought staff shortages; sometimes the information is hard to find; and processing a large request takes a long time. Sometimes in sensitive cases, the bureaucrats with an eye on their political masters may try to stonewall or delay a request as long as possible.

Under the U.S. federal FOIA, it is possible to request an expedited review of the material. To be granted an expedited review you have to either demonstrate "compelling need" (such as a life-threatening situation) or compelling "public interest" (if you are in the media).

The political level

A sensitive Freedom of Information request may trigger a response on the political level. Bureaucrats formally or informally inform the political level about requests that could cause controversy.

In some cases, including a notorious case of an investigation into misconduct by Canadian troops in Somalia, an FOI request can actually trigger an attempted cover-up. In other cases, knowledge among politicians that the media or a scholar has made a request may start the spin machine working, and you will find yourself and your research being spun almost as soon as it is released.

Tip: Canadian reporters used to the parliamentary system routinely request *ministerial briefing notes* as part of a request. These notes are supplied by bureaucrats to a minister who has to answer questions in the federal parliament or provincial legislature. In U.S. jurisdictions similar briefing notes on current issues are regularly supplied to senior members of the executive branch and sometimes to members of the legislative branch. On any subject that may have political ramifications, always include a phrase such as "briefing notes for the minister," "briefing notes for the Secretary and senior officials," or "legislative briefing notes" in your definition of all records in a request. The briefing notes will often give you a good summary of the information and perhaps provide alternative avenues for your research.

Exemptions

Every Freedom of Information law provides for exemptions, and information can be denied or redacted (taken out) on the basis of those exemptions.

These generally include:

- **National security, national defense, and foreign policy.** This includes items classified under appropriate federal laws, rules, and executive orders.
- **Privacy.** Information that could violate privacy statutes or would be an unwarranted invasion of an individual's privacy is exempt.
- **Police investigations.** Information that would tend to reveal police investigation methods, may reveal the identity of confidential informants, could interfere with an accused's fair trial rights, or could endanger the life or safety of any person is exempt.
- **Trade secrets.** Many business are required by law to provide business, financial, technical and scientific information to the government. In many circumstances that information is also exempt.

- ❑ **Interagency, intra-agency, and government operations.** This exemption covers such things as draft reports (not final reports), internal consultations, and internal agency rules, as well as some personnel and administrative matters.

Most Freedom of Information and privacy acts outline exemptions to some exemptions, when information can be released, under strict procedures, if there is a strong public interest in releasing the information. Under some circumstances, an agency has the discretionary power to release some information that would otherwise be exempt.

In most cases, a Freedom of Information act requires that only specifically exempt material be redacted from your request. So information not covered by the exemption is released to you.

That could mean that you receive some pages with a few sentences blacked out and others with whole pages (with the exception of page numbers) blacked out.

Some agencies are fairly strict in their interpretation of the exemptions, while others are more easygoing. When I was working on my Prohibition books, the FBI used exemptions on tending to "disclose techniques and procedures for law enforcement investigations" to heavily censor reports from 1925 on the activities of bootleggers in Buffalo.

Fees

Your request will normally cover a certain amount of search time and a minimum number of photocopies. Under the U.S. FOIA, noncommercial educational institutions and the news media are charged only reasonable duplication costs, and even that can be reduced to nothing if you are granted a waiver.

If you are dealing with a large amount of material, it is sometimes a good idea to inspect the documents in the agency offices. The material you see will already have been screened for exemptions before your visit, so you will be seeing photocopies. Then you can choose which photocopies you want to have copied for you and reject the rest.

Appeals

If you are denied access to any or all of the information you want, you can appeal. The agency usually sends you a letter outlining the reasons for the denial and outlining the appeal procedures.

You then have a limited period of time, usually about 30 days, to launch an appeal. Under U.S. federal and many state jurisdictions, the appeal is to a panel of senior bureaucrats. In Canada, the appeal is to an independent commissioner or commissioners independent from the agency. Some U.S. states, such as Connecticut, also have similar quasi-independent review agencies.

Whether the appeal is to a senior bureaucrat or to an independent agency of some kind, the government can still generally refuse to release information. The last resort, if the appeal is denied, or unsatisfactory, is to the courts, which can often be a long drawn-out and expensive process.

Links

Canada

Freedom of Information Research Project

qsilver.queensu.ca/~foi/

Guide to Canadian federal and provincial freedom of information from Queen's University School of Policy Studies.

Open Government Canada

www.opengovernmentcanada.org/

Home page for a campaign for better freedom of information in Canada.

Links page

www.opengovernmentcanada.org/resources.htm

Canadian Access and Privacy Association Home Page

www.capa.ca/

Info Source: Main Menu

www.tbs-sct.gc.ca/gos-sog/infosource/Info-Srce-Menu_e.html

Official guide to information resources from the Canadian federal government.

United States

The Reporters' Committee for Freedom of the Press

www.rcfp.org

Excellent site for information on U.S. Freedom of Information.

FOI Handbookpage

www.rcfp.org/foiact/index.html

Freedom of Information Center at the University of Missouri

web.missouri.edu/~foiwww/

University of Missouri FOI center.

Freedom of Information Clearinghouse

www.citizen.org/litigation/foic/foic.html

An extensive guide to U.S. FOI from Ralph Nader's Public Citizen advocacy group.

Society of Professinal Journalists Resource Center

spj.org/foia/index.htm

FOI information from the Society of Professional Journalists.

Federal FOI Contacts

www.spj.org/foia/foiresources/fedcontacts/index.htm

List of FOI contacts in the U.S. federal government from the Society of Professional Journalists.

State FOI Contacts

spj.org/foia/foiresources/states/index.htm

State-by-state guide to FOI laws from the Society of Professional Journalists.

FOI Resources

web.syr.edu/~bcfought/foires.html

FOI resources site from Syracuse University.

U.S. Dept. of Justice Office of Information and Privacy

www.usdoj.gov/oip/oip.html

U.S. Dept. of Justice guidesite for the Freedom of Information and Privacy Acts.

Access Reports, Freedom of Information Act, and Privacy Issues

www.accessreports.com

Provides the most comprehensive coverage available of access issues in the United States, Canada, and abroad.

Access Reports: Links

www.accessreports.com/links.html

Links to key U.S. and Canadian FOI and privacy sites.

Other

Access to Information

www.info.gov.hk/isd/acc_e.htm

Hong Kong access to information page.

Freedom of Information Act Part 1 (Edited Version)

www.irlgov.ie/finance/free1.htm

Ireland's Freedom of Information Act.

Campaign for Freedom of Information

www.cfoi.org.uk

Site outlining the British campaign for Freedom of Information.

open.gov.uk

www.open.gov.uk/

British site that offers links to all UK government sites that post information on the Net.

Privacy International—World FOIA Survey

www.privacy.org/pi/issues/foia/foia-survey.html

Privacy International's survey of Freedom of Information in 40 countries around the world.

Chapter 26

A Picture Is Worth...

When you are doing picture or video research for your project, you have to remember that a picture is not only worth a thousand words, it is also often worth a lot of money. While you can paraphrase text or use a minimal quote under the fair use/fair dealing copyright laws, for most pictures and video, you have to clear the rights and often pay for the right to use the material.

You should always keep pictures in mind as you do your research. If you are working on a book, you should decide early on, in consultation with your editor and publisher, how many illustrations you are going to include and have a rough idea of the format. In almost all cases, with the exception of a cover shot, the publisher will opt for less expensive black-and-white pictures rather than color.

For a documentary and even a feature, footage is the essence of what you are seeking. It usually takes a greater effort and costs a lot more. Original illustrations, pictures, or film or video that tell *the story you are researching and telling* are always better than stock stills or footage.

That's not to say that stock stills or footage are not important, as long as they illustrate the actual story and are not just what television news producers call "wallpaper."

As with library and archival research, the World Wide Web has increased the accessibility of film, video, and picture services by letting them put a search engine online that lists their holdings.

Starting out

In picture and video research, the professionals have exactly the same advice as their counterparts who work with words: Do your pure research first.

"Get your facts straight whenever possible," says Bill Brewington of the Grinberg Worldwide Images film library in Los Angeles. "If you are doing historical research, you need dates and anything else that helps you get a grasp on the subject. Often things are pretty vague because of the way they were filed years ago. Filing methods changed over the years. If you don't have a show title to go on, you need a fact of some sort to start."

CBC video research Sonja Carr says, "You have to have a good background knowledge in history or politics or arts, or whatever the topic that you're going to be asked to research. You don't want to waste time asking for things that aren't necessary. If you don't have that general knowledge base, you should do some background research before you launch into the project."

Knowing what is available is crucial for film and video. "Do as much research as you can before you write," Brewington says. "See what's out there first and write around that. So many people take the opposite approach. They have a script and have to go out and find the footage to match. Then they're in a jam and can't find what they want or it takes forever to get it out of the place that has it."

Obtaining material

When I work on a project, I am always on the lookout for pictures. Commercial picture and video collections should always be your final choice.

Photographs

For my research into the Prohibition era in the United States and Canada, the best photographs were not in the actual picture collections of the archives in Washington, Ottawa, and Toronto, but included in the case files themselves. It was a simple matter of getting the pictures copied.

The 1926 mug shot of gang boss Rocco Perri was found in the case file in the Ontario Archives, not the picture collection.

I was able to get a prize collection of photographs of undercover Mountie Frank Zaneth from his relatives in Massachusetts. To make sure nothing went wrong, I hired a local photographer to make copies. (A good idea it turned out, because after the book was published, the publisher lost the pictures while moving offices.)

Other photographs for my books were obtained from the picture collections of various archives, mostly for only the cost of reproduction and a credit. Other archival collections will charge a usage fee, especially if the archives hold what was once a private collection. You should always check with the archives about what rights are available and what the charges are (if any).

Depending on the policy of the archives, you may actually be supplied a negative of a picture for a file rather than a print. Other archives will supply you with a print, keep the negative, and add it to their collection. Credits from many archives and other picture collections require you to include the picture or negative number so other researchers can find it quickly.

Another good source for still pictures is the news media. Newspapers and magazines are a good source of still pictures, although you have to know how far back the collection goes. Some newspapers have archives going back to the 1920s, when the picture-based tabloid became popular and profitable, or even further. Many newspapers, however, have only scattered material in the era before World War II, and some picture collections didn't get organized until the late 1950s.

For pictures that are in the files of a newspaper, you will have to pay for both the print and for the rights to use it. For a book, many newspapers sell the usage license for a small flat fee, while others charge a fee for each edition of the book.

If the pictures are *not* available from the newspaper itself, you have two choices. If a local or national library has a bound hard copy of the newspaper, you can pay the library's photographic service to copy the picture from the newspaper. If hard copy doesn't exist, go to the microfilm. You then have to find the original source of the microfilm; often it is a national library for older newspapers. Frequent use of the microfilm in a local library leads to scratches on the film. The original source, however, will have a master copy, either positive or negative, and it is usually possible to order a print of the photograph directly from the pristine microfilm.

If you obtain the pictures this way, you usually have to do a double credit with the name of the newspaper (whether or not it still exists) and the name of the library. It is a good idea, as a courtesy, to write to the newspaper and ask permission to reproduce the picture. In every case I have done this, permission was granted and there was no charge for the rights.

Black-and-white drawings and text

Always be on the lookout for black and white drawings, posters, text, or other items that add to your research and your story.

These days, books, magazines, and newspapers are all reproduced by scanning or a photographic process. That means that two-color or black-and-white illustrations can be pasted (either physically or by computer) right into the text and don't count as part of your quota of photographs.

In my books I have included posters, editorial cartoons, old newspaper ads, and handwritten police reports.

Finding video

A good video researcher is always on the lookout for original material and for ways of finding material as cheaply as possible.

"There are a lot of alternative sources out there you can go to and they are usually cheaper," Sonja Carr says. "They are not as quick, because they are not a commercial business. A lot of the material out there is public domain....That way you only pay for the duplication charges, you don't pay for the licensing.

"You have to be a creative thinker to try and think, 'Who might possibly have footage?' You know the commercial newsreel places have it. But you want to get stuff that's cheap. So, you could try, depending on how much time you have, local organizations. Local museums are a great place, local libraries are a great place, universities are a great place. So are local TV stations. If you have got a lot of time you can put ads in the newspaper for people's home movies.

"Some museums have footage and they haven't a clue what it is. Sometimes they just don't have the resources to look at it or transfer it to video. So find a lab, find a reliable courier, and send it over to the lab. Pay the bill yourself. Get their film transferred. Ensure they get a copy of the footage on a video tape and then they allow you to use it.

"It can be very complex and in another way it could be quite simple. It could be as simple as phoning somebody up, finding out they have home movies, [asking to] borrow them, transfer[ring] the videotape, and [offering to] give a copy of the videotape as a courtesy. Or it could be so obscure that you're looking for some obscure German politician, and you don't know where to go to.

"A lot of it's word of mouth. If you phone somewhere and they don't have it, you ask, 'Well can you recommend somebody who does?' Never be afraid to ask that. Most people are quite helpful."

The researcher's point of view

The aim of video and picture research, Carr says, is "to give someone quality pictures for a project."

"Sometimes it's right in front of your nose and a lot of times it isn't. Sometimes you really do have to go in the back door to find something. Public libraries are completely underused. So public libraries are the best place to start. You do your background research. You'll get an idea of what photos have already been published. They have huge video collections and you get an idea of what's already been on a tape....Look at the creditor list and find out what sources might be able to give you some footage."

The library is also a good source for photo research. Carr suggests looking at published books in your subject area and using these photos if possible.

Carr points out that technical quality and editorial suitability are key considerations when selecting visual aids. Ownership of an image is also critical. "There can be copyright on any kind of moving image or still image. The copyright may have lapsed....It may be considered public domain."

Photographs, audiotapes, and videos in the public domain should be free for anyone to use. But you may have to pay a licensing fee if the only copy of your sought-after image is in the hands of an individual who says he "owns" it. Commercial sources also charge licensing fees, even if they are providing footage or photographs that are public domain, according to Carr.

Carr says that copyrights can sometimes be tricky. "An image [or piece of footage] can have different rights....Sports and performance footage are tricky because not only is there the copyright on the filming of the event, but [also] on the performance....Some of the commercial footage places take care of all that for you. You pay one straight licensing fee...you should have a basic idea of what copyright means but you don't have to be a real expert."

Going commercial

If you have been unsuccessful in finding material, you should go to a commercial film or video house, remembering that even as you research, that, for the sake of your budget, you should be looking for alternative sources.

"Back when they were doing newsreels they tended to share a lot of footage," Sonja Carr says. "So you can buy a Pathé newsreel from 1936 from one source, and then you'll find the same exact footage in a Paramount newsreel from another source."

It's the same with commercial still houses; the further you go back in time, the more alternative sources you may find. Some of the pictures come from old magazines such as the *London Illustrated News* or *Harper's Weekly*, which are easily found in a library. Other material that a commercial picture library may have will be unique and may be worth a reasonable price.

Inside a commercial film house

"There are different ways to handle different searches," Bill Brewington says. "Newsreel or historical research is different than picture research for a feature movie. Most film and video houses have online catalogs, so it is easy to do a basic search.

"When someone has a very lengthy search...I will tell them to go on the Internet and do the search themselves. It is a lot easier," Brewington says. "But if they were [here in Los Angeles] I would tell them to come in and go through my card file....It's a lot faster to go through 100 cards than to go through 100 screens."

Brewington says that while the Internet is a good source for footage and stills of significant events, the more obscure happenings may not have been covered by the media and are therefore unavailable. "The Internet is good for things [such as] finding the speech when [Franklin Delano Roosevelt] was inaugurated, but if you're looking for some obscure speech...that may or may not have been covered by a newsreel."

If your research is a major project, Brewington suggests that you "hire a local researcher familiar with the material. They can save you time and a lot of money....chances are they've done it before and they will have their notes on it."

Sonja Carr has similar advice. "You can go through online databases, but every online database gives you a warning that it only describes a portion of what's in there." Carr suggests sending your request in writing to a researcher, outlining your project and what you're looking for. "Usually there is a small research fee, maybe $50. Sometimes it's a minimum of an hour of research. But they can do a hell of a lot of research in an hour. So it's sometimes worth your while to have them do that."

Searching online

If you cannot find the pictures or video for your project during the pure and applied research phases, and you haven't been able to find them from sources such as libraries or archives, then it is time to turn to commercial sources, remembering you are going to have to pay for both the print or tape and licensing.

Even if you do search online, Carr says personal contact is still essential. Although sites do have an e-mail contact, it's always a good idea to follow up by phone and fax.

"I have...sent the request...but it hasn't gotten there at all because someone is not reading her e-mail or the person responsible has changed. So use the telephone. It's always good to make personal contacts. You can do the research without ever talking to a real human being, but it's always a good idea to pick up the phone at one point and try to talk to someone."

Footage.net, which calls itself "the stock, archival, and news footage network," uses a meta-search engine as a gateway for searching the online video archives of organizations such as ABC News, NBC News, Associated Press Television News, CNN Imagesource, Grinberg Worldwide Images, National Geographic Television, and stock-footage houses. It also has contact lists for other news archives and stock houses that don't yet have online catalogs.

Corbis is one of the world's largest photography, image, and picture agencies. It offers a variety of services for both the consumer and the professional. The company now owns the Bettman Archive, which includes many historic images, plus the UPI photo library, and the famed picture agency Sygma. Images can be purchased and licensed for commercial use, including publication. Other royalty-free images are available online and can be purchased for a nominal price, or in some circumstances, such as e-cards, obtained for free. Site registration is required.

Many news organizations and magazines also have still-photo services and some are searchable online. In many cases you have to register with the site before searching.

The Mary Evans Picture Library in London is a major source for still pictures from Britain and Europe.

Ditto.com is an image search engine that crawls the Net looking for pictures on sites and then presents the viewer with a page full of thumbnail images, on which you can click to get to the original site. The major search engines also offer image searching. Hotbot allows you to click a box on its search page to find an image. AltaVista also allows you to search for images.

Links

Photographs

Corbis—The Place for Pictures on the Internet
www.corbis.com
Corbis Picture service.

Regional Breakdown of PACA Member Agencies
www.pacaoffice.org/paca1b.html
Site listing links to picture agencies.

Time Inc. Picture Collection
www.thepicturecollection.com
Time and Life's picture agency page.

Magnum Photos
www.magnumphotos.com
One of the world's leading picture agencies.

Mary Evans Picture Library
www.mepl.co.uk/index2.shtml
One of the world's largest commercial picture libraries with a lot of historic material.

Wieck Public Search
www.wieckphoto.com
Commercial site; some public access.

ditto.com—the place for pictures
www.ditto.com
Search engine for online pictures.

AP/Wide World Photos
www.apwideworld.com/main.html
AP Wide World photo service.

Video

Grinberg Worldwide Images
www.grinberg.com
A Los Angeles and New York based commercial film and video library.

FOOTAGE.net Search
www.footage.net/search/
Online gateway to search for stock shots and historical footage.

Demo Reels

www.footage.net/demoreels/online_clips.html

Footage.net links page lists sites with online demo reels.

Newsfilm Library at The University of South Carolina

www.sc.edu/newsfilm/index.html

Holds the old Movietone newsreels.

Newsfilm Library FAQ page

www.sc.edu/newsfilm/faq.htm

Chapter 27

The Mirror Up to Nature

"...the purpose of playing, whose end, both first and now, was and is, to hold as 'twere the mirror up to nature..."

—*Hamlet*, advice to the players [ACT III, Scene 2]

What is the role of research when it comes to drama, whether dramatic nonfiction or fictional drama? It's a subject that has been debated for years, with some saying that research can get in the way of dramatic freedom, the aim to tell "a truth."

A badly researched drama usually fails because the audience often knows that the "truth" behind the story rings false, just as the actor William Shakespeare refers to in *Macbeth*:

> ...a poor player,
> That struts and frets his hour upon the stage,
> And then is heard no more, it is a tale
> Told by an idiot, full of sound and fury,
> Signifying nothing.
>
> [Act V, Scene 5]

That could describe some of Hollywood's pictures. A recent blatant example is Universal's *U-571*, a fictional concoction where American sailors save the world by stealing the Enigma code machine from a Nazi U-boat.

The historic reality is that it was British seaman from the destroyer *HMS Bulldog* who got the Enigma code machine from U-110.

At other times Hollywood succeeds, despite holes in research so big you could sail the *Titanic* through the crack. Yes, the history purists hated *Titanic* but it was a terrific movie.

Why? And what does that mean for research?

First, let's remember that an creative writing, fiction or nonfiction, is essentially a crapshoot. As screenwriter William Goldman put it in his famous phrase from *Adventures in the Screen Trade*: "Nobody knows anything," adding, "Not one person in the entire motion picture field *knows* for a certainty what's going to work. Every time out it's a guess—and if you're lucky, an educated one." Goldman, I should note here, wrote *Butch Cassidy and the Sundance Kid*, and he says, "Most of the movie was made up." But behind that creative imagination was eight years of research on Butch and Sundance, which Goldman summarizes in *Adventures in the Screen Trade*.

The answer is simple: *Good research gives you more choices.*

Good actors will tell you that a great performance is a series of choices, choices made moment by moment, choices that bring a character to life on stage or film. It's called the *magic if*, "What would I do if I..." was Hamlet, King Lear, Romeo, Juliet, on the *Titanic*, on the beach on D-Day?

A superficial research job *always* means a superficial story. A superb research job simply means that the writer, actor, musician, or artist has more tools to command, more choices of where to go and what to do.

The secret no one knows is what you do with those choices. Talent certainly helps. So does experience. So does serendipity.

The bow of the *Titanic*

So if a few historians and some *Titanic* enthusiasts didn't like James Cameron's *Titanic*, why was it a blockbuster success?

There were two objections to James Cameron's *Titanic*. The first was a major part of the plot, the fact that Leonardo DiCaprio's Jack Dawson would never have been allowed "upstairs" in that class-conscious era. The second is that no one would be allowed on the bow. So the famous scene with DiCaprio and Kate Winslet's characters would have never taken place.

Both situations are, in my view, acceptable dramatic license.

Cameron, the director, said in media interviews that he wanted to tie the contemporary undersea shots of the bow of the sunken *Titanic* with the ship he created for the movie. So with the discovery of the wreck at the bottom of the sea, the bow itself became a key character in the picture.

As for Leonardo DiCaprio's wooing of the rich Kate Winslet, that works because it is part of the traditional story of rich and poor falling in love.

In both cases, the scene and the story pass the lie detector inside our minds. We know that Jack Dawson would never be allowed upstairs to first class, but we allow the suspension of disbelief.

In the history of movies just about the *Titanic*, two have been successful: James Cameron's 1997 film, *Titanic*, and the 1958 British film *A Night to Remember* (based on the book by Walter Lord). The 1953 Twentieth Century Fox production of *Titanic* is unremembered and the 1980 film *Raise the Titanic!* sank like a stone at the box office.

A Night to Remember is a docudrama, grounded in the research by author Walter Lord. Cameron's *Titanic* is more about the myth of the *Titanic* that has grown year by year since 1912. As myth, a feeling of authenticity supported the film. The script was nothing to write home about—Cameron was not nominated for a screenwriting Academy Award—but the supporting research that went into the direction and production was superb. So it too was able to pass through the filter in the orbiofrontal cortex.

Making choices: nonfiction

To put it simply, if you are writing journalism or dramatic, narrative nonfiction, *don't make anything up!*

In recent years, dramatic nonfiction has come into its own, and many books are selling well. True, real-life stories, dramatically told and well written, as Mark Bowden does in his masterpiece, *Black Hawk Down*, are more appealing to the public than 99 percent of novels.

But there is also a growing controversy because some authors use composite characters or invent fictional characters as Edmund Morris did in *Dutch: A Memoir of Ronald Reagan*.

The trouble in making anything up is this: If the story is supposed to be true, and one thing is made up, one character is composite, then you are always wondering what is true and what isn't. The very fact that part is made up does not improve the drama of the narrative.

Remember again: *Good research gives you more choices.*

Sometimes, however, you need help in making those choices. The original publisher of our biography of Frank Zaneth wanted more material, more about his personal life, and when we couldn't find any, rejected the book. We then took it to an astute outside editor, John Robert Colombo, who told us we had a casebook, not a biography. It was easy to change the focus from a biography of Frank Zaneth to our subtitle *Cases of the RCMP's Most Secret Operative.*

But unfortunately, the controversy means that you have to prove to the reader that you didn't make anything up. In "A Note to the Reader" in the front of *Undercover*, we wrote:

> Undercover is both history and investigative journalism. Nothing fictional has been added. All scenes and conversations are based on accounts in police files, trial transcripts, letters, newspaper reports, and other accounts. All material in quotation marks is accurate.

Writers of dramatic nonfiction now know to be fair to the reader, they have to prove that the story is true. So the authors are now insisting that their books have pages of source notes at the end, attributing each fact. *Black Hawk Down* has 23 pages of notes; G. Wayne Miller's *King of Hearts* has 19. (There is a note on citations in the Appendix).

If you are about to embark on a nonfiction narrative, whether for a magazine or a book, be prepared to fight for the facts. If you follow the advice early in this book, you should have a premise, a focus statement to guide you. But if that focus doesn't pan out, follow the facts, and change your premise, and keep going.

If you find you can't, then don't call your book nonfiction. Write a novel and call it such; say it is a novel based on certain events.

Making choices: fiction and drama

If you choose to write fiction or drama, how does research help you make choices? Will research interfere with dramatic vision? Or make that vision sharper?

For a moment forget about the script, and take a look at another area of dramatic research: the costume worn by actors on stage or screen. Perhaps it is with the dilemma faced by the costumer that an answer can be found.

Kathryn Sherwin is a tailor at the Stratford (Ontario) Festival and designs for a private costume house called The Merchant's Wife, which specializes in Tudor and Elizabethan costumes. She has also worked on the Toronto production of *The Lion King*.

"Finding the right way is trial and error, discovering what the wearer will accept and what the audience will accept," Sherwin says. "It's always a compromise between modern expectation and historical accuracy."

For example, Sherwin says, the modern audience expects brighter colors. "The vegetable dyes from the old days would probably look 'muddy' to a modern audience, so we use modern dyes.

"Today we fit the garment to the body. Then they fit the body to the garment. People in past eras often had restricted movements. Queen Elizabeth had stiff garments; she probably couldn't touch her toes. Today, we try [to] find a comfort level."

Culture and economic changes also affect what the costumer does. Today both in the theatre and for reinactors of the Renaissance, "Women in particular want to show a lot of bosom in playwear and that was not necessarily true of everyday wear in the past," Sherwin says.

So if your research project is to be a fiction or drama, you might consider it not as your play, your book, your movie, but as a costume that each of audience will wear. Actors know that putting on a costume, whether it is a police uniform or Roman armor, helps create the new "you" of the character. Reinactors, whether for the Battle of Gettysburg or a Renaissance fair, take great pains to ensure that the "compromise between modern expectation and historical accuracy" works.

The researcher/writer of fiction and drama should do no less for their audience.

Shakespeare: the master of research

If you want to use a model of "the compromise between modern expectation and historical accuracy" you only to have to look at William Shakespeare. His *Macbeth* was based on Holinshed's *Chronicle of Scotland, Hamlet* on an old Norse legend recounted in a history of the Danes by Saxo Grammaticus (although Shakespeare's actual source is unclear, because it is believed Hamlet was performed before the English translation was published). *Antony and Cleopatra* came from *Plutarch's Lives,* as did *Julius Caesar, Coriolanus,* and *Timon of Athens*.

Shakespeare saw in those thin pages of historical research stories and characters. He was a genius who knew that secret of making the right choices more often than most of us.

And you may ask, what about a character such as *Richard III*, one of Shakespeare's greatest characters and a clear distortion of history? First Shakespeare was playing to the "modern expectations" of his time in his characterization of Richard. He did it so well that today, when we know more about Richard, we can still sit back and suspend disbelief, because the character draws you in, keeps your attention, and leaves you satisfied as Richard cries "My kingdom for a horse" and gets what he deserves.

If Shakespeare did it, why can't someone else? Sure you can, if you can do it as well. If not, your audience detects the distortion and decides the work is "sound and fury, signifying nothing."

Suit the word to the action, the action to the word

How do you do the research so that you—the writer, the actor, or the director—can take more of Hamlet's advice and "suit the word to the action, the action to the word?"

Let's go back to my idea that the modern researcher is on a journey of discovery and that when the researcher writes or directs or performs, becomes a guide. Just as an actor discovers moments during the rehearsal process, just as ideas coalesce and characters take on a life of their own during the writing process, each fact you uncover during research passes through that router so that when you're creating the output, conscious and subconscious come together. C. S. Forester, the creator of the *Hornblower* novels and other books, in an autobiography, used the analogy of a log that sinks to the bottom of the ocean, only to rise again at the right moment.

The facts you find during your research are those logs, and the more logs you have, the more choices. It is as simple as that.

Fiction: substitution

An actor is taught to use *substitution*. To find each moment of a performance, they take a moment from their own lives, an emotional experience, and substitutes it for what the character must feel in that moment on the stage or set. The search for that substitution in one's own life is in its own way research.

The fiction writer does the same.

Steven Pressfield used both research and substitution for *Gates of Fire*. "I pretty much use old-fashioned research," he says. "I am near UCLA, so I go to the UCLA library and take out books and one book leads me to another book. I read as much as I can. I'll copy a lot of it into my computer, and organize just as any traditional research person would."

He also drew on his experiences in the Marine Corps. "That is one of the other things that sparked my interest in the Spartans. Before I wound up in the Marine Corps, my image was of these brutal guys, and when I got into the corps, I found it was wonderful guys, not at all like my image.

"So when I was writing about the Spartans, I thought the same thing. They've had a bad rap, these brutal militaristic guys....It can't be the way it is."

In the book there is a scene where the Spartans make a night raid on Xerxes' camp. That raid is not mentioned in Herodotus but it is retold by Diodorus. "I've read various scholars," Pressfield says, "where some of them will scoff and say 'this never could happen,' and others say 'of course, it happened.' What motivated me to use it was for reasons in the story and my belief that in real life it would have happened. Why not take a shot, you're all going to die anyway."

Fiction: morphing

When a computer graphics program takes two images linked at key points and then blends the two into something new, the image is said to be morphed. Similarly, when two metals are mixed to create an alloy, often something stronger is created, as bronze is created when copper is mixed with tin, or when titanium is mixed with steel or glass.

That is what good fiction writers and dramatists often do: They take something they know and morph it with something else.

A well-known example from a great movie is Robert Towne's *Chinatown*, in which he takes the 1900–1906 destruction of Owens Valley so Los Angeles could get water and morphs it into Los Angeles in 1937. Los Angeles in the late 1930s was a contemporary setting for some the great private eye stories about Sam Spade and Phillip Marlowe. There is still something magic about that period for an audience almost 40 years later. Again, it's a case of research giving you more choices.

Acting and directing: "the idea gleaner"

"Creative thinking is different from critical thinking," says director and actor Duncan McIntosh. "Critical thought has a destination, to prove or disprove a thesis. Creative thought is often finding an unarticulated feeling. You find scraps and fragments of existence and then use that material to come to a new understanding of how life can be different."

McIntosh was directing a production of Shakespeare's *Twelfth Night* when he discovered that a Web search can be what he calls "an idea gleaner."

"During the development of the play," he says, "finding ideas is kind of fun. In a search engine, you put in key words and it sends you to a destination. So put in ideas, thoughts, even colors, and see what turns up."

For *Twelfth Night*, McIntosh came to the conclusion that the play was about grief and desire. "The characters are lost in mourning," he says. So he used a search engine and put in the words "grief" and "desire."

"Among the entries came Fado, a form of music from Portugal, which originated in the Islamic tradition and had joy, melancholy, and sensuality. The composer then worked with Fado to create the music for the production."

Advice to the players

Experienced and prominent actors have the clout to get access to sources to do research. But many of the younger and struggling actors I know complain that they can't get the access they need, nor are they taught the basics of research. Actors are taught voice, movement, substitution, and sense memory, but unless they are in a university where they have other courses as well, little attention is paid to research.

It is the responsibility of the director to give the actors clues about their characters and roles, but often the good actor wants more.

"All I get is an overview, never anything specific," one actor complains. "I never get very much, [because] the director is always so busy with other things," another says.

Yet even a little research makes an actor's choices better. Once between a book and a television job I was a researcher and assistant to the director on a Toronto Equity Showcase production of *'Tis Pity She's A Whore.*

In that play, one character is poisoned, a second stabbed with a poisoned sword. A quick trip to the library found a guide to poisons written during the late Middle Ages. I found a poison that matched Hippolita's burning sensation as she died and a poison the author recommended for swords and daggers. The description of the symptoms gave the actors better choices.

Everything that a writer or journalist uses in this book can be used by an actor. Library research, interviews in person or by e-mail, and in some cases even archival research, can all help.

The personal Web pages can be a guide to any creative individual, an actor or writer. There are many Web pages by veterans from World War II, Korea, Vietnam, the Gulf War, and peacekeeping/peace enforcement.

"My major characters have something wrong, they are not 100 percent; that's a quirk of me as a writer," says author Robert J. Sawyer. "If you are going to have a character who has Huntingtons Disease, ideally what you want to do is stumble across a person's Web site, where they happen to have that particular condition and have put their heart on the Web.

"When you're building a character, you don't want to violate reality. You hit paydirt when you find somebody who says my Dad died of this. It was horrible but these were his good moments.

"I just recently stumbled on a site that was about what is was like to be an abused wife. It told how many times she had been beaten, how many times she had tried to leave, how she finally got out.

"She put it on the Web and changed a few names, but she said, "This is my life story." This is people opening up to you in a way if you were there face to face, it's almost there for free, for mining."

But there is more. Acting, McIntosh says, is an "exchange of energy" and interplay of emotional response between characters.

McIntosh advises actors to "look for insight into the manner of things."

"The actor," he says, "is interested in what are the sparks? So look not just at what is on the Web pages, but what lays behind the decision to post the account on the Web. The poster has recorded a vision he wants you to believe. Look for what is hidden."

That's advice all researchers should heed.

Omnes: being there II

Whether you are an actor or a writer, there is no substitute for being there, for personal contact with people and places. Actors hang out with people who have the same job or life experience as their character. It's now common in Hollywood to hire professional advisers, such as the one for

Saving Private Ryan, whose stars experienced a version of bootcamp to give authenticity to their performance and build a sense of *esprit de corps.*

Writers of both nonfiction and fiction look for more than "local color"; they strive for authenticity.

Mark Bowden had to go to Magadishu and "left with a feel for the place, for the futility of its local politics and some insight to why the Somalis fought so bitterly against American soldiers that day."

Martin O'Malley spent two years at Toronto General Hospital. "I call it hanging around journalism. Experiential. I kind of metaphorically see myself sawing a large circular hole in the roof above me, until the information just falls in my lap," he says. "I got to a point after a year researching Toronto General that I just asked my publisher for another year because I knew I was only at the point where I was now accepted. I became nicely invisible. I was part of the scenery. I was really getting top-notch stuff. Before that I was getting reportorial stuff—you know, they would give me stuff like they would a newspaper reporter. But after sitting, standing though many many operations and many overnight shifts in emergency, I became almost like one of the residents. Then they really confide, tell me stuff that was sometimes almost diametrically opposed to the stuff they would give me when I was perceived as a kind of newspaper journalist. After a year I sort of became more an author than a reporter. And the good stuff just came."

Omnes: find a training officer

When I was on my first job as a police reporter in Sudbury, Ontario, in 1975, the city hired a new fire chief, who had a great idea.

After he had been on the job a month or so, he proposed that the members of the media who covered police and fire stories spend a day with the fire department's training officer, so that reporters could get a basic idea of how firefighters worked and what exactly went into fighting a fire. "That way you can be accurate," the chief said.

As a newspaper reporter, I was often self-assigned, and after I filed my morning stories, I went over to the firehall. I was the only one who showed up. My broadcast colleagues, who could not be spared, were busy elsewhere. I spent the rest of the day getting the basic rookie's lecture on how a fire is fought, learning the parts of a pumper, trying on a Scott air pack and helmet, lifting a rolled hose, visiting the tower where the hoses were dried, and I was told what can go wrong when things go bad.

It was every 5-year-old's dream. Although I did not get to ride the fire engine, it did make me accurate when covering fires. It also helped me to get to know some of the fire crews better.

Spending that day with the training officer was a brilliant idea. The training officer's job is to make sure that the people he trains do their jobs safely and properly.

If more fire and police chiefs provided a day or so of training to the media, and if the beancounters in the media allowed their staffs the time to take the training, the caliber of that day-to-day reporting would improve considerably.

So if you're a reporter or a writer of long-form fiction or nonfiction, or an actor or director, try your best to contact a training officer in the field you're researching. If you do get access and they can help you out, either formally or informally, at the end of a day or two you'll know the basics, and then you go on to do better research.

Links

Robert J. Sawyer (Author)

www.sfwriter.com

Robert J. Sawyer official site.

Afterword

Research is a journey, and on some projects, for some people, it is an all encompassing one. In some moments of research, you can be so focused on your task, that you enter the mythical "zone" that athletes and mystics speak of.

At other times, you are mind-numb, checking file after file, book upon paper upon article upon book.

Then there comes the time when you have done as much as you can.

If you have planned well, you are at about the time you hoped to complete your research. Or, if the experience of most people is any guide, you may be behind and scrambling to meet a deadline.

Now is the time to take a few days off, to relax, to recharge your batteries, to give your mind and body a rest, to relax, and to let your subconscious take over and synthesize all you have learned during the research journey.

As you turn your attention from input to output, to write, to compose, to rehearse on the way to performance, new questions will arise, as the information is synthesized, as characters are built, as the writing progresses. If you have done your work well, answering those questions will be at your fingertips. If in the process, there is a new and expected question—or something you forgot to do or thought was not important at the time— it may mean a return to the Web, to the library, to e-mail and telephone follow-up calls. If so, the experience you gained on your journey should make any return quick and easy.

That is your task now: to move on and bring what you have learned to others. Your research has given you more choices. Now is the time to make those choices, to do the best job you can with what you have gleaned.

But wait, what's that? A little thought at the back of your mind, an idea, a hunch; you've seen an intriguing news article, read a new scholarly paper, or overheard a fascinating story.

Even you before complete what you are doing, a new project is being born.

And so the research journey begins again.

But the experience you gained stays with you and helps guide you on the next journey, you know when to use the shortcuts and when to take on the challenging peaks.

Does it get easier? No, not really. It's hard work. But most of the time it's fun.

Then comes the moment you've worked so hard for, the day of book publication, opening night, the album release, the movie premiere, the awarding of the degree.

You have the grail, the Golden Fleece, Aladdin's lamp.

Congratulations.

Good luck.

Appendix

Citations

Citing sources is an important part of research. First it proves what you have done and second it is a resource for future researchers who are following in your path.

There are several styles of citations, depending on who your publisher is. And within that citation style, almost every journal and publisher has a house style. As one freelance editor, who specializes in academic editing told me, "I just follow the general guidelines, the editor at the journal will change it anyway."

The same style guides may also dictate the use of numbers, quotes, spelling and other often-contentious issues.

For citations and bibliographies the most common and widely used is based on the *Chicago Manual of Style*, which has a general style and one for the humanities. The Modern Language Association (MLA) sets the rules for academic literary criticism and the American Psychological Association (APA) is used in the social sciences, engineering and health fields, the Council of Biology Editors uses yet another style for other areas of science. Then, of course, lawyers have their favorite way of doing legal citations. The *New York Public Library Writer's Guide* is another general alternative.

As for notes, there are three types: the classic **footnote**, the classic **endnote**, and the **informal source note**. Generally you will find the classic footnote and endnote in academic publications and books from university presses.

The informal source note, which I use in this book, is preferred by commercial publishers, and the actual style usually depends on the preferences of the individual author. Many of the marketing people in commercial publishing believe that academic footnotes or endnotes are a turnoff to the public and reduce sales. Many general source notes, such as the ones I use in this book, use quotes and are not geared to specific page numbers to save time in the publication process. Some publishers, however, prefer to tie a source note directly to a page reference.

For this book I created the source notes manually, but used Scholar's Aid to generate the bibliography. Scholar's Aid can also produce references using the APA, MLA, and Harvard University styles. Other bibliographic programs have a similar functions.

Notes

Full bibliographical information for the books and articles listed here is also found in the Bibliography.

Introduction

Tim Berners-Lee, *Weaving the Web,* Enquire Within...p. 1; *"The Web arose...,"* p. 3.

NSA. "Biggest U.S. spy agency choking on too much information," CNN, November 25, 1999.

The Library at Alexandria, Matthew Battles, "Lost in the Stacks," *Harpers,* January, 2000, p. 36.

Porteous, *Washington Quarterly,* Autumn 1996, p. 201.

Chapter 1

Full details of the life of Frank Zaneth and details of the documents can be found in the author's *Undercover: Cases of the RCMP's Most Secret Operative.*

Kim. *The Best Fiction of Rudyard Kipling*, p. 131, 110.

Todd Lewan, Telephone interview, November, 1999.

Ira Silverman Telephone interview, November, 1999.

Trevor-Roper's account of how he obtained the manuscript and his subsequent research is found in the Prologue of *Hermit of Peking*. "enchanter" p. 367. "fantasy and fabrication" p. 369.

Chapter 2

Campbell, *Hero with a Thousand Faces,* p. 245.

Tuchman, *Practicing History*, p21

Egri, *The Art of Dramatic Writing,* p. 2-3.

Lord, *A Night to Remember,* p. 66.

Biel, *Down with the Old Canoe*, p. 8.

Pressfield, telephone interview, December 1999, *Gates of Fire*, p. 380.

Franklin, posted on Writer-L, January 7, 1998, reproduced by permission.

Tracy Kidder. Talk at the Narrative Train II conference, Boston University, Dec. 4, 1999.

John Sawatsky, telephone interview, December 1999.

Lynn Franklin, posted on Writer-L, Sept. 28, 1999. Used with writer's permission.

Baldwin, quoted in *James Baldwin, Artist on Fire,* p. 2.

Chapter 3

Nora Paul. I originally adapted my version of Paul's 5Ws from a handout she distributed in 1994. To see a complete and updated version of Paul's 5Ws see her *Computer-Assisted Research*, fourth edition, p. 8-16.

Roy Peter Clark Talk at the Narrative Train II conference, Boston University, Dec. 4, 1999.

Chapter 4

Zaneth. For complete details of the Bronfman money-laundering scheme, see the author's *Undercover: Cases of the RCMP's Secret Operative*.

Bowden. Talk at the Narrative Train II conference, Boston University, Dec. 4, 1999, plus personal conversations.

Berners-Lee, *Weaving the Web,* p. 18.

Chapter 5

Dean Tudor, comment in *Finding Answers,* p. 97.

Sam Porteous, interview, December, 1999.

Tuchman, *Practicing History,* p. 78.

Ted Anthony, telephone interview, November, 1999.

Chapter 6

Campbell, *Hero with a Thousand Faces*, p. 30.

Star Trek. The episode was "Parallels," written by Brannon Braga from Season 7; original air date November 29, 1993.

"Congenial truth," a term originated by Andie Tucher, former associate editor of *Columbia Journalism Review.*

Tuchman, "Practicing History," p. 21-22.

"Act of propaganda," Righelhof, *The Globe and Mail*, April 22, 2000.

"Infinite," Demos, *Unredeemed Captive,* p. 10.

Chapter 7

Karp, Jonathan. "Rules for the nonfiction author," *IRE Journal,* Oct/Nov, 1999, p. 11.

Zinsser, William, *On Writing Well, Fifth Edition*, p. 165.

Tuchman "Undigested Facts," *Practicing History,* p. 18.

Tuchman, "Stop," p. 20-21.

Martin O'Malley, personal interview, November, 1999.

Chapter 8

English Teacher's Revenge, Franklin, *Writing for Story,* p. 110.

Harvey Cashore, personal interview, December, 1999.

Chapter 9

Jerome Loving, telephone interview, November, 1999.

Martin O'Malley, personal interview, November, 1999.

Cashore, personal interview, December, 1999.

Mark Kramer, personal interview, December, 1999.

"Immerses" *Literary Journalism,* p. 22.

Egri, character "bone structure," *Art of Dramatic Writing,* p. 49-59. Although Egri's bone structure is still considered the classic, you will find another approach created by Nancy Kress in her book, *Dynamic Characters*, which is loosely based on a FBI profiling form, she calls it a character dossier, p. 149-155. See also Uta Hagen's classic, *Respect for Acting,* p. 81-85.

Chapter 11

Robert J. Sawyer, personal interview, December, 1999.

Chapter 13

Steve Lawrence, phone interview, November, 1999.

C. Lee Giles, phone interview, November, 1999.

Chapter 15

Ted Anthony, telephone interview, November, 1999.

Jerome Loving, telephone interview, November, 1999.

Collins, e-mail to author.

Chapter 16

Bjarnason, personal interview, November, 1999.

Kramer, personal interview, December, 1999.

Chapter 17

Tuchman, "Bias in a primary source...," *Practicing History,* p. 19.

Tuchman, "Show me," *Practicing History,* p. 36.

Tudor, checklist, *Finding Answers,* p. 27-28.

Trites URRC, boundaries *Impact of Technology,* p. 15-18 19-29, 58, 66-68.

Polyani, *Globe and Mail,* November 9, 1999.

Gerber, "You cannot trust anything that's on the" interview, December, 1999.

"NEJM conflict of interest," Associated Press, February 22, 2000.

Chapter 19

Tuchman, notes *Practicing History*, p. 20, interviews, p. 68.

Ted Anthony, telephone interview, November, 1999.

Chapter 20

Sliverman, telephone interview, November, 1999.

Kalushner, personal interview, November, 1999.

Belgraver, personal interview, November, 1999.

Chapter 21

Pappworth quote is from A *Primer of Medicine,* p. 9. I found the quote in Belton, the *Good Listener*, p. 183.

Sawatsky, telephone interview, December, 1999.

Sawyer, personal interview, December, 1999.

Kevin Donavan, presentation to my class, March, 2000.

Silverman, personal interview, November, 1999.

Mike McGraw, telephone interview, December, 1999.

O'Malley, personal interview, November, 1999.

Eric Nadler, Loosening Lips, photocopied handout.

Shaver, Lecture to the Canadian Police College, photocopied handout.

Kramer, personal interview, December, 1999.

Chapter 22

Face to face; Kiesler and Sproull, 1986, "Response effects" p. 404; "found more," p. 411.

Illicit drugs; Sussman and Sproull, 1999, "Straight Talk" p. 153.

"Self-absorbed," "Response effects," p. 411.

Kiesler, Walsh, and Sproull, 1992, "Computer surveys," "Computer networks," p. 247.

Sussman and Sproull, 1999, "people find," "Straight Talk," p. 153. "Cushioning the blow," p. 163; "higher levels of comfort," p. 162.

Sussman, e-mail to the author, December, 1999.

Chapter 24

"are to be considered as enemy," "hundreds of civilians," war, "American soldiers machine-gunned hundreds," Associated Press, Sept. 29 1999.

Bob Port, telephone interview, November, 1999.

Mendoza, "Digging into History," p. 6.

Bullock case, my article in *Hamilton This Month,* April, 1989.

Chapter 26

Sonja Carr, personal interview, November, 1999.

Bill Brewington, telephone interview, December, 1999.

Chapter 27

"Nobody knows," Goldman, *Adventures in the Screen Trade,* p. 39.

Goldman, "Butch Cassidy and the Sundance Kid," *Adventures,* p. 283.

Sherwin, telephone interview, November, 1999.

Forester, *Long Before Forty,* many references.

Pressfield, telephone interview, December, 1999.

Duncan McIntosh, personal interview, November, 1999.

Sawyer, personal interview, December, 1999.

Bowden, "left with a feel for the place," *Black Hawk Down,* p. 344.

O'Malley, personal interview, November, 1999.

Bibliography

Books

Baldwin, James. 1989. Notes of A Native Son. Chap. in *James Baldwin: The Legacy*. Edited by Quincy Troupe. New York: Simon & Schuster.

Barzun, Jacques, and Henry F. Graff. 1988. *The Modern Researcher*. Boston: Houghton Mifflin Company.

Belton, Neil. 1998. *The Good Listener Helen Bamber: A Life Against Cruelty*. London: Orion Publishing Group.

Berners-Lee, Tim. 1999. *Weaving the Web: The Past, Present and Future of the World Wide Web by its Inventor*. London: Orion Business Books.

Biel, Steven. 1996. *Down with the Old Canoe: A Cultural History of the Titanic Disaster*. New York: W.W. Norton & Company.

Bowden, Mark. 1999. *Black Hawk Down: A Story of Modern War*. New York: Atlantic Monthly Press.

Campbell, Joseph. 1968. *The Hero With A Thousand Faces*. Second Edition. Princeton, N.J.: Princeton University Press.

Davis, Cullom, Kathyrn Back, and Kay MacLean. 1977. *Oral History From Tape to Type*. Chicago: American Library Association.

Demos, John. 1995. *The Unredeemed Captive: A Family Story from Early America*. New York: Vintage Books.

Dubro, James, and Robin Rowland. 1991. *Undercover: Cases of the RCMP's Most Secret Operative*. Toronto: Octopus Publishing Group.

Dubro, James, and Robin Rowland. 1987. *King of the Mob Rocco Perri and the Women Who Ran His Rackets*. Markham, Ontario: Penguin Books.

Egri, Lajos. 1960. *The Art of Dramatic Writing*. New York: Simon and Schuster. Touchstone, 1946.

Field, Syd. 1982. *Screenplay: The Foundations of Screenwriting*. New expanded edition. New York: Delta.

Forester, Cecil Scott. 1968. *Long Before Forty*. Boston: Little, Brown.

Franklin, Jon. 1986. *Writing for Story: Craft Secrets of Dramatic Nonfiction*. New York: New American Library Mentor.

Frites, Gerald D., Gergory M. Gallant, and Alex Young. 1999. *The Impact of Technology on Financial and Business Reporting*. Toronto: Canadian Institute of Chartered Accountants.

Goldman, William. 1984. *Adventures in the Screen Trade: A Personal View of Hollywood and Screenwriting*. New York: Warner Books.

Hagen, Uta, and Haskel Frankel. 1973. *Respect for Acting*. New York: MacMillan Publishing Company.

Kiesler, Sara, John Walsh, and Lee Sproull. 1992. Computer networks in field research. Chap. in *Methodological Issues in Applied Pyschology*. 239268. New York: Plenum Press.

Kipling, Rudyard. 1989. *The Best Fiction of Rudyard Kipling*. John Bennett, editor. New York: Doubleday.

Kress, Nancy. 1998. *Dynamic Characters*. Cincinnati: Writer's Digest Books.

Lord, Walter. 1963. *A Night to Remember*. New York: Bantam.

Loving, Jerome. 1999. *Walt Whitman: The Song of Himself*. Berkeley and Los Angeles: University of California Press.

Mann, Thomas. 1998. *The Oxford Guide to Library Research*. New York: Oxford University Press.

Metter, Ellen. 1999. *Facts in a Flash: A Research Guide for Writers*. Cincinnati, Ohio: Writer's Digest Books.

Miller, G. Wayne. 2000. *King of Hearts: The True Story of the Maverick Who Pioneered Open Heart Surgery*. New York: Random House.

O'Malley, Martin. 1989. *Gross Misconduct*. Toronto: Penguin Books.

O'Malley, Martin. 1986. *Hospital: Life and Death in a Major Medical Centre*. Toronto: Macmillan of Canada.

Pappworth, Maurice. 1960. *Primer of Medicine*. London: Butterworth Heinemann.

Paul, Nora. 1999. *Computer-Assisted Research: A Guide to Tapping Online Information*. Fourth Edition. Chicago, IL and St. Petersburg FL: Bonus Books, Poynter Institute for Media Studies.

Pressfield, Steven. 1999. *Gates of Fire*. New York: Bantam.

Quittner, Joshua, and Michelle Slatalla. 1998. *Speeding the Net: The Inside Story of Netscape and How It Challenged Microsoft*. New York: Atlantic Monthly Press.

Richie, Donald. 1965. *Films of Akira Kurosawa*. Berkeley and Los Angeles: University of California Press.

Rowland, Robin, and Dave Kinnaman 1995. *Researching on the Internet.* Rocklin CA: Prima Publishers

Sawatsky, John. 1998. Interviewing. Chap. in *The VJ Handbook*. 49-61. Toronto: Canadian Broadcasting Corporation, Training and Development.

Shenk, David. 1997. *Data Smog: Surviving the Information Glut*. San Francisco: HarperEdge.

Shilts, Randy. 1987. *And the Band Played On: Politics, People, and the AIDS Epidemic*. New York: St. Martin's.

Sims, Norman and Kramer, Mark. 1995. *Literary Journalism: A New Collection of the Best American Nonfiction*. New York: Ballantine Books.

Trevor-Roper, Hugh. 1978. *Hermit of Peking: The Hidden Life of Sir Edmund Backhouse*. Harmondsworth & New York: Penguin Books.

Tuchman, Barbara. 1981. *Practicing History*. New York: Ballantine Books.

Tudor, Dean. 1993. *Finding Answers: The Essential Guide to Gathering Information in Canada*. Toronto: McClelland & Stewart.

Vogler, Christopher. 1992. *The Writer's Journey: Mythic Structure for Storytellers & Screenwriters*. Studio City: Michael Wiese Productions.

Articles

Affleck, John. 1999. Managers like e-mail—to demote, discipline or fire. *Associated Press*, July 1.

Atkinson, William Illsey. 2000. Bird Brains. *The Globe and Mail* (Toronto), February 17, R9.

Battles, Matthew. 2000. Lost in the Stacks, The decline and fall of the universal library. *Harpers* (New York), January, 36-39.

Chiose, Simona. 1999. Takin' it to the Net. *Globe and Mail* (Toronto), December 6, R4.

Choe Sang-Hun, Charles J. Hanley, and Martha Mendoza. 1999. Bridge at No Gun Ri—Condensed. *Associated Press* (New York), September 29.

Evans, Mark. 2000. Lycos leader aims high. *Globe and Mail* (Toronto), February 5, B8.

Hanley, Charles J., and Martha Mendoza. 1999. No Gun Ri—Legal. *Associated Press* (New York), October 1.

Johnson, Linda. 2000. Medical journal apologizes for conflicts of interest in choosing doctors to review treatments. *Associated Press*, February 22.

Karp, Jonathan. 1999. Rules for the nonfiction author. *IRE Journal* (Columbia, Mo) 22, 8 (November): 11-13.

Keisler, Sara: Sproull, Lee S. 1986. Response effects in the electronic survey. *Public Opinion Quarterly* (Chicago) 50: 402-413.

Lawrence, Steve: Giles, C. Lee. 1999. Accessibility of information on the web. *Nature* 400 (July 8): 107.

Mendoza, Martha. 2000. Digging into history AP investigates U.S. actions during Korean War. *IRE Journal* (Columbia, Mo) 23, 1 (January/February): 6-7, 31.

Polyani, John. 1999. The bottom line: excellence. *The Globe and Mail* (Toronto), November 9, A19.

Porteous, Samuel D. 1996. Looking out for economic interests: an increased role for intelligence. *Washington Quarterly* (Washington) 19, 4 (Autumn): 191-204.

Reaney, Patricia. 1999. Ancient Chinese flute still plays sweet music. *Reuters*, Sept. 23.

Rigelhoff, T. F. 2000. Reconstructed Pilate delightfully disturbing. *Globe and Mail* (Toronto), April 22, D5.

Rowland, Robin. 1978. Kit's Secret. *Content* (Toronto), November, 30-31.

Rowland, Robin. 1978. Kit of the Mail: The world's first accredited woman war correspondent. *Content* (Toronto), May, 12-20.

Rowland, Robin. 1989. Intent to kill Matthew Bullock. *Hamilton This Month* (Hamilton, On), April, 35-38, 62.

Sproull, Lee. 1986. Using electronic mail for data collection on organizational research. *Academy of Management Journal* 29, 1: 159-189.

Stith, Pat. 1995. These people are not your friends. Do not hand them sticks to hit you with. *IRE Journal* (Columbia, Mo) 18, 4 (July-August): 7-10.

Sussman, Stephanie Watts, Sproull, and Lee. 1999. Straight talk: Delivering bad news through electronic communication. *Information Systems Research* 10, 2 (June): 150-166.

Walsh, John P., Sara Kiesler, Lee Sproull, and Bradford Hesse. 1992. Self-selected and randomly selected respondents in a computer network survey. *Public Opinion Quarterly* (Chicago) 56: 241-244.

Weinberg, Steve. 1999. Getting sources to talk. *IRE Journal* (Columbia, Mo) 22, 6 (August): 12.

Wypijewski, JoAnn. 1999. A boy's life. *Harpers* (New York), September, 61-74.

Wypijewski, JoAnn. 1998. The secret sharer. *Harpers* (New York), July, 35-54.

Reports

Postel, J. 1993. The U.S. Domain. *RFC 1480*, Internet, Network Working Group. June. Available in various locations.

Demco, John. 1997. The CA Domain: An Introduction. *CA domain registrar*, Internet, University of British Columbia. May 31. Available in various locations.

Middleburg, Don: Ross, Steven S. 1999. *The 1998 Middleburg/Ross Media in Cyberspace Study*, New York, Middleburg + Associates. Fifth national (U.S.) survey.

Nadler, Eric. ND. Loosening Lips The Art of the Inteview. Training handout.

National Library of Canada. 1989. *Publisher's Path*. Supply and Services Canada

Postel, J. 1994. Domain Name System Structure and Delegation. *RFC 1591*, Internet, Network Working Group. March.

Shaver, Claude. 1982. Use of Non-verbal Communication in Interviewing., Ottawa, Canadian Police College. Unpublished lecture (handout).

Web sites

Berucson, David. 2000. Damn Yankees!. *National Post Arts & Life*. www.nationalpost.com: National Post, April 21.

Dow Jones Business News. 2000. Dow Jones, Excite At Home To Launch Work.com Business Portal. dowjones.wsj.com/i/media/SB951232222581671165-media-more-news.html:February 22.

Elder, Sean. 1999. How they got the Korean War atrocity story. *Salon.com Media*. www.salon.com/media/feature/1999/09/30/ap_korea/index.html: Salon.com.

Note: This list was generated using Scholar's Aid.

Index

D

E

F

Q

R

S

T

U

V

W

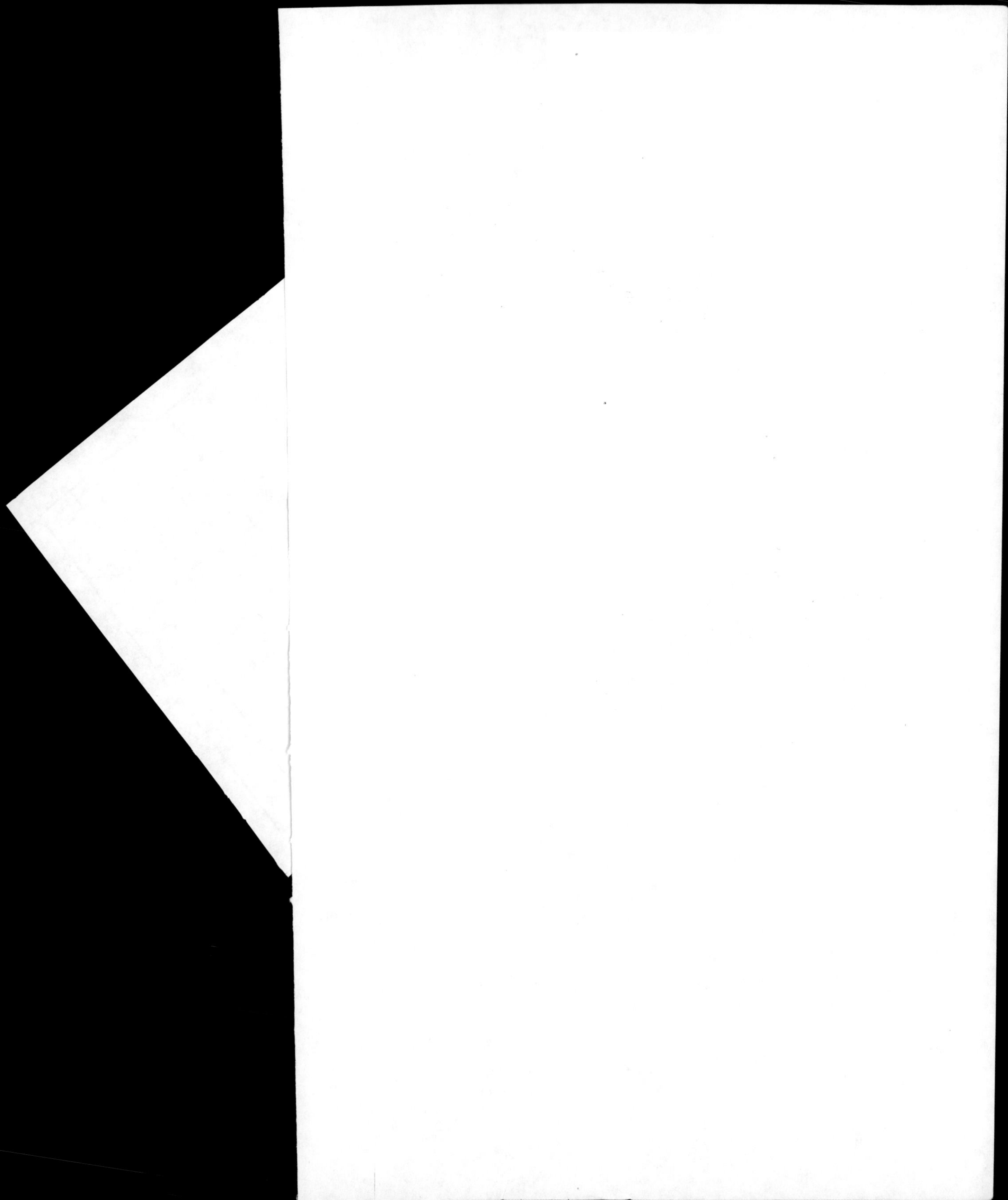

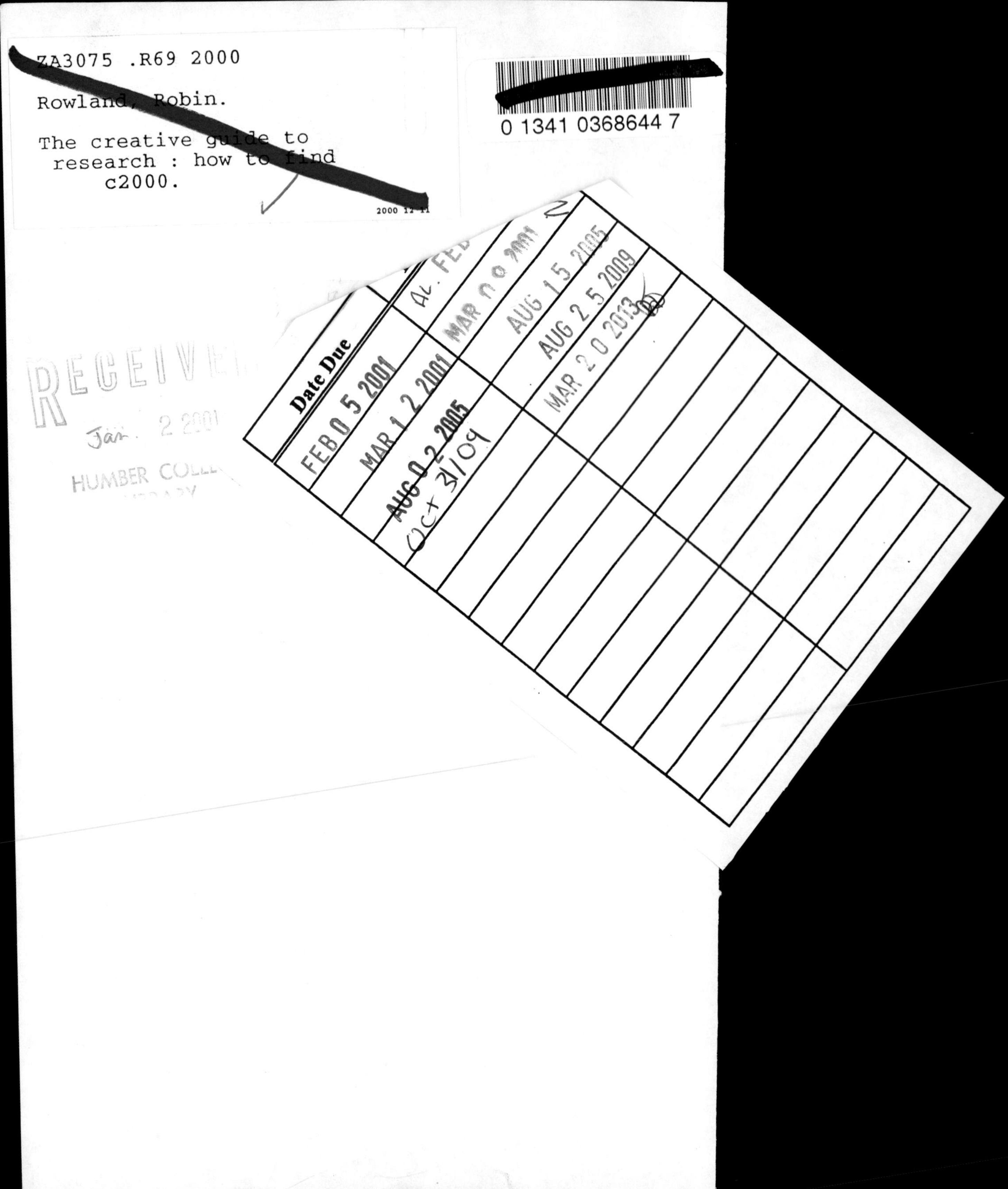
ZA3075 .R69 2000
Rowland, Robin.
The creative guide to research : how to find
c2000.
0 1341 0368644 7
RECEIVED
HUMBER COLL
Date Due
FEB 0 5 2001
MAR 1 2 2001
AUG 0 2 2005
Oct 31/09
AUG 1 5 2005
AUG 2 5 2009
MAR 2 0 2013